# LOVE AROUND THE CORNER

---

## AMANDA WEAVER

carina
press

**carina press®**

Recycling programs
for this product may
not exist in your area.

ISBN-13: 978-1-335-14688-5

Love Around the Corner

First published in 2020. This edition published in 2024.

Copyright © 2020 by Amanda Weaver

For questions and comments about the quality of this book, please contact us at CustomerService@Harlequin.com.

® is a trademark of Harlequin Enterprises ULC.

Carina Press
22 Adelaide St. West, 41st Floor
Toronto, Ontario M5H 4E3, Canada
www.CarinaPress.com

**Printed in U.S.A.**

This is dedicated to the millions of immigrants who, for the past four centuries, have come to New York seeking a better life and have made this the best city on earth.

## Chapter One

One of Gemma Romano's earliest memories was of her mother perching her on a bar stool at Romano's Bar. She must have been really little, because it was before Livie or Jess had been born. A patron had just given her his police badge to keep her busy while her parents handled a small rush of customers, and she remembered turning it back and forth, watching the red and yellow lights from the neon Michelob sign in the window dance across the shiny surface.

Twenty-five years later and not a damned thing in Romano's had changed. Sure, she had two grown sisters now, and their mother had been gone for more than a decade. But Romano's carried on, the same Michelob sign in the window, the same cracked leather bar stools, even the same cop, although Frank was retired now, that shiny badge gathering dust in a drawer somewhere.

She loved Romano's. Every nick in the wooden bar, every chipped floor tile, was as familiar to her as her own face. She loved the light glinting off the liquor bottles, reflected in the big wall-size mirror with Romano's Bar in flaking gold paint. She loved the feel of the taps in her hand. She loved their regulars, a handful of cops and firefighters—now almost all retired—

who'd been hanging out at Romano's so long they were nearly family.

But on sleepy Tuesday nights like this one—when there were so few customers to wait on she had time to get inventory done and wash an entire rack of glasses, when she was here alone while her two younger sisters were living their new adult lives, both happy and in love, when even her *father* was off on a date—it was hard not to feel—just a *teensy* bit—like life was passing her by.

"Can I get a refill, Gemma?"

Gemma jolted out of her daydream. "Sure thing, Frank. Dennis, you good?"

"You can top me up, too, hon." Dennis and Frank spent so much time parked side by side that those bar stools bore permanent imprints of their butts.

The problem, she decided as she refilled Frank and Dennis's glasses, was that she spent all her time surrounded by a bunch of men old enough to be her grandfather. Carroll Gardens in Brooklyn had gentrified enormously in the past decade or two, filling up with well-off families and hip young people. But Romano's was a holdover from the neighborhood's working-class Italian roots. None of the people frequenting those fancy restaurants and wine bars a few blocks up Court Street ever found their way to Romano's. In here, time stood still. Nothing much had changed since her great-grandfather, Angelo Romano, had opened the place in 1934.

And Gemma liked it that way. Really, she did. But it was an undeniable fact that some handsome, age-appropriate stranger was never going to wander into Romano's and fall in love with her across the brass rail.

"You're pretty quiet tonight, Gemma," Frank said.

"Just realizing all the Prince Charmings seem to have moved out of Brooklyn, Frank."

"A pretty girl like you should be beating them off with a stick," Dennis said.

"Yeah, well, I don't see a line forming outside, do you?"

"You should do the online dating thing," Frank said. "You'd be surprised how many people there are out there. Your sister helped me with my profile. Maybe she could do yours, too."

"Been there, done that, Frank, and it wasn't pretty."

Her attempts at online dating in the past had been nothing but a litany of disasters. There had been the guy who spent their entire date reading her the text exchange he'd just had with his ex-girlfriend and asking her what he should say to win her back. Then there was the guy who asked her, over appetizers, if she was into threesomes. Then there was the guy who still lived at home—which wasn't a problem…this was New York, rents were crazy. Gemma still lived at home, too. Except that he brought his *mother* on their date. And that didn't cover all the guys she never even went on dates with after enduring bizarre, creepy, or downright disgusting text exchanges.

Yeah, the modern dating pool was grim, and Gemma was in no hurry to jump back in.

Turning away, she dumped some dirty glasses into a plastic bin behind the bar and examined herself in the big mirror. Okay, so maybe her look—messy ponytail, minimal makeup, a tank top, and jeans—was a little uninspired. But there hardly seemed any point in dressing up every day just to stand behind the bar and pour refills for Dennis and Frank.

"Maybe I need to step up my game," she mused out loud, turning to the side to examine her profile. Her boobs still looked as good as they always had, and her ass was still pretty perky. "I mean, I *am* thirty."

"You're *thirty*?" Dennis exclaimed. "How is that possible?"

"I remember her when she was no higher than my knee," Frank said with a wistful smile. "Where do the years go?"

"Exactly," Gemma muttered under her breath. "But I'm holding up pretty well, right guys?"

"You haven't changed a bit."

But that wasn't Dennis or Frank, or any of the other old-timers in the bar. That was a much younger and hotter voice, one that set off an avalanche of memories and emotions. Her eyes sought out the front door in the mirror.

*No.* This could not be real. That was not *him*, in her bar, after all these years.

She spun around to look at him face-to-face. He hadn't changed either. No, that wasn't true. He'd filled out some since high school, with broader shoulders than she remembered. And his face had lost every inch of boyish softness. Now he was all hard edges and chiseled hotness and *oh my god* Brendan Flaherty was *back*.

## Chapter Two

Brendan walked across the bar and Gemma was catapulted back in time to Sacred Heart Catholic High School. The school uniform of Brendan's teenage years had been replaced by a suit—a sharp gray spendy-looking one. His once-unruly head full of golden ginger waves was shorter, darker. Money looked good on him.

His eyes were focused on her with a fierce intensity as he advanced on her. She couldn't believe this was happening. After all these years, he just *showed up* in her bar? Bold of him to assume she'd be okay with that. She'd just squared her shoulders and lifted her chin in preparation to toss him out when Dennis and Frank swiveled around and caught sight of him.

"Brendan Flaherty? Is that you, son?"

Brendan's eyes slid away from Gemma as he turned to face Dennis and Frank. "Yes, it's me. How are you, Dennis?"

"Ah, fine. Same old, same old around here."

Did he have to make it sound so dreary? Good ol' Romano's Bar, slowly crumbling into the ground, along with everyone in it.

"Frank." Dennis clapped his buddy on the shoulder.

"You remember Brendan? Mike Flaherty's kid, God rest his soul."

"Sure, I remember you! Look at you all grown up. It's been…what?"

"Fourteen years." Three sets of eyes turned to look at her. "It's been fourteen years," she repeated, then cleared her throat. "What brings you back to these parts, Flaherty? Slumming it for old times' sake?"

His gaze shifted back to her, sending an unexpected shock of electricity down her spine. He'd changed a lot, but those eyes were just the same. The color of melted milk chocolate, and just as beautiful as the rest of him. It had been a long time since she'd been on the receiving end of that look of his. Like he was irritated and impressed by her all at once. How dare he come in here flashing that look at her like it would still work after all these years? After what he'd done?

"Actually, Gemma, I came to see how you were doing."

Bracing her hands far apart on the bar, she leaned forward and smiled. "Here I am, right where you left me."

Because that's what he'd done fourteen years ago. He'd left and never looked back. And there was no way she was going to make his sudden return easy for him by pretending everything was fine, pretending they were just old friends catching up. Because they weren't.

Dennis and Frank might be delighted to see him again, but she intended to make this as unpleasant as possible for him. He'd earned it.

Something flickered in his eyes and his smiled faded slightly.

"Can I—"

"Walk out the way you came in? Sure. There's the door."

"Get a drink," he finished after a beat, staring her down.

"Sure, sure!" Frank answered for him, absolutely oblivious to Gemma's simmering antipathy. He pointed to the empty bar stool next to him. "Sit down and have a drink. Tell us what you've been up to."

"Brendan's been busy making his millions." She flashed him another bright, false smile. "Isn't that right, Brendan?"

"Ahh... I've been working in building construction."

That was an interesting way to put it. Because she knew, from ill-advised Google searches guiltily done in the middle of the night, that he'd been working for his uncle since he left, developing multimillion-dollar luxury high-rises all over Chicago and the Midwest. Building construction was a laughably quaint way to describe it.

"Well, let me and Dennis buy you a drink and you can tell us all about it. What'll you have?"

Damn. There went her plan to kick him out as quickly as he'd come in.

He glanced back at her. "I'm not too sure Gemma wants me hanging around, guys."

Oh, of all the transparent, manipulative ploys. He knew Dennis and Frank were going to back him up. And sure enough, Frank charged in to do so.

"Oh, sure she does. You kids went to high school together, didn't you?"

Gemma let out a snort of laughter. Sure, she'd gone to high school with Brendan. She'd spent months following him around like a lovesick fool, sneaking kisses in every corner and stairwell in Brooklyn, spinning ridiculous fantasies about true love and happily ever afters. Oh, yeah, she also lost her virginity to him. And then…he left.

But Dennis and Frank didn't know all that backstory. Almost nobody did. And she knew when she'd been beat.

"Fine," she exhaled, rolling her eyes. "Stay and have a drink."

Brendan smiled at her. She didn't return it, staring him down until he turned his attention to the taps instead. "I thought you might have—"

"Moved to Paris? Become an astronaut? Married Gavin Rossdale? Nope, just a bartender in Brooklyn, thanks for asking."

His eyebrows hiked. "I thought you might have more beers on tap."

"Just Michelob, Bud, and Bud Light. Works just fine for the regulars around here. We've got Sam Adams in bottles, if you're too fancy for that now."

Brendan gave her another one of those tight exasperated-turned-on smiles, which she knew must have been fake because there was no way Brendan Flaherty was turned on by her. Not anymore.

"Bud Light," he said at last.

"You got it."

"So what you been up to, kid?"

Brendan sat on the stool next to Frank, folding his hands together on the bar. God, did she remember those hands. During the intervening years, she'd been disappointed to discover not every man was as talented or creative in using theirs as Brendan had been. It sucked that her first had been some sort of freaking sex prodigy. No man since had ever measured up, and she still hated him for that.

"Oh, you know. Nose to the grindstone and all that," he said with a dismissive shrug.

"You work for your uncle, right?"

Gemma set his beer down in front of him just as he said, "Not anymore." His eyes flashed up to hers and she started. He left his uncle's company? That was surprising. Last she'd heard they'd been conquering the world together.

"Did you get a better job offer?" Frank asked.

"No, I went into business for myself."

Dennis whistled in appreciation. "I bet you'll outdo your uncle, huh?"

"Well, we'll see," Brendan said modestly. Gemma suppressed the urge to roll her eyes. "It's new. We're just getting our feet under us. But I hope it does well. How are things around here?"

"Oh, well, you know, Antonelli's closed—"

"And Lou Bertoni died last winter—"

"They sold the old First Federal building. Turning it into condos—"

"John Romano's got a girlfriend now—"

Gemma tuned out Frank and Dennis's recital of Carroll Gardens minutia, watching Brendan as he smiled politely and nodded at all the appropriate places. What the hell was he doing here? From the look of the suit and that seriously expensive titanium watch he was wearing, he'd found all the money and success he was chasing when he left Carroll Gardens. And here he was, back again, and sitting in Romano's. Why?

If he was just back visiting old friends, then the last place he'd have wandered into was Romano's. Because the way they'd left things, they *definitely* weren't friends anymore.

Was he just there to take a victory lap through the neighborhood? Flash his cash at everyone who hadn't made it out like him? If so, then coming to wave his success in *her* face was particularly vicious. But somehow she didn't get the feeling that was it. Frank and Dennis had given him plenty of openings to brag and he had shut them down, deflecting their questions.

His sudden reappearance was a total mystery, and even more mysterious was the fact that she was standing there trying to puzzle him out. Why should she care why he came back? Brendan Flaherty was most decidedly not her problem. He didn't deserve to take up real estate in her brain. That had all been over and done fourteen years ago.

He hadn't spared a thought for her as he sailed off into a glorious future she couldn't begin to imagine. Now he was back, transformed and hotter than he'd ever been. And she was still there, right where he left her, and exactly the same.

Suddenly the timeless atmosphere of Romano's felt a little bit like a tomb.

"Hey, Gemma," Frank said. "Can we get another round? On me."

"Sorry, Frank, it's closing time."

Brendan eyed her skeptically. "It's barely eleven."

"I'm in charge, I decide when we close. And it's now."

"Oh, sure, sure." Frank fished his wallet out of his back pocket and threw a few paltry bills on the bar. "Time for us old stiffs to clear out."

Gemma scooped up the cash. Tonight's register receipts probably wouldn't even cover the cost of turning on the lights, never mind paying her anything for the hours she'd spent there.

"I bet you got a hot date, right, Gem?" Dennis asked, hiking himself off his bar stool.

She had a hot date with a glass of wine, some episodes of *The Great British Bake Off*, and her dog, but she'd be damned if she'd admit that in front of Brendan.

"You know it, Dennis."

"You're really closing up?" Brendan asked, fixing her with that stupid, melting-chocolate gaze. He still had a hint of the freckles he'd sported in high school. She hadn't noticed until now, when he was staring at her from two feet away. They didn't make him look boyish anymore, though. They made him look burnished, dusted with bronze, gilt-edged and gorgeous. Definitely too expensive for her.

She cleared her throat and waved a hand at the empty room behind him. "No reason to stay open. So out you go."

He watched her in silence for another moment. She refused to look away, even though her stomach was in knots. *Oh please, just go back to your penthouse in the sky and let me be*, she prayed.

"Guess I'll see you around then, Gemma."

"You know where to find me."

He smiled, a small, private smile. "Yes, I do."

Then he turned and left, Frank and Dennis talking his ear off the whole way out. Gemma let out her breath for the first time in what felt like hours.

# Chapter Three

Gemma took her time closing up, drying the last of the glassware after washing it instead of leaving it to air-dry overnight, and checking the levels on the kegs before emptying the register and shutting off the lights.

Outside, the neighborhood was quiet and dark. Good thing she'd closed up early. There would have been no more customers tonight anyway. Reaching over her head, she grasped the bottom of the steel roll gate and gave a massive pull to get it moving. It didn't budge, as usual. The goddamned thing was a menace. It needed to be replaced, but for now, that stayed on a long list of upgrades they couldn't afford. She blew out a frustrated breath and pulled harder.

"Need a hand?"

"Jesus," she gasped as she spun around and spotted Brendan leaning on the lamppost on the corner. "Don't sneak up on me like that."

"I wasn't sneaking up, I was waiting."

"Why?" She turned her back on him, reached for the stubborn security gate and yanked on it again. Brendan came to join her, grasped the security gate and got the stupid thing moving with one effortless tug.

"I got it started for you," she grumbled, crouching to lock the padlock.

Brendan cast a look up and down Court Street. "Do you always close up alone? It doesn't seem safe."

"I'm a big girl," she replied as she stood.

"I can see that," he murmured. And damn if his eyes didn't dart down the length of her body as she straightened.

Gemma ignored that frank once-over. Plenty of guys looked. It didn't mean anything. Hoisting her bag onto her shoulder, she planted her hands on her hips. "One: I'm not always alone. Dad's off tonight. Two: half the guys in this bar are cops, along with most of my extended family, and everybody around here knows that. And three: I'm armed."

Brendan choked on a laugh. "Really?"

"Really. You're lucky I didn't blow a hole in you when you snuck up on me like that." Not that he'd been in any real danger. She'd been in gun safety courses since she was a teenager. But nothing wrong with keeping him on his toes.

"I told you, I wasn't sneaking, I was waiting."

"And I'm asking again, why?"

"We didn't get a chance to catch up earlier."

"Catch up? What exactly are we supposed to catch up about?" She thought she'd played it pretty cool when he came in earlier, but she wasn't sure she could maintain this front of disinterestedness one-on-one. They had way too much history together.

"How are your sisters?"

"Seriously?"

"Seriously."

"I need to get home." She turned away and started

off down the sidewalk, tugging her jacket closed against the cold.

"No problem," he said, turning to follow her. "I'll walk with you."

Gemma stumbled to a halt. "What are you doing?"

"Walking with you. I remember the way." He stuffed his hands in his pockets and grinned, the first full smile she'd seen on his face in years. Oh, she'd forgotten the power of that smile—his bright white teeth, those dimples that were more like slashes bracketing his mouth. Brendan's smile had always been disarming. Now it was downright deadly.

"Suit yourself," she muttered, turning around and stomping away. He caught up. Of course.

"So…" he tried again. "Your sisters?"

Okay, *fine*. Maybe if she satisfied the fleeting burst of nostalgia and curiosity that had made him seek her out, he'd go away and leave her in peace for another fourteen years. Or forever.

"My sisters are doing great. Jess is a reporter for the *Brooklyn Daily Post*. Oh, and she's engaged."

"Jessica's *engaged*? She's just a kid!"

"It's been fourteen years. Kids grow up."

"Who's the guy? You like him?"

"Alex? What's not to like? Rich, handsome, polite, and heir to a media empire."

Brendan processed that for a moment. "Alex…as in Alex *Drake*?"

"That's the one."

"Jessica is engaged to *Alex Drake*?"

"Yep. You know him?"

"I know *of* him." His elbow brushed against hers as he dodged a teenager walking a dog.

"Of course you do," she said under her breath, putting some space between them again. "The rich hang together, I guess."

He ignored her biting comment. "What about Livie?"

"Grad school, getting her PhD in Astrophysics. She's in Colorado. She's got a guy, too, now. Some rich-as-sin computer expert. He followed her out there." She still wasn't sure how much to trust Nick DeSantis, but Livie was head over heels in love with him, and everything Nick had done indicated he felt the same about Livie, so…she guessed that meant the little criminal was sticking around.

"Wow, Livie, all the way out in Colorado. Hard to imagine. You must miss her."

How dare he ask the questions about her life that were sure to press on all her tender spots? Like he still knew her or something.

"I do." She missed Livie so much it was hard to breathe sometimes. It was inevitable that her sisters would grow up and move on with their lives. She was so proud of both of them. And if sometimes the echoing silence of their house was enough to drive her crazy, that was her problem to deal with.

"How's your dad?"

Her elbow brushed his. This time she was the one who'd drifted closer. Adjusting her bag on her shoulder, she moved away again. "Fine. Great. Dad's great."

"Did I hear one of the guys say he's dating?"

"Teresa. His girlfriend."

"She the first one since your mom died?"

"Yep."

"That's a long time."

"Well, Mom was Dad's first love. Sometimes you

don't get over that." Thank God she hadn't spent years of her life hung up on Brendan Flaherty the same way. He wasn't worth that kind of devotion.

"He did, though."

She shot him a quick look, unsure how to interpret that expression on his face. "Eventually, yeah. He did." At the corner of her street, she paused. "This is my block."

He stopped too, watching her. The orange glow of the sodium streetlight did unfair things to his bone structure. "Yeah, I remember."

"You don't need to walk me home."

"I know."

She huffed in frustration. Why wasn't he leaving? After all, Brendan Flaherty was a pro at leaving. "You're really just gonna keep following me?"

"Unless you tell me to go. Are you telling me to go?" He slid his hands into his pockets and hiked an eyebrow. His lips twitched as he suppressed a smile.

Cocky bastard. She should tell him to go fuck himself all the way back to Chicago and enjoy his gilded life there. She had no idea why she hadn't done it yet. Sick, morbid curiosity, maybe? The same curiosity that fueled those shameful late-night Google searches. Maybe she needed this peek at his adult self so she could quit wondering once and for all.

"Ugh, whatever."

His grin broke free. She turned and stomped up the sidewalk, just to avoid being blasted with another dose of that irritating, intoxicating smile.

He followed, easily matching his stride to hers. They'd always been physically in sync. In a whole lot of ways. He'd moved with a sort of barely restrained exuberance when he was younger, all boundless energy and physical power. That had been tempered by the years. Now he walked like a man supremely comfortable with his place in the world. Easy, confident, infuriatingly sexy.

"So," he asked. "Is Kendra still around?"

"Yep. Kendra's still around. She's exactly the same." Her cousin Kendra had been an irrepressible force of nature in high school, and hadn't changed a bit in that regard. She was also the only person in Gemma's family who knew about Brendan.

When she and Brendan had first collided in that white-hot blaze of teenage passion, it had only been a couple of months since her mother had died. Their family had still been shell-shocked. Her father had been barely holding things together. Jess and Livie had been ten and eleven, respectively—far too young to lose their mother forever—not that it had been any easier for Gemma. But they'd needed her more and suffered more when she'd died. Gemma's job was to be strong, to help hold them all together, to take care of her sisters as her father did his best to fight his way back to the land of the living.

Falling in love with Brendan had felt unspeakably selfish. How could she bring him home to her family, all full of happiness and hearts and flowers, when they were still deep in the throes of mourning? So she never brought him home, at least not when anybody had been there to meet him. She didn't keep him a secret so much as she just didn't tell anyone about him. It was harder to hide what was between them when they were in school together, though, especially since Kendra was in the same year as her. Luckily, Kendra was good at keeping secrets and a sucker for drama.

Gemma had planned to tell her family all about Brendan eventually, when things were less raw. She'd desperately wanted to bring him home and introduce him to everyone, certain that they'd love him as much as she did. But he left town before that could happen. And after he was gone, there hadn't seemed much point in telling anyone about him, so he was still her secret.

"Hasn't changed much, has it?"

His voice startled her back to the present. That eighteen-year-old boy in a Catholic school uniform faded away, replaced by this grown man in an expensive suit, inexplicably walking at her side again after all these years. She shivered in discomfort.

"The new people have more money." She tipped her head toward one of the row houses they were passing. The new owners had ripped up the old front yard and replaced it with a formal Japanese garden in miniature. "Things change."

He gestured to Mrs. Maratelli's house across the street and the icon of the Virgin in her front yard. "And some things don't."

She wasn't interested in whatever point he was trying to make. Time to turn the tables and put him on the spot for a while. "So what about you?"

"What about me?"

"What prompted this trip down memory lane after all this time?"

"It's more than a trip down memory lane."

"Please don't try to sell me a timeshare or get me to join Scientology. It's not gonna happen."

Brendan threw his head back and laughed. "I pity the timeshare salesman who tries to get one past you, Gemma."

"What's that supposed to mean?"

"Just that you're one of the smartest, most streetwise women I know. You always have been."

She scowled, uncomfortable with his compliment… if that's what that was.

"Okay, so you're not forming a cult. Why are you slumming it back in Brooklyn?"

"Because I live here now."

Her stomach turned over in slow motion and the ground suddenly felt unsteady. She stopped, absorbing his words. "What?"

"I told you I wasn't working for my uncle anymore? That I founded my own company?"

"You told Frank, not me, but yeah. So?"

"It's here. In Carroll Gardens. And so am I. My apartment is right around the corner." He grinned at her again, unabashedly enjoying her shock. "Guess that makes us neighbors again."

Brendan turned around and kept walking. Gemma gaped after him. He glanced back over his shoulder. "Gemma? Your house? It's this way."

Slowly, she started moving again, still processing this colossal piece of news. Brendan wasn't just back for a visit. Brendan was *back*. And apparently living right around the corner from her. This wasn't just one uncomfortable night to be endured. She'd see him again. Maybe a lot. Oh, God…there wasn't enough scathing snark in the world for that.

He probably still had family here and had to have come back for a visit now and then. But as the years passed and they'd never crossed paths, she'd figured he wasn't back for very long…or that maybe he'd avoided her on purpose. But tonight was no accident, no unlucky crossing of paths. He'd come to her bar seeking her out on purpose. Fuck. Maybe she wished he'd stayed invisible after all.

"It's not often Gemma Romano is speechless," he teased. "Guess I played that one right."

"Don't pat yourself on the back too hard, Flaherty. You just surprised me, that's all. Why here?" She needed to get herself together. This didn't matter. Not one bit.

He shrugged, looking around at the row houses with something she'd have been tempted to describe as longing if she didn't know better. "Why not? It's home."

"It hasn't been for fourteen years!" she blurted out, with a lot more passion than she'd intended. She might be still nursing some bruised feelings where Brendan Flaherty was concerned, but he didn't have to know that. In fact, she'd die if he did.

"This never stopped being home," he said, eyes on his feet. "It just took me a while to realize that."

"So…what? You just quit your uncle's business, walked away from all that, to open up shop in Brooklyn?"

"Pretty much."

She didn't know what to make of that. It didn't jive at all with everything she'd thought she knew about Brendan Flaherty. Then again, when he'd decided to leave fourteen years ago, that hadn't made sense to her either. Maybe it just meant she hadn't really known him all that well back then, and she still didn't.

"This is me," she murmured, stopping in front of the rusting black wrought iron fence in front of their narrow patch of front yard. She was uncomfortably aware of how scruffy the place looked in comparison to many of their newer, more upscale neighbors. The windowsills all needed repainting, and the windowpanes were grimed with a post-winter gray film. She'd meant to clean up their little front yard last spring, maybe plan out some actual landscaping for once. But spring had come and gone, and so had summer, and she'd never gotten around to it. Now another spring was right around the corner and the front yard was still just a mess of patchy grass and half-dead shrubs. Landscaping cost money and took time, and both were in short supply. The bar ate up everything.

She turned back to face Brendan, chin lifted in defiance, but he wasn't looking at the house or the yard. He was looking straight at her.

Behind her, on the far side of the yard, the house was dark and silent, and would stay that way. Livie and Jess had both moved out, and her father and Teresa were visiting Uncle Richie on City Island. Tonight, there would just be Gemma, all alone in that big, empty house.

Once upon a time, Gemma and Brendan and a house that would remain reliably empty for the night would have been the start of a sex marathon that would shock the world. But that was then.

Brendan looked over the worn red brick facade. "Nobody's home?" he said, like he could hear her thoughts. Once, it had felt like he could, and she could read his. She'd been wrong. The whole time, they'd had very different ideas about the future. And now here she was, living hers, the one she'd once thought would include him. And Brendan had been happily living his, the one that had never included her.

"Just me and Spudge," she said, without thinking.

Brendan went still. "You still have Spudge?"

She cleared her throat, keeping her eyes on her feet. "Sure. He's our dog. It doesn't matter where he came from."

*Brendan.* Spudge had been a gift from Brendan. God, it had been so long and Spudge had become such an integral part of the Romano family that she'd almost forgotten.

# Chapter Four

*April, fourteen years earlier*

"Can I come over?" Brendan's voice sent a shiver down Gemma's spine the second she answered the phone, all deep and rumbly and so hot.

"Now?" Gemma glanced furtively over her shoulder, which was ridiculous because she knew she was alone in the house.

"Come on, Gem. Just for a few minutes." He paused, breathing heavily into the phone. "Although if we've got more than a few minutes, I know how to use them."

God, how did he *do* that? One sentence and her knees had turned to liquid and her nipples had gone hard. He wasn't even *there*.

"We don't," she said, tucking the phone under her ear so she could use both hands to move the pot of sauce she was heating up to the back burner. "Dad's at the bar, but Livie and Jess will be home from their afterschool programs in less than an hour."

"We can do a lot in an hour, Gem."

"Stop!"

Brendan burst into laughter. "I'm kidding. That's

not why I want to come over. I have something for you. A present."

"You got me a present?" The idea set off a little burst of warmth in her heart. There hadn't been much celebrating around the Romano house since Mom died. Even Christmas had been barely acknowledged.

"Yes, so can I come by and give it to you?"

It would be cutting it close. If anybody found him there, she had no good explanation ready. But she couldn't help it. She needed to see him, touch him, kiss him, even if it was just for a few minutes. "Hurry."

Ten minutes later, she was rushing through the house to let him in before any of the neighbors spotted him. But she still paused to glance in the mirror in the entryway to smooth her hair down. She threw open the door, already smiling. It was hard to believe there was anything on earth that could distract her from Brendan, looking so incredibly hot in his white uniform shirt, green and navy repp tie, and dark pants. But there was one thing that could, and he was holding it in his arms.

"A puppy!"

As if he knew he was being spoken about, the floppy little brown dog in Brendan's arms began wiggling with delight, scrambling frantically to get to her. Laughing, she plucked him out of Brendan's hands and gathered him to her chest. The little guy immediately strained to lick her chin, her cheeks, anything he could reach.

"He's so cute! Whose is he?"

"Yours, if you want him," Brendan said, grinning as the dog licked her chin.

"He's for me?"

"You and your family. I thought your sisters might like him." He stuffed his hands in his pockets, sounding unsure of himself. Everybody thought Brendan Flaherty was so cool and confident. They overlooked this side of him, so sweet and thoughtful, eager to please. It was her favorite thing about him.

"Like him? Jess and Livie are going to *freak*. They need a happy surprise. Brendan, this is so nice. You don't even know them."

He shrugged, suddenly bashful. "I know, but I feel like I do. And I… Well, I mean, I hope I'll know them soon."

Gah. He was just the sweetest. She shifted the puppy in her arms and reached for his hand. "You know I want that, too. There's just a lot—"

He held up a hand to silence her. "I get it. It's okay. Dead dad, remember? Families are complicated."

It was the first thing they'd connected over. When she'd gone back to school after Mom's death, after the time off, after the holidays, it seemed nearly everyone in the school avoided her. It wasn't their fault. Teenagers weren't equipped to deal with unexpected deaths, especially of a parent. It wasn't that they didn't care. They just didn't know what to say or do, so they said and did nothing. Still, feeling the crowds in the hallways part like the Red Sea when she passed didn't make coming back to school any easier. During that first week, when she'd been hiding in the stairwell to eat lunch because she couldn't take one more sad, sideways glance or whisper in the cafeteria, Brendan had stumbled on her. Instead of skirting around her and avoiding eye contact, he sat down and started talking.

She'd known who he was, of course. Everybody did. Brendan Flaherty was a senior, smart, popular, well liked…and one of the hottest guys in school. He was on Sacred Heart's championship soccer team and made the honor roll every semester. Girls wanted to date him, guys wanted to be him, and the nuns who taught school all thought he walked on water.

Gemma had spoken to him once or twice in passing, but they weren't really friends. That day, unprompted, he sat down next to her and started telling her all about losing his firefighter father on the job. Not in 9/11, like Gemma's Uncle Vincent and so many others. Just a run-of-the-mill warehouse fire in Bushwick a few months before 9/11, one that went badly wrong. His dad went to work and by the end of the day, he was gone, leaving Brendan, just twelve, alone to support his grieving mother and his bewildered younger brother. He knew exactly what Gemma was going through.

Overnight, Brendan became her emotional safe space. While she put on a brave face at home, being strong and getting through it, with Brendan, she could cry. She could get angry. She could be selfish. He understood.

It hadn't taken long for their fragile new friendship to turn into a romance. And once it had, it had become nearly all consuming. After she'd stumbled through the previous weeks half dead in a fog of grief, Brendan made her feel intensely, completely alive. He'd healed her heart and, in the process, stolen it completely for himself.

Gemma buried her face in the puppy's warm, silky brown fur. "Where'd you get him?"

"A guy on the soccer team. His dog had puppies. They were up for grabs. You like him?"

"I *love* him. And I love *you*."

Grinning, he stepped forward, settling his hands on

her hips and drawing her in. When his lips met hers, she melted, so completely in love and in lust with him that she could barely remember her own name. He teased her lips apart, his tongue slipping in to touch hers, and she moaned. His hand slid over her hip, down her thigh, to the hem of her pleated plaid uniform skirt. His long, talented fingers toyed with the hem, tickling the sensitive skin of the back of her thigh.

"Gem," he groaned into her ear, and desire twisted through her body like a live wire. That voice of his, the way he said her name, it just wrecked her every time.

God, she wanted him, too. She wanted his hand sliding up the inside of her thigh. She wanted him to stroke her and tease her until she was shaking and undone.

The puppy broke the moment, wiggling in her arms, reaching up to lick Brendan's cheek.

They reluctantly broke apart. Brendan blew out a breath of pure sexual frustration and raked a hand through his sandy red-blond hair. Gemma felt just as tied in knots.

He glanced up, meeting her gaze. "Can you get away today?"

Ugh, it was impossible. Jess and Livie would be home soon, and there was homework to get through and dinner to make. Dad would come home briefly for dinner, but he had to go back to the bar for the evening shift, so she had to stay home with her sisters and get them off to bed. Then there were tomorrow's lunches to pack, and then her own homework to do. But after all that…maybe. Maybe if last call wasn't too late, she could sneak out after Dad got home for the night.

"I'll try. After last call, if it's not too late. The backyard."

There was a little run-down garden shed in Brendan's

tiny backyard. They'd made use of it so often, Brendan had it practically fully furnished at this point.

His hand tightened on her hip briefly before he released her.

"I'm going to have to explain where he came from," she said, trying to clear her head. As badly as she wanted him, it wasn't going to happen for hours, if at all.

"Tell your dad he's a present from a friend. A special present. And wait until your sisters have seen him first. Once they're in love with him, he won't be able to say no."

"Guilt. That'll work. He'll have to let us keep him if he's a gift. What's his name?"

"He's your dog. You name him."

Gemma held the puppy up under his front legs, looking into his liquid brown eyes. He squirmed in delight, trying to lap at her face. "A special present for Gemma," she said. "Spudge. What do you think? How about it, Spudge?"

Spudge wiggled in agreement.

"Spudge?" Brendan laughed. "What the hell does that mean?"

"Special present for Gemma," she explained. "S.P.G. Spudge. Every time I say his name, I'll remember he was a present from you."

He grinned, lowering his face to kiss her again. "Then Spudge is perfect, because I never want you to forget."

## Chapter Five

She forgot.

How could she have forgotten where Spudge got his name? She said it every day, without once remembering that moment with Brendan.

When she looked up at him again, he was still watching her. That moment from fourteen years ago felt like a heavy fog, still clinging to them both in the here and now. "How is Spudge these days?"

"Tired," she said, with a little more force than necessary. "He's getting old."

The corner of Brendan's mouth ticked up, a flicker of a smile. "But he's hanging in there, huh? Maybe I'll come visit him soon."

*Visit him?* Like he was going to waltz into her house after all these years and just *visit* her dog? "Hey—"

"I'd better go," Brendan said, cutting her off. And when she would have continued anyway, he stepped forward, suddenly filling up her personal space. And stealing her breath. "It was good to see you again, Gemma."

"I—" She had no idea what to say to that. Had tonight been good? Disturbing. Not in the troubling sense. In the sense that all sorts of memories and feelings that were supposed to have long ago been laid to rest had been disturbed. Now she was lost in the stirred-up dust cloud, not sure which way to go to get out. And Brendan standing there close enough to touch wasn't helping to clear the air.

He was so tall. She used to love that about him. She'd hit five foot ten by the time she was fourteen. She was used to looking guys in the eye—and forget about heels. But Brendan towered over her. When he'd stood near her like that, he'd made her feel protected, like she was sheltering behind a large, sturdy tree out of the wind. What a ridiculous idea. There had been nothing safe or secure about Brendan.

This place, this moment—the dark street in front of her house, the hot guy standing inches away—was messing with her head. It sent her tumbling back through time, and she was awash in the emotions of a younger Gemma, full of all sorts of giddy longing. But all that was over, just leftover memories from another time in her life. None of it was real.

She shook herself and straightened. Time to go inside and clear her head. "I'd better—"

"Gem?"

Nobody had ever said her name in that particular tone and timbre. Just the sound of his murmured, deep, throaty "Gem" brought back an avalanche of sense memories, most of them incredibly filthy.

"Yeah?"

He dipped his face toward hers and her heart took off at a gallop. He was going to kiss her. Again, she fell back in time, swept away in emotions that she'd long ago left behind. The emotions might be gone, but the memory of them was surprisingly potent. It was the only thing that explained why she stood there, letting him get closer, letting him move in. Grown up, savvy Gemma would have shoved him away—maybe slapped his face for good measure. But grown up Gemma had fled, leaving behind a trembling shadow of her teenage self.

Every nerve ending in her body tingled with anticipation. Her lips parted, waiting for the pressure of his mouth on hers. He was no more than a breath away, so close she could feel the heat of his body. Then, just as her eyes slid closed, she felt it. But not on her mouth. He left her hanging there in a stunned tangle of lust and confusion as he pressed a chaste kiss *to her cheek*.

She blinked, her eyes fluttering open again. Brendan was smiling down into her face, his eyes gentle, his expression soft, an echo of another boy in another time.

"I'll see you around the neighborhood, Gem."

Then he turned and walked off down the sidewalk.

Gemma stayed frozen, stunned by what had just happened, one hand gripping the wrought iron fence behind her for support like she'd collapse without it, shaking with reawakened lust, and the bastard had just casually strolled off into the night.

"Ugh!" Muttering angrily to herself, she stomped up the path through the front garden, and up the steps of the front stoop. "Asshole!" she growled, stabbing her key into the lock and letting herself in. Spudge was there, right inside the door, sitting in a saggy brown heap, his tail thumping on the wooden floor as he gazed up at her in hopeful adoration. He let out a doggy groan of greeting and pressed his graying muzzle against her hand.

"Yes, he's back," she told him. "And no, you traitor, you are absolutely not allowed to have him over to visit!"

## Chapter Six

As Brendan neared the house he'd grown up in, he could see the work that needed to be done. Flying in once or twice a year for a day to check in hadn't allowed him to keep an eye on the place, so he paid a guy, someone for his mother to call if there was a leak in the roof or a problem with the plumbing. But big old houses needed constant upkeep, stuff you could only do if you were there full time.

He sent money, but it was obvious he was going to have to be hands-on if anything was going to get done. He'd need to get someone in to check the roof, the furnace, maybe update the electrical… The list was long enough to have him feeling exhausted before he'd even begun. After so many years of shouldering the responsibility on his own, he should be used to the weight by now.

It felt strange, to knock on the door of the house he'd grown up in, but he hadn't lived there in fourteen years. It wasn't his home anymore, despite the money he'd poured into it. That wasn't for him, though, that was for his mother.

"I got it, Mom," Tim said, approaching the other side of the door. "Hey! It's my big brother!"

"It's Doctor Flaherty!" It was still hard to believe that his little brother was all grown up and saving lives. If he ever started feeling bitter about the hand fate had dealt him, thinking about Tim and all he had and would accomplish was enough to turn that around. Brendan might have made his share of mistakes, but Tim was the one thing he'd gotten right.

Tim lightly punched his arm. "Nah, cut it out with that stuff. You can just call me Doctor Tim."

Brendan laughed, pulling him into a brief, backslapping hug.

"How's it going?" Tim asked when they pulled away.

"Good. Can't complain."

"How is it being back in the old neighborhood?"

Brendan took a brief look around at the street he'd grown up on, but he wasn't thinking of the familiar brownstones and storefronts from his childhood. He was thinking about Gemma Romano, glaring at him across the bar last night with those flashing dark eyes, looking somehow a thousand times hotter than she had at sixteen. "It's been interesting," he finally said. Interesting and exciting in ways he had never expected.

"Come on in. Mom's waiting for you."

He'd been home to visit in the intervening years, but something about being back for good made him see the place with new eyes as he followed Tim through the living room and dining room, to the kitchen in the back of the house. It was like time stood still in there. Nothing had changed since he was a kid, with the exception that everything was older, more worn out.

His mother turned away from the kitchen counter, her face lighting up with a smile when she saw him. "Brendan!" she cried brightly.

She looked good. There was a time, years ago, when she'd looked far older than her years, her face creased with worry and sadness. But Brendan had worked his ass off to make sure she had nothing to worry about anymore.

"Hey, Mom." He leaned down to kiss her cheek. "How are you doing?"

Her hands fluttered around her face like little birds. "Oh, I'm fine. You look like you've lost weight, Brendan."

"No, Mom, I haven't." She always thought he'd lost weight. It was the one worry about him she never seemed to shake.

"Oh, well…" She looked momentarily confused before she shook her head. "I thought we could eat outside since the day is so nice."

It was early March, but the day was unseasonably warm, a taste of the spring soon to come. "Sure. Let's enjoy the warmth while we can, right, Tim?"

"We just got another foot of snow in Buffalo, so I am all about soaking up a little sunshine."

"Just give me a minute to finish up," she said, turning back to the counter.

"Can we help with anything?"

"Oh, no. It's just sandwiches. Nothing fancy. I just don't cook all that much anymore."

"It's fine, Mom." He and Tim exchanged a brief look. When they were kids, his mother's cooking had been so legendary in the neighborhood that their friends had begged them for invites to dinner. Just one of the many things from their childhood that had been lost when their dad died. In a lot of ways, they'd lost Mom then, too.

She'd never been the same after Dad died. Losing him the way she had would throw anyone. But what he understood now that he hadn't when he was a kid was that she just wasn't someone good at handling her adult life, or any of the problems and catastrophes it could throw at you. While she'd been married, she hadn't really had to handle anything. Dad had dealt with the bills, maintained the house, made sure the car ran well. Mom raised the kids and spent her days volunteering at school and cooking for her husband's firehouse buddies.

Then Dad was gone in an instant, and she hadn't just lost her husband and the father of her children, she'd had the supports knocked out from under her entire life. She'd been thoroughly unprepared to handle it all herself. Then the hits just kept coming at them, and by the end of it, Claire Flaherty was a shell of herself. If she'd been bad at coping with life before, by the end of their trials, she was utterly incapable of it. Brendan had spent the intervening years doing all that he could to make sure she didn't have to. It was the least he could do.

As he watched her puttering between the counter and the fridge, frequently forgetting what she'd gone to get and having to turn back around, she seemed more disconnected than he remembered. She'd been okay while Tim had still been living at home, going to medical school at Columbia. But since he'd left for his residency, she'd been alone most of the time, and it wasn't good for her.

Tim was chatting with her, keeping her entertained, so Brendan took the opportunity to check out the rest of the house and see how things were holding up. Upstairs, apart from her bedroom, the rest of the rooms looked untouched. His old bedroom was like a time capsule of his senior year in high school. Running his fingers along the dusty surface of his dresser, he wondered idly if any mementos of his time with Gemma had survived in here.

But he'd satisfy his curiosity about that some other day. Right now, he was trying to get a feel for how Mom was doing on her own. First off, he definitely needed to hire a cleaning person for her. She seemed to have let that go, along with cooking. Up the next flight of stairs, the third floor felt like a tomb. His shoes left imprints in the dust on the stairs. How long had it been since she'd been up there? Maybe the house was just too much for her to manage now.

For most people, coming home was comforting. It was supposed to make you feel safe and taken care of. But it hadn't been that way for Brendan since his father died. Home just meant responsibilities, people to worry about. Sometimes he wished it had been different, that he'd been the one to be taken care of. But it hadn't been and never would be, and that was okay. He'd made sure Mom and Tim had a home they could count on, and that was enough.

Back downstairs, Mom had finished making lunch, and Tim was just coming back in from clearing off the table in the backyard.

"Don't get out there much, do you, Mom?"

She shrugged. "Seems like a lot of bother when it's just me."

Brendan made himself useful carrying plates and glasses outside and then held her chair out for her as his mother got settled.

She smiled tremulously at them. "It's so nice, having both you boys home for a visit."

Brendan glanced quickly at Tim. "Mom, I moved back, remember? I'm here for good now." Had she forgotten that already?

She let out a soft scoff. "Buy yourself a place in the city if you want, but your job is in Chicago, Brendan."

He set his glass down. "Mom, I don't work for Walsh anymore. You know this."

Across the table, his mother stared at him in dismay. "Brendan, you just can't do that. Not after everything Jimmy has done for you."

"I'll always be grateful to Jimmy for the opportunities he gave me."

"So grateful you'd quit your job and leave him in the lurch?"

Brendan couldn't help but laugh. "Mom, he's not single-handedly running the place like it's a deli or something. There are a thousand people lining up to take my job. Look, I got invaluable experience with Jimmy—"

"He taught you everything you know."

He took a deep, measured breath through his nose. She couldn't help it, he told himself. After his father, her brother, James Walsh, was the man she relied on most, and she was lost without a man to rely on. He'd made sure he was that man now, arranging her life for her so that she never encountered an obstacle or a difficulty, but she still couldn't help seeing her brother as her personal savior. "I won't forget it. I haven't. But I'm interested in going in a different direction than Walsh, so I started my own company."

"That's gratitude. He trains you and you stab him in the back by becoming his competition."

"Mom, Walsh could buy and sell my company a dozen times over. I'm not his competition."

"But he relies on you. You know he doesn't have any kids of his own. You're supposed to take over."

That allegation stung a bit, because it was true. Jimmy had been grooming him to helm the corporation for fourteen years. But his eyes had been opened about who and what Jimmy Walsh was, and he couldn't close them again, no matter how much money he could have made with him. Some things mattered more than money.

"He'll find somebody new to rely on." Besides, the day Jimmy Walsh was sentimental about family... But he wouldn't say that to his mother. She would just refuse to hear it. Her adored older brother could do no wrong in her eyes.

"Mom, have I told you about my rotation through pediatrics?" Tim interjected, trying to divert her attention.

"Pediatrics?" she echoed.

"I loved it. I'm thinking of specializing in pediatrics. Of course that'll require an additional residency, and another three years."

Brendan watched their mother as Tim outlined his plans. She'd always been dreamy and a little distracted, but she seemed to be retreating further into herself. She was alone too much. Now that he was back in the neighborhood, he could make sure she got out more and engaged with the world.

After cleaning up from lunch, Brendan slipped out into the backyard again while Tim put on a pot of coffee. The old garden shed was still there, tucked into the back corner of the yard, sliding more into decay with each passing year. The house on the street perpendicular to theirs had a driveway that ran along their back fence. That was how Gemma had slipped into his backyard and into the shed. Such a sad little heap of wood, but it lived on in his memories like a shrine.

The first time they'd had sex, it had been in that shed. The many subsequent times had all happened there, too. Over the months they'd been together, he'd snuck old cushions and blankets out there, attempting to make it more comfortable. It had still been freezing, dirty, and dark. They hadn't cared. In those heated moments, nothing had mattered beyond getting their hands on each other. Some of the best sex of his life had happened in that run-down shed. Other, less pleasant memories were made there, too. That's where he'd told her he was leaving. That's where she'd cried and begged him to change his mind, to choose her instead. What he hadn't been able to explain at the time was that he'd had no choice but to break her heart.

Over the years, he hadn't let himself remember too often, because dwelling on what he'd lost, what he'd never have again, just made it worse. But that didn't mean he didn't think about her. Maybe it was because of the way it had ended, or maybe it was because it had been that kind of hot, intense first love that left a permanent scar— whatever the reason, he'd never been able to fully exorcise her from his mind. He'd sought out Gemma hoping to finally lay the memories to rest. He'd been so sure he'd find her happily married, maybe raising some kids, that brief high school romance with him just a hazy memory for her. Maybe then—finally—his own memories would start to fade.

But she *wasn't* married. And that crazy electricity they'd shared as teenagers had unexpectedly come roaring back to life last night when he'd walked her home. She was different than he remembered. Of course she was. Thirty was a whole different ball game than sixteen. She had more hard edges and sharp points now. In all fairness, he was probably the person who'd put some of them there. That biting wit was new, too, although maybe that was just for his benefit. Her tough yet sweet sass was just the same. Last night, all she'd shown him was her anger, which was understandable. But he'd seen flashes of the tenderness he remembered when she'd dealt with Dennis and Frank. And when she talked about her sisters, the nurturing Gemma from before made a brief appearance. He suspected her heart was still as big as it had ever been, even if it was now closed to him.

Last night, a thought had been planted in his mind that he was having a hard time ignoring. He'd come back to Brooklyn to fix what had gone wrong in his life. He'd thought that meant his work and his mother. But there was one other terrible wrong he'd committed, and maybe he could fix that, too. He certainly wanted to try. He hadn't realized until he saw Gemma again that he'd never stopped missing her. He'd spent twenty years working for everyone else's happiness. Maybe it was finally his turn. He still wanted to lay to rest memories of high school Gemma, but now he wanted to fill that space up with who she was now, if she'd let him get close enough to discover it.

Behind him, the back door opened and Tim came out, carrying two cups of coffee, one of which he passed to Brendan.

"Still black?"

"Still black," he said, taking a sip. "Where's Mom?"

"Lying down for a minute. I think the excitement of having us both here wore her out."

Brendan sat down on the top step of the old wooden deck. Tim settled next to him, looking out over the back-yard, bare and scraggly after the winter. Brendan took after their father, tall, with the same red-gold hair and Irish freckles when he was younger. But Tim had Mom's coloring. Smaller and thin, with black hair, pale skin, and bright blue eyes. When they were kids, people had always been stunned to discover they were brothers.

"She's getting older," Tim said quietly.

"Yeah, I noticed. She seems a little out of it."

"So when we were doing our rotation through the Psych ward, this buddy of mine from my residency told me about his mother. She has dementia."

"You think Mom has *dementia*?"

Tim held up a hand. "No. Not that could be diag-nosed. But my friend, he told me that once they got the diagnosis for his mom, looking back, he could see warning signs that were there years earlier, long before anything became a problem."

"And you think Mom has warning signs?"

"I think," Tim said carefully, "that we should keep a close eye on her as she gets older."

Brendan sighed and ran a hand over his face. "I guess it's good I moved back."

Tim made a face. "I'm sorry, man. If I do this pediatrics specialty, I'm looking at four years of residency still to go, and—"

"Hey." Brendan cut him off. "Go do your residency. Don't worry about this. I got it." The last thing he'd do was truncate Tim's dreams. He'd worked too hard to make them possible.

Shaking his head, Tim clutched his coffee cup in both hands. "You've had it for way too long, Brendan. Getting me through college, sending money for Mom..."

He'd done a lot more than just send money to his mother, but if Tim knew the extent of it, he'd just feel worse.

"I was the one with the opportunities that allowed for that. I don't regret any of it." Which was true. He could be sorry for the way things had turned out fourteen years ago, but he couldn't regret what he'd done, because he'd never really had a choice. "I think the house is getting to be too much for her," he added.

"I noticed. What do you think we should do?"

Brendan thought through the idea he'd had during lunch. "I'm planning my next development, six units right here in the neighborhood, as soon as I secure the right properties. I was going to move into one unit myself. Maybe we could move Mom into another. Then she'd be right next to me, in a smaller space that would be easy to manage. I could take care of everything."

"What about the house?"

Brendan craned his head around, glancing up at the back of the three-story brick townhouse his father had inherited from his grandfather. "Maybe it's time to talk to Mom about selling up."

"What do you think it would go for?"

"Three million, easy."

Tim choked on his coffee. "Are you serious? Three million dollars? But nothing's upgraded."

"Yeah, which means original tiling and claw-foot tubs in the bathrooms. All the original hardwood floors. Four working fireplaces with period enamel tiling. I've been learning the market since I got back. A three-story, one-family house in Carroll Gardens, built in 1907 with all its original detailing? Three million is the bottom for this house."

Tim let out a low whistle. "That's a lot of money. Plenty to take care of Mom when the time comes. There are organizations I'd like to work for, nonprofits…places that do good work but pay for shit. I haven't really been considering it because I needed to help you out with Mom—"

"You don't need to worry about that. The money from the house will cover everything."

"You sure?"

"Mom will be fine. I'll make sure everything's set up for her when she needs it."

"When do you want to talk to her about selling?"

"We have time. I haven't even secured properties for my development yet."

Tim clapped him on the shoulder. "You will. I'm beginning to think you're Superman, Brendan."

He chuckled and shook his head. "I'm no superhero."

He didn't need to be a superhero. He was just trying to be one of the good guys after spending far too many years on the wrong side. Maybe he'd never really be able to do it. Sometimes the scale felt too far tipped in the wrong direction. But he was going to try. He wanted to be happy for once. He wanted his life back. And he wanted Gemma Romano back, too, even if he wasn't sure if he deserved her. He'd just have to do whatever it took to earn the chance.

## Chapter Seven

If there was one time of the week at Romano's that was sleepier than a Tuesday night, it was a Wednesday afternoon. The stillness, broken only by the background hum of some long-forgotten Mets game replaying on ESPN3 on the flat screen, did nothing to banish memories of the night before from Gemma's mind.

Her brain was in overdrive, replaying every moment of it, from the second Brendan had walked in the door until the second he'd kissed her cheek and walked off into the night. She was so *mad* at herself. For fourteen years, she'd been imagining revenge fantasies, practicing the epic "screw you" speech she'd give him in her head, ego crushing and ruthless. Then last night he'd finally been standing right there in front of her, all hot and confident and sexy, but instead of unloading on him like she'd so often dreamed, she froze, like a deer in headlights. Instead of telling him to go to hell and stay there, she'd gone all weak kneed and soft brained, and she'd actually let the bastard *kiss her cheek*. It was disgusting.

In an effort to distract herself from last night's disaster, she restocked every liquor bottle on the shelves. She even dusted them. Then she Windexed the mirror behind the bar, eliminating a year's worth of finger-prints and smudges. Then she polished the taps, which absolutely didn't need polishing. Nothing helped. The whole embarrassing, infuriating night ran on a constant loop in her head.

As the afternoon light faded in the front windows and the streetlights began to flicker on in the twilight up and down Court Street, the front door shrieked on its hinges—next she'd oil those bad boys—and Dennis shuffled in.

"Afternoon, Gemma. Get me a beer, would ya?"

"Sure thing, Dennis." She wiped her hands on the bar towel tucked into the waistband of her jeans. "Where's Frank?" She couldn't remember the last time she'd seen one of them without the other.

Dennis heaved himself up on his regular bar stool. "Got a *date*. Can you believe that?"

"What? Frank's got a *date*? Who with?"

"A lady he met online." Dennis slurped the foam off his pint glass as soon as Gemma set it down in front of him. "Veronica. He says he likes her."

"Wait…he's seen her before?"

"Oh, yeah. Only for lunch. That's what they do now. Lunch. Then the ladies don't have to worry about—" Dennis blinked, a blush suffusing his ruddy cheeks.

Gemma chuckled. "You mean women don't have to worry about being pressured for sex at the end of the night? You forget, Dennis, I've been dating online, too."

"Ah, you know I forget you're all grown up, Gem."

"Yep, I know the ropes." And once again, she was thinking about last night, about standing there on the sidewalk with Brendan, her dark empty house behind her, burgeoning with promise, and the wicked temptation of the hot man in front of her… Yeah, not gonna happen. "Well, I hope Frank has a great time with Veronica. He's been divorced for, what?"

"Fifteen years."

"Fifteen years! It's time, Dennis, don't you think? I mean, even my dad is dating again. Hey, we should sign you up!"

"Eh." Dennis shrugged. "My daughter wants to introduce me to someone. Some woman who lives near her. A widow like me. Marjory."

"See, there you go!"

"Nah, they live all the way down in Toms River."

"New Jersey isn't the moon, Dennis. Go visit your daughter and meet this woman."

Dennis seemed to consider this for a minute, so Gemma pressed her advantage.

"When was the last time you went to visit your daughter?"

"Too long," Dennis acknowledged.

"There you go. Plan a trip."

"Maddie's on me to move down there," Dennis said, rubbing a hand across the back of his neck.

"To Toms River?" That gave Gemma an unexpected pang. When she'd been urging Dennis to take a chance on love, she'd imagined him bringing a lady love home to Brooklyn. It hadn't occurred to her that Dennis might ever move away. But of course, that's what everyone was doing now. Why would a retiree move back to this neighborhood of skyrocketing rents and perpetual change? The old-timers were moving out, not in.

"Ah, that stuff's not for me. My place is here." Although Dennis sounded less certain of that than the words implied. What kind of place was this for Dennis anyway, Gemma suddenly wondered—all alone in some bar at six o'clock on a Wednesday? Maybe he'd be better off with his daughter in Toms River, chatting up the widow Marjory.

"Hey, Dennis, I made lasagne bolognese," she said briskly, dispelling the gloom. "Want some?"

Dennis's grin was bright enough to banish any pesky doubts or fears Gemma might have felt. "You know I'll eat cardboard if you cook it, Gem."

"Well, I can promise you, it's better than cardboard. Hang on."

She'd just returned from the back room with Dennis's plate when the front door shrieked open again. Damn, she really did need to get on those hinges.

"Oh. My. God."

"Hi, Kendra. Come on in. I'm serving dinner."

Gemma's cousin Kendra strolled across the bar with a loose-limbed, sexy confidence that would have turned every head in the room, had there been any heads to turn.

"Gem." Kendra dropped her enormous leather hobo bag on the bar with a clatter. "You know you're not a restaurant. We've been over this."

"I'm not selling food. I'm sharing personal food with friends. You're a friend, right, Dennis?"

"Been a friend of the Romanos for thirty-five years."

"There you go. Here, eat your dinner."

Dennis happily tucked into the plate of food she slid in front of him.

"It's okay if I don't charge," Gemma told Kendra.

"It was okay when you were cooking for your family and you *had* to," Kendra pointed out. "There's no family here tonight. Who are you cooking all this food for?"

Wow, that stung. There was no family here. Livie and Jess both gone, her father off with Teresa as often as he was here. In all of Gemma's life, that had never been the case. She kept cooking meals out of habit, for a bunch of people who were never going to come eat them.

"There's always someone who needs to eat. Since you're here, why don't you make yourself useful and take a plate of this food upstairs to Mr. Mosco?" Mr. Mosco had lived in the rental apartment above Romano's for so many years it was hard to even think of him as their tenant. He was just *there*…a fixture, like the old Michelob sign in the window, or the mirror behind the bar.

"You're feeding your *tenant* now?"

"He's old," Gemma protested. "And he doesn't have any family."

"That doesn't mean you have to sign up as his caretaker, Gemma. You've spent your whole life taking care of people. The last thing you need is one more to worry about."

"I'm not his caretaker. He still gets around okay. But what's wrong with bringing him a home-cooked meal now and then? It's just a nice thing to do."

"You were always a nicer person than me." Kendra sighed. "Too nice."

"Did you come here just to bust my chops, Kendra?"

Kendra shook back her long blond hair. She spent a fortune on that color and it was worth every penny. "I've heard a very juicy piece of gossip and I came straight to the source for confirmation." Her voice dropped another register. Kendra's dark cat's eyes, golden mane of hair, and wicked curves were what initially drew men's attention, but it was her voice that brought them to their knees—throaty and low, like whiskey on the rocks.

Gemma bit back a groan. She should have known this interrogation was coming. "Yes, he's back."

Kendra scrambled up on the bar stool usually occupied by Frank and propped her chin in her hands. "Tell me *everything*."

Although she had two sisters, they were younger than her—Livie by four years and Jess by five. And since Gemma had been more or less left in charge after their mother's death, confiding about her personal life with Livie and Jess had always felt a little weird. Kendra, on the other hand, was her cousin, and only a few months younger. She'd grown up a few neighborhoods away and they'd gone to the same high school. As a result, Kendra knew more of Gemma's secrets than pretty much anyone else.

"Nothing to tell," she lied nonchalantly. "He showed up last night, chatted with some of the guys, and then I tossed him out."

"You threw him out?"

"Well, it was closing time. I threw everybody out." Gemma kept her eyes on the bar as she scrubbed at a particularly stubborn sticky spot, muttering under her breath, "All three of them."

"That's it?" Kendra looked crestfallen. She'd clearly been hoping for a much more explosive reunion than Gemma was fessing up to. Gemma was wishing she had more fireworks to report, too, but only the kind where she set his ass on fire and sent him packing. Instead, she hadn't even managed to light the damned match.

"Dennis, need a refill?" Gemma swept Dennis's glass away without waiting for an answer.

"Ha!" Kendra crowed, pointing a finger at her. "I knew it!"

"Knew what?" Gemma scowled as she tilted the glass under the tap.

"Something happened."

"No, it didn't," she insisted, setting Dennis's refilled glass in front of him. His attention was entirely on his food. No hope for a change of subject there. Reluctantly, she turned back to Kendra. "Okay, fine. He hung around after closing."

Kendra abruptly hopped off her bar stool, reached across the bar to grasp Gemma's elbow, and bodily hauled her down to the end of the bar, far out of Dennis's earshot. "Tell. Me. Everything."

Gemma huffed, looking away out the window at the well-dressed people flowing past on Court Street, headed to all the chic new restaurants and bars a few blocks away. "When I closed up, he was waiting outside. He walked me home."

"Oh. My. God."

"Will you stop saying that? We walked. We talked. End of story."

"What did you talk about?"

"Um…" What *had* they talked about? Not the past. That had been off limits. The present? Sort of. "We just caught up."

When she didn't say anything more, Kendra's eyes widened. "And? What's he up to? Is he married? Kids?"

"Well…" Actually, she hadn't asked him any of those things, which, in retrospect, seemed like a bit of a lapse, really. "I don't think so. To either one."

Kendra leaned back and blew out a breath. "Well.

This is an interesting development. Brendan Flaherty is back in town and single."

"No! You get that look off your face right this second, Kendra Giordano. It's not gonna happen." Even though it nearly had last night. Whatever. He was just teasing her. He'd never intended to kiss her. He'd just been winding her up.

"But he's single, you're single…"

"*Nope.* I may be hard up for a date, but I would date literally anybody else in Brooklyn before I considered Brendan Flaherty again."

Kendra raised a perfectly penciled brow and tucked her tongue into her cheek. "You're hard up because you're too picky."

"I'm hard up because I spend all my days in this bar for geriatrics."

"I find guys for you all the time."

"Kendra…"

"Look, I have a great guy for you right now."

"Oh, no," she groaned as Kendra produced her phone from the back pocket of her skin-tight jeggings. "He's a cop in Chris's precinct."

"Of course he is." Kendra's brother, Chris, was a cop, along with about half of the family.

"Look. He's cute, right?" She presented her phone with a flourish.

Gemma squinted at the photo of two uniformed cops in front of a squad car. "Kendra, he's old enough to be my father."

"No, not him! The other guy."

"And that one's young enough to be my kid!"

Kendra tsked. "He's twenty-two. Totally old enough."

"Old enough for *what*?"

The grin on Kendra's face was purely X-rated. "All the good stuff."

Ending up with a cop wasn't so hard to imagine. In her family, you either became a cop or a firefighter or you married one. When she was younger, that had been her plan, too. Hers and Brendan's—the plan they'd made together. After his graduation, he'd take the classes he needed at community college and study for the firefighters' exam. He'd wanted to be settled in his first firehouse by the time Gemma graduated from high school, hopefully with a little money saved up. Then they could afford to get a place of their own nearby and get married—

Well.

None of that had happened. By the time Gemma had graduated, Brendan was long gone, working with his uncle, a thousand miles away in Chicago.

Still, even after Brendan, Gemma had figured eventually she'd end up marrying a cop or a firefighter. And she'd certainly dated plenty of both.

But one by one, sparks never materialized, guys flaked, relationships fizzled. One day she looked around to find herself thirty and everyone else in her generation had paired up, gotten married, and settled down. It was like a game of musical chairs she hadn't realized she'd been playing until the music stopped, leaving all the chairs filled and her still standing there alone. There were a few guys back on the market after their first marriages crashed and burned, but she'd figured out pretty quickly why those marriages flamed out. Usually it was because the guy was too dysfunctional to manage a relationship more complicated than his Netflix membership.

It was different for Kendra. She wasn't interested in any relationship that lasted longer than her roots touch-up, and she wasn't the least bit bothered that all the single guys kept getting younger. She dated them just the same, partying with them like she had when she was eighteen. Gemma was just too old for all that. Not old in years, old in experience. She'd been all but raising a family since she was fifteen, tending her sisters, her father, the bar. All that stuff young guys were into—clubbing, weekends on the Jersey Shore, all-day boozy music festivals—Gemma had worked right through that phase of her life, and she had no interest in going back to try it now.

"Kendra, I'd have absolutely nothing to say to some twenty-two-year-old kid."

"Who said you have to say anything at all?"

"There's more to dating than sex."

"Doesn't have to be." Kendra picked at one of her long, perfectly polished nails. "Seriously, Gem, when was the last time you got laid?"

Ugh. It didn't bear thinking about. And that last time had been nothing to shout about. "It's been a while," she conceded.

"So? Maybe all you need is some mindless physical fun. It doesn't have to mean anything."

"Maybe, but I just can't see sleeping with that kid. He's younger than my baby sister. It would be weird."

Kendra's glossy pink lips curled up in a grin. "There's another age-appropriate option that's suddenly become available."

"I told you, I'm not going there. He messed me up enough already. I'm not that much of a masochist."

"He can only mess you up again if you care."

"Are you suggesting I hook up with *Brendan*?"

"Didn't you say he was fantastic in bed?"

Better than fantastic. Mind-blowing. *Still* the best she'd ever had. "Yeah, but that was high school."

"And now he's all grown up. That's a skill that tends to get better with practice."

Well, there was a thought. Yeah, she'd been thinking about him ever since last night, remembering what it had been like in high school. But it hadn't occurred to her that he'd be *even better* at it now. Ugh. Another thing to plague her every waking moment. It was bad enough she hadn't managed to tell him off last night, now she was going to start having sexual fantasies about him. For a tough, no-nonsense woman who took no shit, she was having a very hard time banishing Brendan Flaherty to the mental oblivion he belonged in.

"Well, it doesn't even matter because I'm not at all his type."

"What are you talking about? The boy was obsessed with you back in the day."

"That was then. He's changed, and I'm still exactly who I always was. I've got nothing he'd be looking for."

"Quit selling yourself short, Gem. Unless he's had a brain transplant, I'm sure he'd still do you in a hot minute. He was crazy about you when he was eighteen."

"Yeah, he was," Gemma said. "But now he's all rich and fancy, and I'm still a bartender from Brooklyn. High school is over and so are we. It's ancient history."

"Except he came looking for you. Maybe he's interested in repeating a little history."

"Yeah, well we can't always get what we want," she snapped. But inside, she didn't feel quite so sure of herself. The idea that Brendan might still want her, after all these years... She wasn't as immune to it as she'd thought she'd be. As she'd *hoped* she was. Damn him for still being so goddamned hot. And damn her for noticing.

# Chapter Eight

"Gemma, you here?"

Gemma smiled to herself as Spudge hoisted himself to his feet and shambled out to the front door to greet Teresa, Dad's girlfriend.

"In the kitchen, Teresa," she called back.

Teresa had her own key to the house now, a sign of just how serious Dad was about her. She'd reconnected with Dad years after they'd gone to high school together, after her first marriage ended in divorce and she'd moved back home to take care of her mother, who had cancer. Teresa's mother had died just after Thanksgiving last year, and since then, Teresa had been spending more and more time at the Romano house. She'd even spent Christmas with them this year.

It was a little strange, adapting to having a new member of the Romano family after it had just been the four of them for so long. But Teresa was so nice, and she was trying so hard to get to know them all, making such an effort not to overstep or erase their mother.

"What are you cooking?" Teresa asked as she came into the kitchen. "It smells fantastic."

"This short ribs thing with polenta. Grab a plate. You're just in time."

"You want a glass of wine?" Teresa asked, retrieving a glass for herself from the cabinet.

"I'd love one, thanks."

Teresa poured her a glass of Montepulciano from the bottle that lived on the sideboard and set it next to the stove where Gemma was finishing up dinner. It was nice, having someone do little things like that for her. Not that her sisters and father weren't nice to her, but she was the oldest, usually taking care of people rather than being taken care of. Teresa didn't have the same dynamic with her, and she fussed over her a little like a mother might have. Gemma found she didn't mind so much.

After plating two servings of short ribs, she joined Teresa at the kitchen table. "How was City Island?"

Dad and Teresa had spent a long weekend out there with Dad's brother, Uncle Richie. Dad had gone straight to the bar to relieve Clyde, their one part-time employee, for the night shift.

Teresa sighed happily. "Just great. I love it out there. When you're out on Richie's boat, it's like you're not even in the city anymore. He and Sheila are getting pretty serious, you know."

"Seemed like it when she came to Thanksgiving last year. I like her."

"Me too. She's so good for Richie. You should see how well the business is doing. They're thinking of buying another boat."

"Another one? They just bought the second one a few months ago."

"And it's already booked for most of the summer. They could expand to a third boat, easy."

Uncle Richie had been kind of a mess for years. He

hadn't handled it well when Uncle Vincent had died in 9/11. He drank too much, lost his job, and then lost his wife when she took their two boys and moved to Maryland. Danny and Tommy eventually moved back to the city—Danny was a cop (of course), and Tommy was an E.M.T.

When he realized he'd lost his family, Richie pulled it together and quit drinking. Still, it had seemed like a gamble when he'd asked Dad to buy him out of his share of the bar and the house so he could buy a boat and open a charter fishing boat business on City Island. That was after Mom had died, and they'd just gotten the legal settlement from the health insurance company, so Dad did it, because Richie was his brother and he was trying to turn things around, but nobody really thought Richie would make a go of it. He'd surprised them all, though, and made good. The business was expanding and doing so well Sheila had quit her nursing job to help him run it.

"That's great. I'm really glad he's doing so well."

"Gemma, this is amazing," Teresa said after taking her first bite. "Where'd you get the recipe?"

"No recipe. Well, I read a few but then I tried it my own way."

Teresa shook her head with a smile. "What a gift."

"It's just cooking."

"This is *not* just cooking. Boiling pasta and sauce out of a jar, which is all I can manage...*that* is just cooking. This, Gemma...this is a whole lot more than 'just cooking.' Don't sell yourself short."

"Come on, Teresa."

"I'm serious. You should think about pursuing this."

"What, like being a cook?"

"Like being a *chef*."

"Nah, I have the bar," she demurred. Teresa's lips tightened into a line, but she didn't say anything else.

It wasn't as if Gemma hadn't thought about it. She loved cooking. It had started out of necessity when their mother had died. Someone had to feed the girls while their dad was trying to keep the bar afloat single-handedly. Over the years, it had become, well, calling it a passion sounded silly. It was just food. But it was her favorite thing to do, and she spent pretty much all her time outside the bar in the kitchen.

But doing it for a living? How would that even work? Which of her two sisters were going to give up their brilliant careers to come take her place in the bar? Besides, she loved the bar. It was more than just some job. It was home. It was her history—her legacy. Cooking for friends and family was enough for her.

At her feet, Spudge lifted his head and wuffed softly. A second later, she heard Jess's key in the lock. Funny, she could always tell which of her two sisters it was just from the sound the lock made, although she couldn't pinpoint why. Of course, it had to be Jess. Livie was all the way out in Colorado. Jess had moved out, too, but she often came by after work if Alex was going to be working late. Home was still home.

"Anybody home?" Jess hollered from the entryway.

"Kitchen!" Gemma hollered back.

"Of course," Jess said, when she appeared in the doorway. "Two floors and five bedrooms, but this family lives in the kitchen. Hey, Teresa. How was Uncle Richie's?"

"Great, thanks. Grab a plate. Gemma made dinner and it's fantastic."

"I need wine first." Jess swiped her long dark hair out of her face and dropped her messenger bag on the sideboard. She splashed a healthy pour of wine into a glass before moving to the stove to serve her plate.

"Hang on, Jess." Gemma scrambled out of her seat to grab some fresh chopped rosemary from the cutting board and sprinkled it over Jess's plate. "It makes all the difference."

Jess sniffed at it. "If you say so. You know I trust you." She dropped heavily into the chair next to Gemma.

"Long day, babe?"

"An eventful one. You'll never guess what happened."

"The government has been taken over by shape-shifting aliens and Alex is about to break the story."

"No, although you're right about the government. This is juicier. Dan has proposed to Mariel."

"What?"

"Dan?" Teresa interjected. "That's Dan, your boyfriend's dad?"

"And owner of half the world's media outlets," Gemma added.

"And Mariel, your boss?" Teresa pressed.

Mariel was much more than Jess's boss. When their mother had first gotten sick, their insurance company abruptly dropped her coverage over some bullshit technicality. Poor Dad had to deal with his wife's terminal illness and a mountain of medical debt, too. Even at ten years old, Jess had been an idealist, out to right the world's wrongs. She wrote an impassioned letter to Mariel Kemper, her favorite investigative journalist… because Jess had been the kind of kid who had a favorite journalist. Mariel had taken that letter to heart and ended up writing a multi-part story on the company's shady dealings. She'd won a Pulitzer and the Romanos won a settlement from the insurance company. Mariel was the editor at Jess's paper now, but she'd been in the Romano circle long before that.

"Yep." Jess took a hefty swig of her wine. "He popped the question when he whisked her off to his estate in St. Croix this weekend."

Gemma shook her head. Dan falling in love. Who'd have guessed? "So the greatest womanizer the world has ever seen has been tamed. What did she say?"

"She's thinking about it."

"Ouch," Teresa said. "I'm guessing Dan wasn't expecting that."

"Mariel's no dummy," Gemma said. "She knows Dan's rep just like the rest of the world does. He wasn't exactly subtle. I don't blame her for being cautious."

"I know it's hard to believe, but he hasn't so much as glanced at another woman since he and Mariel got together. I think he really loves her."

"She's too good for Dan," Gemma said.

"She's brilliant, for sure," Jess said. "But Dan has his good points, too."

"I don't believe it. Are you finally warming up to Daddy Drake?"

Jess waggled her left hand, the diamond of her engagement ring flashing in the light from overhead. "He's going to be family. I have to. But seriously, Dan's not all bad. He's a lot to take. And he can be an arrogant ass sometimes. But he's really generous with the people he loves."

"He tried to give you a whole townhouse in Manhattan as an engagement present."

"His heart was in the right place," Jess said staunchly. "He just didn't understand how Alex and I would feel about it. It's fine now."

"Why didn't you take the house, Jess?" Teresa asked. "That's a hell of a gift."

"It's just not right for me. I wouldn't feel comfortable in a place like that. Alex and I wanted to live someplace a little more modest."

Her baby sister would stand by her principles to the death. Gemma didn't always understand her, but she was proud of her confidence, her passion. It was going to serve her well when she married the son of one of the richest men in America. That world could devour some people, but Gemma wasn't worried about Jess. She'd hold her own just fine.

"So do you think Mariel will say yes?"

Jess sighed, her gaze turning a little dreamy. "Yeah, I think she will, eventually. Dan drives her crazy, but you can't help who you fall in love with."

No, that was for damned sure. Jess had hated Alex Drake before tumbling headlong into love with him. And Livie—brilliant Livie—had to go fall in love with some irresponsible hacker felon who was about as wrong for her as a guy could be. And then there was Gemma, so besotted at sixteen that she didn't see Brendan Flaherty's ability to devastate her until it was too late.

How much pain could she have saved herself years ago if she'd been able to avoid falling in love with him? But the years since had made her smarter. That was never happening to her again.

On the counter, her phone vibrated with an incoming call from her father.

"Hey, Dad. Need me to come in and help out?" Football season was over so Mondays were usually dead, but it was possible he could have gotten a little rush of customers.

Her father exhaled heavily. "I don't need you behind the bar, but you'd better come over, Gem. It's Mr. Mosco. The ambulance is loading him up now."

Gemma glanced at Jess, who was already on her feet, sensing bad news in the air. "We'll be right there."

## Chapter Nine

"I can't believe he's gone," Jess said, looking sadly around Mr. Mosco's tiny, cluttered apartment over the bar. "He's lived here as long as I can remember."

John Romano rubbed a hand across the back of his neck. "Nearly as long as I can remember, too. Victor moved in when I was still in high school. Damned shame."

Teresa stepped up behind him and ran her hand over his shoulder. "He seemed like a nice man."

"He was the sweetest," Jess said.

Gemma ran her fingers across the spines of a row of brightly colored binders. They contained Mr. Mosco's collection of Broadway Playbills, one from every show he'd ever seen. The bookshelf was entirely full. Sometimes when she'd bring him up some food, he'd tell her about his favorites, name-dropping all the original casts he'd seen perform live. Gemma rarely recognized the names, but she listened anyway, because those memories had been precious to him.

"Do you know how to contact his family?" Teresa asked.

"They, ah, didn't approve of him," Dad said.

"Homophobic assholes," Jess muttered.

"That's terrible," Teresa said, turning in a slow circle, taking in the room where Mr. Mosco had lived the majority of his adult life. She fingered the fringe of an embroidered shawl draped over a side table. "Poor man."

"Guess I'll put a notice in the paper," Dad said. "See if any of them want to come claim his stuff. I remember he had a lot of friends coming and going back when he was younger, but then with AIDS and everything…" He lifted a hand and let it fall. "I think all his friends from the old days are gone now."

Gemma's eyes roved over the room, crowded with a lifetime's worth of possessions—a giant framed poster from *Singin' in the Rain*, another shelf packed with DVDs, a collection of blown-glass figurines entirely covering the surface of two tables, stacks and stacks of gossip magazines. An overstuffed, sagging floral armchair, still bearing the imprint of Mr. Mosco's form, faced the television set. A folding TV table stood before it, holding the remote, a copy of TV Guide, Mr. Mosco's pill box, and an empty plate, scattered with the remains of the last meal she'd brought up to him.

All these years, Mr. Mosco had always seemed so happy, so cheerful, always ready with a smile or a snarky quip whenever she saw him. He'd lost everyone—his family, his friends—and still stayed so upbeat. For a moment, Gemma imagined it, not having her family at her back, losing all her friends one by one, and she felt cold.

"If his family haven't reached out to him in all these years, I can't see why they'd bother now," Jess said. "After all, it's not like he was secretly sitting on millions of dollars."

"He was broke," Dad said. "Getting by on social security. I'd be surprised if there's enough in his account to pay to bury him."

"We'll put a collection jar on the bar to pay for his funeral," Gemma said. "He shouldn't end up buried in some unmarked grave out on Hart's Island." The least they could do was to make sure poor Mr. Mosco had a dignified exit from this world. And maybe he had no family or friends, but he had them, the Romanos.

"That's a great idea, Gemma," Teresa said.

"And we'll make up the rest ourselves if we need to," her father added.

"We should be the ones to pack up his stuff," Jess said, with a decisive nod of her head. "We cared more about Mr. Mosco than any of his stupid family. It's right that we're the ones to do it."

Dad smiled fondly at Jess. "You're right, honey. It should be us. It's the right thing to do." He cast a look around the room. "It's gonna take some time to get this place ready to rent again."

"Hey, if we ask market rate maybe we'll finally make enough to cover the property taxes," Gemma pointed out.

Dad had steadfastly refused to raise Mr. Mosco's rent for a decade, at least, even as the neighborhood skyrocketed in popularity. Gemma completely agreed with his decision, but she had to admit, it would be nice if this building could start paying for itself. God knows, the bar barely did these days.

"It's going to take more than movers to get this place ready for a new tenant." Jess crouched to examine a wall outlet, overloaded with splitters and extension cords. "These outlets are still two-prong. You can't plug a single modern appliance in up here. Dad, when was the last time we had an electrician in?"

Their father looked momentarily flustered. "Hell if I know. We've got the certificate of occupancy, but since the tenant and the business haven't changed, I never had to update anything."

Gemma groaned. "We haven't had this unit inspected since the *eighties*? Electricity, plumbing, insulation… I bet we have to redo everything."

"If it's still got the insulation my grandfather used, then it's old newspapers."

"What?" Gemma turned to gape at him. "Newspapers? Like, *actual* newspapers? In the *walls*?"

Dad shrugged. "That's what they used in the old days."

"Jesus, this place is a firetrap," Jess said. "It's a miracle it hasn't already burned down."

Gemma picked her way through the living room, winding around the closely packed furniture, noting each overloaded outlet and snaking extension cord with growing trepidation. Mr. Mosco kept the wood floors mostly covered with bright, threadbare area rugs, but she could feel the uneven boards of the floors—original to the building—poking through. So much work to do.

She peered through the front windows at the people streaming by on the sidewalk one floor below, trying her best not to scan the crowd for a glimpse of Brendan Flaherty. Now that she knew he was back in the neighborhood, her eyes couldn't help looking for him everywhere she went. She hadn't so much as caught a glimpse of him since that night he came into the bar. Maybe that was it, the one and only time she would cross paths with him, despite his proximity. Good. Let him stay gone. Again.

Jess came to join her at the window, running a thumbnail through the chipped paint of the frame. "These windows look original. Which is quaint and all, but I can feel a draft coming in."

"New windows would cost a fortune." Gemma glanced over her shoulder at her father. He was standing in the middle of the room, looking around himself. She knew that expression on his face so well. She'd seen it ever since her mother died—the face of an overwhelmed man, doing his best to hold his family together all on his own. No matter how hard he worked, there always seemed to be something new popping up to bring that expression back. Taxes, payroll, the liquor supplier's bill, taps that needed to be replaced, plumbing that needed repairs, a dying furnace, two daughters to put through college, and now this. As hard as Gemma tried, she'd never been able to banish that expression of worry once and for all. It seemed she never would.

Property taxes were due May first, which meant they needed a new tenant in this place as soon as possible, preferably paying market rate. But that couldn't happen if they couldn't come up with the money to get it ready to rent in the first place. And that was looking highly doubtful at the moment.

## Chapter Ten

The next day, Gemma was still fretting over what to do about Mr. Mosco's apartment and absently drying a rack of pint glasses when the front door shrieked open. She really had to get on those hinges.

"Hey, Kendra. What are you doing here? Aren't you working today?"

She shrugged as she crossed the bar. "Carlos is out of the country until next Tuesday."

Three years ago, in a typical Kendra-like display of bravado, charisma, and bluster, she'd talked her way into a gig as a personal assistant to a financial guru, despite having zero qualifications for the job. Somehow, she'd turned out to be brilliant at it, and she now had her boss convinced he couldn't breathe from one minute to the next without Kendra there to organize it for him. Gemma didn't know how she did it.

As long as his life ran smoothly, Carlos Hernandez was willing to give Kendra free rein to manage her days as she saw fit, which often included taking two-hour lunches to hit sample sales, get her roots done, or come harass her hardworking cousin in Brooklyn.

"So you decided to spend all your free time at Romano's? Aww, thanks, Kendra."

"I came to see if you'd heard the news."

"What news?"

"DiPaola's is closing."

Gemma's hands stilled as she looked up at Kendra. "Tell me you're joking."

"Mom heard it from Cecilia DiPaola herself this morning. They're closing up and selling the building."

Gemma set the glass down carefully, bracing her hands on the bar. DiPaola's Bakery was their next-door neighbor and had been in business almost as long as Romano's. They were one of the stalwart holdouts from the old days. DiPaola's Bakery, Vinelli's Meats, Russo's Pizza, Sal's Restaurant, Romano's Bar...they were almost all that was left of the old Italian neighborhood. The DiPaolas were like family.

"I have to talk to Maria." Gemma ducked under the pass-through and hurried across the bar.

"What...*now*?" Kendra hustled after her, her high heels clacking on the tile floor.

"What is she *thinking*?"

"She's thinking people don't buy bread at a bakery every day anymore and they can't afford to stay in business. It happens, Gemma."

Gemma hung the Back in Five Minutes sign on the front door and locked it behind Kendra. "Not to the DiPaolas."

Because if it happened to the DiPaolas, it might happen to the Vinellis next, and after that...well, it didn't bear thinking about.

Outside, DiPaola's looked like it always had...like it had since the fifties. The fading green fabric awning was extended, keeping the sun off the three-tiered wedding cake that had sat on display in the front window for the past five years…having replaced an earlier identical display cake. Baskets flanked the wedding cake, holding today's loaves of Italian and semolina bread, wrapped in the distinctive white, green and red DiPaola bread sleeves.

The bell over the door tinkled as Gemma pushed it open. The warm, yeasty smell of the morning baking, which was still done in the ovens in the basement, lingered in the air. Mrs. Burke from around the corner was paying Maria DiPaolo for her small bag of rolls, carefully counting out nickels from her change purse as Maria smiled patiently at her. There was no sign of the apocalypse about to descend.

Gemma hovered near the front door with Kendra while she waited for Mrs. Burke to be finished.

"What exactly are you expecting to accomplish?" Kendra hissed.

"I just want to know what happened."

"Probably nothing. The same shit that's been happening for decades, just a little bit less of it each month until they end up in the red."

Mrs. Burke, who had to be ninety if she was a day, finally made her way to the front door.

"Good morning, Mrs. Burke."

"You girls," Mrs. Burke said with a hazy smile. "You're growing up so fast!"

To Mrs. Burke, they were always teenagers. Every time she saw either one of them, she was surprised all over again at the passage of the years.

Kendra smirked and elbowed Gemma. "We sure are, Mrs. Burke." But she still held the door open for Mrs. Burke, because that's what you did for old people, even if you were a sarcastic smart-ass like Kendra.

Maria DiPaola planted one hand on her ample hip and leaned against the counter. "You heard."

Gemma closed the distance across the shop. "I heard, but Maria, I don't understand. What happened?"

Maria threw up her hands and glanced around the shop. "Nothing. Everything. Every year we make less and running this place costs more." She brushed a tuft of fuzzy black curls that had escaped her ponytail off her forehead. Maria was in her early forties, but Gemma had always thought of her as a contemporary—another fourth-generation kid coming up in the family business. She'd looked up to Maria, expecting to see her eventually take over one hundred percent once her parents retired, just like Gemma expected to take over from her dad someday.

"I didn't realize it was so bad."

"It wasn't just profits and losses," Maria acknowledged.

"Then what?"

"I'm tired of getting up at three a.m. and driving in from New Jersey to open up." Maria sighed. "I'm missing my kids growing up because I'm always here. Since Ma's heart attack, Pops doesn't want to leave her home all day. She's going to need a lot of care as she gets older, and now, with the money from the building, we can afford it. Pops can pay off the house and finally slow down. It's a long list, Gemma. You know how tough business has been lately."

It had been tough for Romano's, but it had been tough for all the other old-timers, too. The neighborhood was changing. The old clientele had largely moved away or died. Hell, even the DiPaolas had fled Carroll Gardens, selling the family house and relocating to Jersey a dozen years ago.

"I didn't even know you'd put the building up for sale."

"Well, we didn't. But we got a good offer, and when we thought about it, we decided the time was right."

"A good offer? Out of the blue? From who?"

Just then, she heard Mr. DiPaola, Maria's dad, laugh from behind the plastic strip curtain that divided the counter from the kitchen in the back of the store. The plastic curtains parted, and Mr. DiPaola, thinner and grayer than he'd been even five years ago, passed through, followed by—

"What the hell are you doing here?"

Brendan Flaherty stopped just on the other side of the swinging plastic strip curtain, a smile slowly growing across his face.

"Gemma. Nice to see you again. Hi, Kendra."

"Hey, Brendan. You're looking good."

"Thanks. You, too."

Gemma elbowed her traitorous cousin then turned back to Maria. "Him? You sold the building to *him*?"

Maria glanced between Brendan and Gemma. "Well, yeah. His company, anyway."

"What are you doing buying the DiPaolas' building?"

Again with the maddening smirk. He was wearing a suit again today, dark navy, with an ice blue shirt and dark blue silk tie...every bit of it so crisp he looked like she could cut her finger on him. "That's what my business does. We buy properties to develop."

"Develop?" A haze of red descended over Gemma's vision at the mention of that dreaded word. Of course, he only came back to Carroll Gardens to wreck it. Like he hadn't done enough damage to her when he left. Now he had to come back and level everything else she cared about. "I should have known," she scoffed. "Nothing good could come from you being back here."

Before he could open his mouth to spew some smarmy defense she had no interest in hearing, she turned on her heel and stomped out, leaving Kendra, Brendan, and the stunned DiPaolas staring after her.

## Chapter Eleven

"What the hell is a Gritty anyway?" Dennis groused.

"I think he's like a Muppet or something," Frank replied before taking a swig of his beer.

"Scariest damned Muppet I ever saw. What kind of a mascot is that?"

"Do I need to remind you, Dennis, that you root for the Mets?" Gemma set his refilled beer in front of him.

"And?"

"Our mascot is a baseball with feet."

"Fair point."

Halftime ended and the game resumed, drawing Dennis and Frank's attention back to the TV. Hockey didn't draw in the customers the way football and baseball did, so business had stayed light tonight. Gemma had chased her father out an hour ago. There was no reason they both had to waste an evening standing behind the bar and staring into space. Dad had Teresa waiting for him, and Gemma just had...well, she had Spudge and the Food Network.

The door shrieked open, so she plastered on her most welcoming smile and turned to greet the newcomer. Her smile evaporated when she saw who it was.

"We're not for sale," she said flatly.

Brendan paused just inside the door. "I'm not here to make an offer."

"Good."

She started wiping down the bar, even though she'd just thoroughly wiped it down not ten minutes earlier, just so she'd have something for her hands to do and someplace for her eyes to rest. Someplace that wasn't Brendan Flaherty, looking practically edible in a pair of weathered jeans and a white button-down with the sleeves rolled up. The suits were bad enough. Bared forearms were just unfair. His forearms had always had the ability to make her weak in the knees.

"What do you want, Flaherty?"

"Just dropped in for a beer, Romano."

She flicked a disbelieving look at him. "Here?"

"Why not here? Hey, Dennis. Hey, Frank."

Frank and Dennis swiveled on their stools to greet Brendan, and under the cover of their effusive hellos, he insinuated himself right up onto a bar stool at her bar. Sneaky bastard.

When Dennis and Frank had finished telling the neighborhood golden boy how much he'd always be welcome to share a pint with them, he finally turned to Gemma.

"Can I get a Bud Light, Gemma?" Those melted-chocolate eyes locked with hers, daring her to refuse him.

She should. She should kick his traitorous, faithless ass straight out of her bar. She should tell him to never darken her door again. But Dennis and Frank would ask a million questions, and the gossip would be all over the neighborhood before morning. It wasn't worth all the drama.

So instead of telling him to shove his Bud Light someplace interesting, she wordlessly turned on her heel and poured it for him. At least she'd get four bucks out of him for the beer, and she'd enjoy handing off his tip to the next homeless person she passed.

She half-listened to Dennis and Frank filling him in on all the latest, peppered with some bitching about baseball spring training.

"All I gotta say is Vargas looked strong in spring training. The Phillies better watch their asses this year," Frank said, draining his glass. "Can I get a re-fill, Gemma? And you got any more of that pork stuff hiding in back?"

"For you, Frank, anytime." She whisked away his empty glass and plate.

Brendan was watching her closely as she returned and set Frank's refilled plate in front of him.

"Since when did Romano's start serving food?" he asked.

"Since never. We're not a restaurant."

"That looks like food to me."

"Tastes like it, too," Frank said, tucking into his second helping. "Nobody in Brooklyn cooks better than our Gemma."

Brendan turned his assessing gaze on her. "Is that right?"

She shrugged dismissively. "I just brought in some leftovers. For *friends*."

Which was a lie. There had been no one home to eat what she'd cooked today. Dennis and Frank were the sole recipients.

"Smells delicious," Brendan said, eyeing Frank's plate.

"It is," she replied smugly. "Too bad you're not a friend."

"I am hungry, though," he said, giving her what she was sure he considered his most winning smile. It was maddeningly effective. "Seems a shame to let the rest of it go to waste."

It was a shame, because, as always, she'd cooked like she was still feeding a whole family. The fridge at home was packed with plastic containers full of her leftover food. She just couldn't help it. Cooking meant cooking for an army.

"I suppose you want me to feed you, too." She sighed.

"I wouldn't complain if you did." He grinned.

She stared him down for another minute. Shameless, hot asshole with his stupid, nuclear missile smile.

"Ugh, fine," she huffed. "Just this once."

As she stomped into the back room and served up his plate, she wondered what the hell had just gotten into her. She certainly wasn't harboring any warm, fuzzy feelings toward Brendan, nor was she interested in becoming his "friend." So why was she feeding the asshole? He didn't deserve so much as a single word from her, never mind a plate of her food.

It was pride, she decided, as she dusted the plate with some chopped parsley from a tiny plastic container and grated a little fresh Parmesan over it. She was proud of today's effort and she'd had nobody to show it off to, except Dennis and Frank. And while they were always appreciative, honestly, they couldn't tell a delicately seasoned red wine reduction from a jar of gelatinous store-bought gravy.

Brendan had his titanium watch and his expensive suits and his loads of money to flash around, but Gemma hadn't arrived at this showdown unarmed. Maybe she never went to college and had no impressive career. Maybe she spent her days pouring beer for geriatric Brooklynites. But her cooking could make grown men cry. How many people could say that?

A couple of twists of the pepper mill and a quick swipe of a napkin around the rim to tidy up the plating and she was done. If she was attempting to impress him, she was going all in.

Doing her best to look nonchalant, as if his opinion meant less than nothing to her, she casually slid the plate in front of him on the bar. Brendan looked down at it, eyes wide.

"You just made this back there?"

"There's no kitchen here. I made it at home and kept it warm in back." Even reheated, it was good, and she knew it.

She turned her back on him under the pretense of checking the levels in the liquor bottles on the shelf behind the bar, but she watched his face in the big mirror behind the bottles as he cut the first piece of pork and lifted it to his mouth. Gemma suppressed a triumphant smile as he took a bite, froze, and his eyes went wide.

Brendan had eaten in most of the Michelin-starred restaurants in Chicago in his day, and what happened when he took his first bite of Gemma Romano's food had never happened in any of those fine establishments. His dick twitched.

He actually had to hold still, not chewing, not swallowing, just tasting and absorbing the shock of awareness that ricocheted through his body. It was a sensory experience one might expect when eating something so sublime, but the rest—the flush, the sudden tightening in his groin—that was not the sort of sensory experience he was used to having during a meal.

Gemma still stubbornly had her back to him as she tinkered with the liquor bottles on the shelf. As he breathed in and registered all the flavors asserting themselves on his tongue, he let his eyes trace her body, from her shapely calves outlined in a pair of skinny jeans worn like a second skin, to her long satiny dark brown hair, caught back in a ponytail, swinging between her shoulder blades every time she moved. The tight tank top she wore exposed a hell of a lot of skin and left no doubt about the shape of the rest of her.

In high school, Gemma Romano had been the hottest girl he'd ever laid eyes on in real life. She'd been tall and coltish as a freshman, then all of a sudden, one summer she'd blossomed, turning leggy and sexy and stunning seemingly overnight. He'd been working up the courage to ask her out when her mom got sick and everything had changed.

The years since then had only made her more beautiful, adding polish to an already-flawless diamond. Fourteen years of experience out in the world and she was *still* the hottest woman he'd ever met.

Reluctantly, he tore his eyes away from her. It was the visual of Gemma, combined with her extraordinary food, causing the inconvenient…tightening. That had to be it. Closing his eyes, he focused on what he was eating, on the tastes and textures of everything.

"Jesus, this is good," he finally said.

She turned around with a shrug. "It's just a riff on saltimbocca."

"There's no 'just' about any part of this. What's in it?"

If he wasn't mistaken, he spotted a flare of pride in her expression before she carefully locked it away from him. "Pork tenderloin. I brined it first with some salt and allspice, to hold in the moisture, then I rubbed it with garlic and fresh sage. I used Parma ham instead of prosciutto, the good stuff from Vinelli's, and layered in some wild mushrooms and fresh spinach."

"But the sauce…" Brendan said, taking another bite. "This sauce is like crack."

"I deglazed the pan with Marsala wine and finished it with lemon and a disgusting amount of butter. There's a few other things in there, but that's the gist of it."

"Where the hell did you learn to cook like this? In high school you barely managed opening a jar of pasta sauce."

Her eyes cooled slightly at the mention of high school. "I taught myself. I had a family to feed."

"You could have fed your family with peanut butter and jelly sandwiches. Gemma, this is fucking amazing."

His compliment clearly unsettled her. She shifted her weight from one foot to the other, arms crossed tightly in front of her. He couldn't help but notice that it caused her breasts to press northward. There was a delectable shadow of cleavage above the scooped neck of her tank. Damn, how he remembered those spectacular breasts.

"Thank you," she finally bit out reluctantly.

He smiled as broadly as he could before taking another bite, reveling in shaking her up. She might be showing him a solid wall of hostility right now, but he'd take that over apathy, or worse, disinterestedness. She was most definitely *not* apathetic to him. She was *bothered*. He could work with bothered.

"So you cook like this every day?" he asked as he polished off the last of his food.

"Most days."

"Great." Fishing his wallet out of his pocket, he dropped some bills on the bar—far more than he owed for the beer—and slid off his bar stool. "Can't wait to see what you come up with tomorrow."

Gemma's eyes flared with temper. God, she was gorgeous. "Tomorrow? What the hell does that mean?"

"It means," he said, bracing his hands on the bar and leaning closer, "that I'm coming back tomorrow, and I hope you'll be gracious enough to share your talents with me again. And I'll be back the day after that, and the day after that, too. Because, Gemma, I'm back, and I'm not going anywhere."

She huffed in outrage, tilting her chin up imperiously. "You think I give a shit?"

He leaned in closer, close enough to note the rapid rise and fall of her chest, the dilation of her pupils, the thrum of her pulse at the base of her neck. "Yeah, I think you do give a shit, even if you wish you didn't."

Then, before she could regroup and come up with another insult to hurl at him, he clapped Frank on the shoulder. "Frank, Dennis, I'll see you guys tomorrow."

He left Gemma staring after him in shock. As he stepped out into the cold, crisp night air, he wondered how long it would take to earn Gemma's forgiveness. Because if he was going to win her back, her forgiveness was critical. And there was no doubt about it; he fully intended to win back Gemma Romano.

## Chapter Twelve

John Romano finished closing out a tab for a customer then tossed his towel on the bar. "Gem, I'm going to bring up some more Seagram's from the basement."

"Great. Can you dig out some Dewar's, too? We've got plenty, but it got buried behind the kegs during the last delivery."

He waved a hand over his head in acknowledgment as he disappeared through the door to the back.

"Are you closing out the register yet?" Jess asked from her perch at the corner of the bar. "Then I can include tonight's receipts in the books."

Gemma cast a look around Romano's, empty except for Willie Fortman, who was nursing his last beer as he watched the end of the Mariners game on TV. He wasn't spending any more cash tonight, and neither was anyone else. Might as well call it a night so Jess could finish up the month's bookkeeping and get out of here.

"Yeah, I'll close out." She sighed.

Maybe at some point they should have upgraded, she thought as she tallied the credit receipts. Then they could compete with all those trendy new places up the street. But turning Romano's into a wine bar or something just felt wrong. Besides, upgrades cost money and they never had any. Romano's on its own was just homey and ordinary—exactly the same as it had been when they opened their doors in 1934. They weren't like the Brooklyn Inn in Brooklyn Heights, with all that gorgeous, dark, hand-carved German woodwork, so impressive that tourists stopped in to see it. And unlike the White Horse Tavern in the city, nobody famous had ever drank themselves to death at Romano's. The closest Romano's had ever come to fame was when Sandy Koufax had come in for a drink in 1956, right after he'd been signed to the Brooklyn Dodgers.

All they had to offer the world was a place to sit, a cold beer, and some friendly conversation. Too bad people didn't seem to be looking for that anymore.

She'd just stuffed the cash from the register into the bank bag when Kendra came in.

"We're closed," she called out.

"Screw you. Family drinks on the house." Kendra dumped her bag on the bar and wiggled onto a stool.

"I don't remember instituting that rule."

Kendra pouted dramatically. "Family drinks on the house when they have shitty days."

Gemma laughed as she poured her a beer. "What's the matter? Carlos made you actually earn your paycheck?"

"Hey, Carlos couldn't tie his own damned shoes without me. He's throwing this party for his investors, and of course, every bit of the planning is on me. Today the caterer bailed. I'm so screwed."

"Sorry, that sucks."

Kendra jolted upright as a light bulb went off. "Hey, why don't you do it?"

"Um, because I'm not a caterer?"

"But you can cook. Honestly, Gem, you're just as good as some of the pros. Why not?"

She ticked off the reasons on her fingers. "One, I don't have a professional kitchen. Two, I don't have any of the permits. Three, I'm kind of busy running a business."

Kendra huffed dramatically and rolled her eyes. "Okay, fine, if you're going to get hung up on the details. Seriously, though, Gem, you should have tasted some of the samples from these caterers who are charging stupid amounts of money. You could cook circles around them."

"So I've been told," she muttered under her breath as she wiped down the bar.

She should have kept her mouth closed around Kendra. Nothing slipped by that girl. A lascivious smile spread across her face and she leaned across the bar. "By anyone interesting?"

She considered lying but Kendra would probably sniff that out, too. "Brendan was here," she said, as offhandedly as she could manage.

"Oh, was he?" Kendra's smile grew impossibly wider. "And what did Mr. Flaherty have to say?"

"Keep your voice down." Gemma glanced over her shoulder at Jess, but she was absorbed in her spreadsheets, and too far away to hear the conversation. As long as Kendra refrained from shouting it. "He said I was a good cook."

"Wait a minute. You *fed* him?"

"Just to shut him up." And to show off. It had worked. He'd been impressed. Somehow she didn't feel like she'd come out of that encounter with the upper hand, though.

She didn't feel like she had the upper hand after tonight either. He'd come in again earlier, and sat next to Frank and Dennis, shooting the shit, barely even speaking to her. When she'd fed Dennis and Frank, she'd wordlessly set a plate in front of him, too, and she still wasn't sure why. Still looking for ways to impress him, she guessed. Still trying to hold her own in a competition that probably only existed in her own head. He'd eaten every bite of what she'd fed him—savored it, was more like it, lingering over each mouthful, watching her with a look in his eyes that made her feel like *she* was being consumed.

For an hour, he'd sat there, chatting to the guys, sipping his beer, and watching her like he was imagining doing a hundred filthy things with her. With each minute that passed, her body grew a degree hotter. She could feel that gaze of his everywhere, and every inch of her responded to it.

Then, when she felt she might snap under the unbearable tension, he stood up, smiled, left a wad of cash on the bar, and left. He'd cleared out even earlier than Frank and Dennis. She wasn't sure what she'd expected from him, but it hadn't been *that*. As a result, she'd been unable to stop thinking about him for the rest of the night, which was probably exactly what he'd intended. Asshole.

"What are you not telling me?" Kendra said, eyes narrowed.

Gemma debated, but really, she needed to talk to someone about this, and there was no one she *could* talk to except Kendra.

"I think he's interested," she said lowly.

"Interested in what?"

"Me. Like…" She waved a hand at herself. "Me."

Kendra burst into laughter. "You idiot. Of course he is. The only question is, what are you going to do about it?"

Gemma snapped her bar towel at Kendra. "What kind of question is that? After what he did—"

Kendra cut her off. "Gem. What he did happened fourteen years ago. You were both still kids."

"So I'm just supposed to forget it and let him back into my life?"

That earned her another eye roll from Kendra. "Geez, it's always all or nothing with you. Nobody said anything about letting him back into your life, drama queen. Just your bed."

"Kendra, he's buying the DiPaolas' building."

"And if he hadn't, someone else would have. You heard Maria. She's done. Honestly, I don't blame her. At least Brendan's from the neighborhood."

"I can't believe you're on his side."

"I'm on *your* side, and *you* desperately need to get laid. And here's Brendan Flaherty, back in the neighborhood, looking all hot and edible, and ready to do the deed with you. I say ride him like the Lone Ranger and get it out of your system."

"I couldn't do that," she grumbled. *Could she?*

Because there was no use in denying it to herself anymore—she wanted him. Despite what he did, despite his fourteen-year disappearing act, she still wanted him. Looking at him made her damned mouth water. While she'd been pouring beers and mixing drinks tonight, she'd also been imagining him naked, imagining herself naked, too, and imagining some really inventive sex she'd like to have with him. It was humiliating and she was furious with herself, but she couldn't seem to stop it.

Part of her wanted to do what Kendra was suggesting, ignore the past and just take, be selfish and indulgent, to use him to satisfy her more lurid fantasies and not worry about the implications of it all. Part of her wanted that real bad. But pride was a bitch and there was no way her pride would give him the satisfaction.

"God, you think too much," Kendra groused before polishing off her beer. "Now, for the reason I came here—"

"I thought you just stopped in to encourage my loose morals."

"Haha. No, seriously, I've got tastings scheduled with four more caterers tomorrow morning and I have *so* many other things to do…"

"Kendra…"

"Please go for me. All you need to do is eat and decide who's best. It'll be easy."

She sighed. "Fine. But you owe me."

"I'm *trying* to do you a solid by throwing you into bed with Tall, Hot, and Irish, but you're too stubborn to play along."

"You are the worst. Text me the caterers' addresses and what time I need to be there."

Kendra smiled in relief as she slid off her bar stool. "You're a lifesaver. What would I do without you?"

That was Gemma. Dependable, reliable, and saving everyone's lives, just like she'd been doing since she was fifteen. "Yeah, yeah. Talk to you later."

"Bye, Jess," Kendra called out as she left. Jess waved a hand without looking up from her laptop.

Gemma leaned on the bar across from her little sister. "How's it going?"

"Not good," Jess replied.

"Got a lot more to get through?"

"No, I'm nearly done with the bookkeeping. I mean the books. They're not good."

"When are they ever?"

Jess's eyes were full of apprehension when she looked up. "Not like this, Gem."

A knot of cold, sticky dread pooled in her stomach. "That bad?"

"There's not enough to cover Clyde's paycheck and the invoice from the beer supplier."

Bracing her hands on the bar, Gemma drew in a deep breath. They'd been in financial pinches before and come through them. So this one was a little more severe. She'd figure something out.

"We'll hold off on paying the beer supplier for a few weeks. We've been good customers for years. They'll give us a little break. I'll call them in the morning."

"And what happens in a couple of weeks when we still can't pay it?"

Gem swallowed around the lump in her throat. "If things don't improve, we'll just have to let Clyde go. Dad and I will split his shifts." She wasn't nearly as disinterested as she sounded. Clyde was a great guy, in his forties and getting his life back on track after running into a little trouble when he was a kid and spending some time behind bars. He'd been working part time for Romano's for five years while he put himself through college. He only had three more classes to go before he earned his bachelor's. This might derail him completely. But what else could she do?

Jess shifted on her bar stool, running her thumb nervously back and forth on the brass rail. "I could ask—"

"No." Gemma didn't even let her finish the thought. "We're not taking money from Alex."

Jess's fiancé was the son of one of the richest men in New York. Hell, one of the richest men in America. But Jess had her pride, and from the start of their relationship, she'd refused to take a dime of Alex's money for herself. Gemma respected her baby sister's sense of integrity. The last thing she'd ever do was let her compromise herself for the bar.

"But Gem—"

"But nothing. Romano's is a business, not a charity. If we can't make it on our own steam, then…" She had to stop and take a deep breath before finishing that sentence. Before saying the thing out loud that she'd scarcely allowed herself to think. "When we can't make it on our own, then it'll be time for Romano's to close."

Jess went pale, staring at her sister with wide eyes. There was no way the same thought hadn't occurred to her before. She was the one who'd been keeping the bar's books since she was sixteen. She knew their financial situation better than anyone. But like Gem, hearing the words spoken out loud felt a little like calling down bad luck. Now that Gem had said it, it was a possibility. It hunkered there on the horizon, a dark black cloud, one that might gobble up everything they'd ever known.

"But not yet," she assured her little sister. It was her job to keep this family on an even keel, and she wasn't quitting now. "I'm not giving up yet. I'll find the money from somewhere."

Her bravado reassured Jess, who smiled and reached for her hand, squeezing tightly. "I know you will."

Privately, Gemma didn't feel the least bit reassured. She feared summoning money out of thin air wasn't going to be as easy as summoning bad luck.

## Chapter Thirteen

The chicken was overcooked, with a dry, stringy texture that stuck in her molars. The pasta was overcooked, too, losing all its firmness and bite. And as for the sauce… would a little flavor hurt? Even some salt?

Gemma set down her fork and nudged the tasting plate of chicken piccata away from her.

"Delicious," she lied.

"Our bacon-wrapped asparagus is a real client favorite," the catering rep said, shoving a plate of it under Gemma's nose. The asparagus was so over-steamed it was almost gray, and the bacon was dark brown and charred in some places, but rubbery and pink in others.

The catering rep smiled encouragingly and shoved the plate closer. It wasn't her fault. She was a chipper girl in her early twenties, who'd cheerfully admitted to being a disaster in the kitchen. The cooking wasn't her job, she'd said airily, waving a hand. That was all done at some industrial kitchen somewhere else and the trays of food were delivered here for refrigeration and eventual reheating and delivery. None of that was the least bit surprising to Gemma. Everything she'd tasted had the texture and flavor of a frozen dinner.

"I'm sure it is," Gemma said diplomatically. "But

I can't eat bacon. The sulfates give me migraines." A lie, but there was no other way to get out of eating that horrible wilted asparagus and unevenly cooked bacon.

"Oh." The girl made a sympathetic face. "Poor you. I couldn't *live* without bacon. Let's move on to desserts!"

Gemma couldn't face it. Watery custards, congealed chocolate mousse, and half-frozen "whipped cream topping." Nope.

"It's a birthday party," she said quickly. "So there'll be a birthday cake for dessert."

"We do those too!" she countered brightly.

"It's already ordered."

"Oh, well then. How many guests should we put you down for?"

*None.* Gemma wouldn't serve Spudge this food. But she smiled pleasantly. "I have to talk to my boss about final numbers. I'll call if we're going ahead."

The girl shrugged offhandedly. "Okay." It made no difference to her if the job got booked or not, which was good, because it was *not* getting booked.

"Okay, well…" Gemma pushed to her feet. "I'll be in touch."

"Sure thing!" Miss Chipper chirped.

Outside on the sidewalk, Gemma sighed and pulled out her phone to call Kendra. Time to issue her less-than-stellar report on the caterers Kendra had sent her to.

Kendra answered on the first ring. "Okay, they're all pretty bad, but I suppose, if you're desperate, I'd go with the first place. I'm reasonably sure they won't give you food poisoning, and I can't promise that about the others."

"We're not going with any of them. I've got someone so much better lined up."

"You could have let me know that, Kendra," she snapped. "I wouldn't have wasted my morning choking down substandard chicken piccata for you."

"I just figured out how to land this other caterer a few minutes ago."

Gemma blew out a breath. "Great. Glad you've got it sorted out."

"It's you."

"Kendra, I already told you I can't do it, even if I wanted to. There are all kinds of health and safety regulations, and I don't have one of these fancy industrial kitchens."

"Yes, you would need all that if you were going into business as a caterer."

"And I don't have any of it, so I'm not going into business as a caterer."

"No, you're not. But you are getting hired as Carlos's personal chef for the night."

"What are you talking about?"

"If you come cook in Carlos's kitchen, you're not running your own business, you're working for him. None of those regulations apply. He can hire you to come cook dinner for his guests. That's totally fine. I am *such* a genius for coming up with this."

"But—"

Kendra cut off her protest. "How much do you want to do it?"

An unexpected influx of cash, just when she was desperate for it. She still thought Kendra was crazy, but she really needed the money. It was only one night. A dinner party wasn't all that different than cooking

Thanksgiving dinner for the Romano clan, right? If she could feed twenty-five Romanos, she could feed twenty-five dinner guests.

Holding her breath, she named a figure, what she needed to cover the liquor distributor's invoice and Clyde's paycheck this month.

Kendra burst out laughing. "Oh, girl. Thank God I'm here to hustle for you, because you're hopeless. We'll triple it, and Carlos covers all the ingredients and any special equipment."

"Kendra! You can't do that!"

"Gem, I'd pay even more than that to hire one of these shitty outfits you visited today. Look, if you do this, you get money I *know* you need and I get a dinner party to brag about for a bargain. It's win-win."

"Are you sure?"

"Carlos won't even flinch at that invoice. Not that he'll see it. So, will you do it?"

There were a million reasons she should say no. She'd never cooked professionally before, and not for anyone outside family and friends. She would be flying by the seat of her pants, and there was a pretty good chance it could all end in disaster. But that tantalizing promise of money…enough to solve all her problems—at least for this month—was too much to resist.

"Okay, God help us both, but I'll do it."

## Chapter Fourteen

When Fig and Thyme, a pricey gourmet grocery store, opened in Carroll Gardens two years earlier, Gemma had loudly railed against it as yet another harbinger of doom for the old-school businesses in the neighborhood. How was Kim's Grocery, the family-run Korean grocery a few blocks away, supposed to survive that kind of competition?

For the better part of a year, she refused to even step foot inside Fig and Thyme. Then, last Thanksgiving, she'd been in the middle of prepping the bouquet garni for the vegetables when she realized she'd forgotten the chervil. As much as she loved Kim's, their fresh herb selection extended to some basil, chives, and only occasionally, a little rosemary.

So she'd swallowed her pride and slunk into Fig and Thyme, only to find a cook's wonderland inside. Produce so fresh she wanted to weep. Spices she'd ordinarily have to hike all the way to Atlantic Avenue to find. Over a dozen kinds of honey. Grains imported from France and Spain. She still hated herself a little bit each time she went in, but she couldn't stay away.

And now, as she furiously prepped for Carlos's dinner party, trying out recipes and honing the menu, she was in there twice a day ferreting through the vast assortment of fresh greens and herbs, looking for interesting new ideas.

She'd thought to finish off the tuna carpaccio appetizer with some fresh chives, but her eye was caught by a bunch of daikon radish sprouts. They had such a fresh green color and distinctive shape. They'd make the plating so much more appealing than a sprinkling of chopped chives. Pinching one off, she gave it a taste. All the powerful flavor of a radish, but with a bright peppery finish. What could she do with this? Maybe punch up the savory, and add a hint of sweetness, something for the daikon to cut through—

"Hi there."

She spun around, only to come face-to-face with Brendan, looking stupidly attractive in his charcoal gray suit, standing in the produce section of Fig and Thyme.

"What are you doing here?"

He held up a bag of coffee. "Ran out of coffee this morning."

It was that Hawaiian stuff that cost thirty dollars a pound, of course, because Brendan might have started out as another working-class neighborhood kid like her, but he clearly swam in a different tax bracket now.

"So what's for dinner tonight?" He peered curiously into her basket to see what she had.

"This isn't for dinner." She resisted the urge to hide her basket behind her back. Catering for Carlos wasn't a secret. She was just self-conscious about it, afraid that anybody who heard what she was about to do would burst out laughing at her audacity.

He hiked one golden eyebrow. "So that's just a snack?" He indicated the bunch of daikon radish sprouts she was still clutching in one hand. The water from the roots was beginning to drip down her forearm. *Nice.*

"I'm trying something new." And she had to hurry. She was due to start her shift at the bar at noon, and she really wanted to make a stab at this new idea for the carpaccio before then. Of course, even if she finished it, she had nobody to try it out on. Dad wouldn't touch raw fish unless it was dangling at the end of a fishing pole, and the midday patrons of Romano's weren't exactly going to warm up to her fancy appetizers either.

Brendan might, though. She looked up at him appraisingly. Brendan had probably eaten at fancy restaurants all over Chicago. He ran in the same crowd as Carlos's ritzy investor guests. If it passed muster with him, then she could rest assured that it wouldn't horrify the dinner party guests.

"Are you free right now?"

Brendan startled before a slow, sexy smile unfurled across his face. "I can be. What did you have in mind?"

"Get your mind out of the gutter. I need a guinea pig."

He spread his arms wide. "Whatever it is, I'm at your disposal."

That was a fairly generous offer, she had to grudgingly admit. She'd been nothing but hostile to him since his return, but here he was, willing to drop whatever he was doing to help her out, no questions asked. He must be really desperate to get into her pants, she decided. Which was why bringing him to the house was maybe a bad idea.

It was no big deal. No different than slapping a plate of food in front of him when he came into Romano's. Except now he'd be in her house. And they'd be alone.

Firmly, she told her sixteen-year-old self to stop getting ideas about that. Nothing would happen except cooking and eating. She needed a taster and here he was, willing and able. That was all.

"Okay. My place."

He grinned again, all hot and sexy. "This gets better and better."

"Dream on, Flaherty. I'm only interested in your taste buds."

"It's a start. At least they're in the right vicinity."

She flushed and ducked her face. *Definitely* a dumb idea.

When Brendan ducked into Fig and Thyme to grab some coffee this morning, he hadn't expected his day to get derailed in such an interesting way. Sure he had work to do, phone calls to make, a bank meeting to set up, but right now, none of that seemed nearly as important as whatever it was Gemma Romano wanted out of him.

They walked in near silence back to her house. He could feel the nerves radiating off her, but if he wasn't mistaken, it wasn't just him and their unresolved sexual tension causing it this time. She'd been jumpy as hell about whatever she was buying in the grocery store. Maybe it had been over a decade since they'd been together, but he still knew Gemma well enough to know she was up to something.

She fumbled her keys twice before getting the front door unlocked and ushering him inside. In an instant, he was assaulted with a wave of sense memories: the faded wallpaper in the entry hall, with its gold stripes and dark green leaves; the coat rack, stuffed with coats and jackets belonging to the entire Romano clan; a pile of snow boots and galoshes by the door, even though it hadn't snowed in weeks; the old sepia-toned photograph in a gilt frame that Gemma once told him was of her great-grandparents; that little glass wall sconce mounted to the wall right at the foot of the staircase, the stairs that led up to Gemma's room… Nothing had changed, not a single thing.

Except for Spudge, who sat in a droopy brown heap in front of him, his tail thumping rhythmically on the wood floor. If she hadn't told him Spudge was still around, he wouldn't have known it was him. The last time he'd seen the little guy, he'd been a wiggly, rambunctious puppy. Now he was an old man, with a graying muzzle and watery eyes.

Crouching in front of him, he rubbed Spudge's head. "Hey, buddy. Long time, no see. How ya doing, man?"

Spudge groaned in delight and leaned into his hand.

Gemma let out a frustrated huff. "First Nick and now Brendan. You're shameless, Spudge."

Brendan straightened and eyed her narrowly. "Who's Nick?" She hadn't mentioned being involved with anyone before, but really, why would she share that kind of information with him? She barely spoke to him if she could help it. It would be a crushing disappointment, but not a surprise to find out she was with someone. Honestly, he'd been stunned to discover she wasn't married. Before he'd left, he'd always felt like guys were lined up to have a chance with Gemma.

But Gemma missed his uncharacteristic flare of jealousy. She was still frowning at Spudge. "Nick is Livie's criminal boyfriend. Spudge is irrationally in love with him, too, for no good reason whatsoever."

Slowly, Brendan let out a breath. Disaster averted. "You don't like him?"

She shrugged and changed the subject. "This way."

She slipped past him into the living room and headed toward the back of the house, where he remembered the kitchen was. He stopped cold at the doorway, surveying the carnage. Every surface was covered with food and kitchen equipment. Three cookbooks lay open on the kitchen table, surrounded by bunches of fresh herbs and piles of vegetables.

Gemma breezed past all of it and cleared a space on the counter for her bag, unpacking it with brisk efficiency.

"Um, what's going on in here?"

"I'm trying out some new recipes," she said, biting her lip.

"Is it always an Olympic event like this?"

Sighing, she turned to face him, a bunch of greens in one hand and a fennel bulb in the other. "Promise you won't laugh."

He held up his hands. "Promise."

"Kendra hired me to cater a dinner party."

He waited for the rest of her confession, the part she seemed to think he'd find ridiculous. "And?" he prompted, when she said nothing more.

"I'm not a caterer!" she wailed, waving her vegetables in the air. "I've never cooked for anybody outside my family. I'm not a professional chef; I just like to cook."

"Okay," he said slowly. "I've eaten your food, Gemma. You're a chef. You've just never been paid for it before. The only thing that makes them professional chefs is that someone pays them for it."

"All these rich people are going to *know*."

"Know what?"

"That I'm just some bartender from Brooklyn."

He huffed in laughter. "Gemma, you've never been *just* anything. Certainly not just a bartender."

"I'm not…" She waved her hands in frustration. "I know what a Meyer lemon emulsion is. At least I've seen a picture of it. But I can't make one! And that's what they're going to expect at a dinner like this. Shavings of this and emulsions of that and—"

"Gemma, stop. So fine, you don't make food in the form of sea foam. Don't try to. I've eaten at places that served dollops of flavored foam. It's not all that. Your food is amazing. Trust yourself and just do what you do. Now why did you ask me for help?"

She watched him apprehensively for a moment, her bout of panic slowly ebbing. "Okay, I need you to taste something for me. And I need you to be *honest*."

He nodded. "Total honesty."

Apprehensively, she nodded, and waved a hand at the overflowing table. "Have a seat. I have to put it together."

Making his way to the kitchen table, he cleared a stack of cookbooks off a chair so he could sit. As she got busy unpacking ingredients and getting out a knife and cutting board, he took a glance at what she'd been reading. Buried amongst the cookbooks was a small binder full of recipes, all written out by hand.

"Did you do this?"

She glanced over her shoulder. "Oh, no, that was my Grandma Romano's. It's all her family recipes. Right after you—" Abruptly, she stopped and cleared her throat. Brendan knew exactly what she'd been about to say. *"After you left."* Guilt twisted in his gut once again. In case he ever forgot for a second, he still had a lot of making up to do.

"After my mom died," she finally continued, "I found it in the basement. I started teaching myself to cook following Grandma Romano's recipes. When I'd come up with something I wanted to add, or an improvement I made, I'd add a note."

He flipped through the book, papered with a sea of yellow Post-Its with Gemma's scribbled notes. The thing was like a family bible of cooking. He knew she was a good cook. One taste had told him that. But clearly it went well beyond that for her. "Looks like you've found your passion, Gem."

"It's just cooking."

He didn't push, even though he disagreed. She'd never been good at taking a compliment. That much about her had not changed.

"So tell me about Livie's boyfriend." He'd momentarily caught Gemma with her guard down, and he wanted to keep her talking.

"Huh?"

"Earlier, when we came in. Sounds like you don't like the guy much."

Gemma shrugged. "He's fine. Wicked smart. Very charming. But the guy had a sketchy past, so I wasn't his biggest fan when she first dragged him home. And then he broke her heart."

"I thought you said he was her boyfriend."

"He is. He figured his shit out and came crawling back to her." Gemma paused and blew out a breath before pouring something else into a little bowl and whisking hard. "Now he seems to adore her, and she's blissfully happy, so I'm coming around. It was hard to watch her get hurt, though."

"Still such a mom to them." It wasn't a criticism. Gemma was tougher and wiser than when he'd known her in high school. He was glad to see her heart was as tender as it had ever been, even if she was keeping it well hidden from him. Knowing he'd hurt her was bad enough. If his abandonment had made her bitter—if it had killed the best part of her—he couldn't live with himself.

"I can't help it. When they hurt, I hurt, even now when they're all grown up. Pathetic, I know."

"That's not pathetic, Gem. It's love."

She made some small sound of acquiescence and turned her attention fully to what she was doing. Brendan leaned back in his chair, happy to be here to watch her work.

There was something sublimely peaceful about Gemma's kitchen. The white-tiled walls, splashed with sunlight from the window over the sink, the brisk, rhythmic "snick" of Gemma's knife against the cutting board as she minced something. And the view wasn't bad, either. Backlit by the sunshine, her body stood out in sharp silhouette. Her hair was up again today…he hadn't seen her with it down since his return, unfortunately. His teenage memories were full of that silky dark hair falling all around him as she… Okay, not right now. She'd thawed enough to ask him for help. He wasn't going to screw it up by pouncing on her.

The ponytail was good, too, though. It left a long expanse of her neck and shoulders exposed. She had great shoulders, fine boned and muscular, like a dancer's. The rest of her was just as gorgeous. Her long, slim torso, her narrow waist and hips, and of course, those endless legs. Gemma's legs were a fucking masterpiece.

"What are you making?"

"Tuna carpaccio. I have this idea…" She trailed off as she sliced into a piece of perfect pink tuna with laser precision. How long did you have to practice something like that to get so good at it? "Are you okay with raw fish?" she asked. "I forgot to ask."

"Love it."

She smirked as she deftly lifted paper-thin slices of tuna on the flat blade of her knife, arranging them on a plate. "Guess you picked that up in Chicago."

He inclined his head. No sense in denying it. The intervening years had changed him in many ways, too, some good, some bad. Hopefully he'd come home before the worst of the bad had a chance to take root.

She paused, staring into a small bowl she'd been adding ingredients to. Spooning out a tiny bit, she dipped a fingertip in and tasted it. He couldn't drag his gaze away from that finger, those lips, if he tried.

"It needs something," she muttered to herself. "Red pepper? No, not heat. It needs…" Another fingertip dip and another taste. "Umami. It needs umami. Oooh, maybe a splash of colatura di alici. And a little honey, to mellow it out and offset the daikon."

She didn't seem to be looking for input from him, so he kept quiet, just watching her work and try things out. Finally, she seemed satisfied and turned to present him with a plate.

It could have been set down in front of him on a snowy white tablecloth in a Michelin-starred Chicago restaurant and he wouldn't have blinked. It looked fantastic, perfect slices of pink tuna, with a pale golden, glistening drizzle of something, and sprinkled with bright green sprouts.

She set it in front of him and shoved a knife and fork in his hand before backing away to lean against the counter to chew on her thumbnail.

He took a bite. Like everything else she'd served him, it was delicious, but this was a serious step above. What she served at the bar was comfort food. Mouthwatering, for sure, but basically family meals crafted with finesse. This...this was sublime.

"Jesus, Gem..."

"You promised. Be honest," she warned him.

"Honestly, it's one of the best things I've ever eaten." He took another bite. "I taste something... What is that? And what did you do to this tuna? It melts in my mouth."

When he glanced up at her, Gemma was fighting back a smile. "Okay, so it's not bad, then."

"Not bad? Gem, this is amazing."

"Don't go overboard, Flaherty," she said, turning back to the counter and beginning to clean up. "These are rich people, and they know good food. I'm just trying not to embarrass myself here."

"This is no embarrassment. Taste it yourself if you don't believe me."

She shook her head. "I can't judge my own food. I'm too close to it."

He stood up and moved in behind her. "Gem, look at me."

She turned back and startled when she registered his nearness. He set his plate on the counter and lifted a bite onto his fork. Then he reached up with his free hand and covered her eyes.

"What are you doing?"

"Giving you some perspective. Now forget everything you've done in this kitchen for the last half hour. You don't even know how to cook."

She huffed in laughter and closed her fingers around his wrist, tugging. "Brendan, come on…"

"I'm serious," he said, keeping his hand over her eyes. "You know nothing about food now. You just know what tastes good. Are you with me?"

Letting out a sigh, her shoulders slumped in defeat. "Yes."

"Now clear your mind and open up."

Her lips parted and Brendan lost himself for a minute, staring at the sensual shape of her lips, the glint of her white teeth, the slick pink of her tongue…

Swallowing back a wild flare of desire, he lifted his fork and slipped it into her mouth. Her lips closed around it, and slowly, he slid it out, reveling in the sensual suggestiveness of it. Gemma had gone still, and the air around them had gone brittle with tension. He stayed utterly silent as she savored the bite, and with each passing second, the electricity crackling between them surged higher.

Her throat worked as she swallowed. He remembered running his tongue along that throat, digging his teeth into her as she shuddered and moaned around him. Her tongue darted out to lick the last of the sauce from her lips and his dick throbbed.

"Well?" His voice was ragged with lust.

"It—it's good," she whispered. "Really good."

Slowly, he slid his hand away from her eyes and down the side of her face. Her eyes fluttered open and fastened on his.

His chest contracted with sudden longing, like it was

something swirling in the air and he'd just taken a deep breath of it. He could see it in Gem's eyes the second it hit her too, an intoxicant they'd both just inhaled. Her smile faded, but her eyes never left his.

Tentatively, he took another step closer, until they were toe-to-toe. Plenty of time for her to slap him, to shove him away, to just say no. Gem said nothing as he edged closer. He licked his lips, too. That fucking aphrodisiac she'd just fed him still lingered there. Her eyes darted to his mouth and she drew her bottom lip between her teeth. That tightening in his chest sank lower.

As he was scrambling for words in his addled brain, trying to figure out how to ask if she wanted this, her eyes lifted to his. Then her hand snaked out, wrapped around the back of his neck, and hauled his head down to hers.

Their mouths clashed together in an explosion of heat and lingering deliciousness and lust. Her lips parted under his and he wasted no time taking her up on that invitation. His hands found her hips just as his tongue found hers, and he moaned at the fucking perfectness of it all. Gemma arched, bringing the long, gorgeous length of her body up against his, and his hands slid north, his arms wrapping around her, wanting to hang on to every inch of her. Up on tiptoes, she wrapped her arms around his shoulders, pulling herself in tight, so tight he could feel the swell of her breasts against his chest.

He'd imagined kissing Gemma again would be like stepping back in time, but it wasn't. Despite the setting— how many times had he snuck over to her house after school and made out with her right here in this kitchen before her family returned home?—this was nothing like high school. Because as good as that was, this was a thousand times better. No teenage fumbling and uncertainty. Now they were two grown adults with full knowledge of what they wanted. And what he wanted was Gemma, every way he could possibly have her.

Suddenly she wrenched her mouth from his, panting and aroused, cheeks flushed. Her eyes flicked between his, assessing, and then she pushed herself back. He waited, breathing heavily himself, to see what came next.

"Umm…" she said, eyes dropping to her feet.

"You kissed me."

"You caught that, huh?" She refused to look up at him.

"Damned hard to miss."

"Okay," she said briskly, stepping to the side and turning back to the counter. "Thanks for your help today. I appreciate it."

He bit back a smirk as she did her best to brush aside what just happened.

"It was no problem. Really. But Gem?"

She looked back over her shoulder.

"What?"

"It turned me on, too."

One eyebrow hiked northward. "Excuse me?"

"The first bite of your food I put in my mouth was almost as good as sex."

"Well, I guess that's a compliment."

"I said 'almost.'" He looked her straight in the eye before she could turn away again. "Because I remember sex with you, Gemma, and it was a thousand times better than any meal, even one of yours."

She said nothing for a long moment. Then she straightened and turned her back on him again. "I have to go to work."

"Sure." He backed away. They'd done enough. He'd laid a few seeds for her to chew on. Best to give her some space to do that.

"Thanks again," she said, making her voice absolutely neutral, as if the last five minutes had never happened. She wanted him; she just hated herself a little bit for it, which meant he still had some work to do.

"Anytime." Leaving, when he could still feel her body against his, when he could still smell her and taste her on his tongue, was the hardest thing he'd ever had to do. But he wasn't rushing the fences with this. He wanted Gemma Romano, and she wanted him, too. He was willing to be patient as she got used to that idea.

"I'll let myself out."

"You do that."

"See you around, Gem."

He turned and left before she could respond. Retreat was what was called for now, to let her come to terms with that absolutely phenomenal kiss. But he'd be back, he promised himself as he made his way back through the house.

Spudge was still by the front door, and he bent to rub his bony head. "I'll see you soon, buddy. Keep my spot warm for me."

Spudge groaned in assent and Brendan let himself out the front door, stepping into the crisp March air, the bright, late-winter sunshine, feeling like a king.

## Chapter Fifteen

Hours after it had happened, Gemma still couldn't quite believe that it had. Not that they'd kissed. That *she'd* kissed *Brendan*. There was no sugar-coating it or trying to paint it in a different light. He'd been standing there in front of her, looking like he wanted to kiss her but not making any move to do it. Before she knew what she was doing, she'd grabbed him and laid one on him.

Maybe she should play it off like it hadn't happened. Actually, she'd tried that immediately and he'd called her out.

So…it happened. The only question left to answer—and it was a big one—was whether or not it was going to happen again. Now, without hormones clouding her brain, she had to figure out why she'd done it, and how she felt about it.

Short answer: amazing.

That kiss had been…damn. She knew the men she'd been with in the intervening years didn't measure up to her memories of Brendan, but now that she'd…ahem… tasted the real thing again, they weren't even on the same scale. It was just a kiss, but it had turned her brain into one of those spinning firecracker things, all bright light and noise and chaos. Imagining what might have happened if they hadn't stopped…well, that made her nearly weak in the knees.

But then there was that long answer to consider.

No matter how wit scrambling his kisses were, he was still *Brendan Flaherty*. She'd trusted him once before—with her whole heart, with every defense down—and he'd walked away from her. Did she really want to roll those dice again?

Then again, maybe Kendra was right. Maybe she thought too much, took it all too seriously. Maybe she should just take what he was offering and stop worrying about the rest. He could only break her heart again if she let him get his hands on it. And while she was interested in letting Brendan get his hands on many, many parts of her, her heart wasn't one of them. Could she do it? Could she act on this almost overwhelming desire and just sleep with him?

But she was only going to have to figure that one out if and when he showed up again. Because she hadn't seen him. The night crept on and there'd still been no sign of him. Frank and Dennis were here, of course, and she'd fed them, as she always did. But Brendan hadn't shown up to join them. As if she needed more reasons to be embarrassed, now she was waiting on pins and needles for his arrival like some obsessed teenager.

"Gem?"

She startled and turned to look at her dad. John Romano was staring back at her, one thick dark eyebrow arched in question. "Where were you? I repeated myself twice."

"Sorry, sorry. Just daydreaming."

"You okay, kid? You don't seem yourself."

"Me?" Her voice was too high, and overly bright. "Sure. Yes. I'm fine."

"You sure? You've been a little distracted for weeks now. Is there something going on you want to tell me about?"

Yes, there was something going on, but her internal debate about the wisdom of getting naked with Brendan Flaherty was certainly not a subject she was going to hash over with her father.

"No, nothing. I'm fine."

He watched her for another moment, his kind dark eyes full of a mix of concern and uncertainty. She called it his Dad-without-Mom expression—when he was worried about one of his daughters but didn't know what to do about it. In the first years after she died, Gemma had imagined those moments were when he missed Mom the most. Lately, since he'd found Teresa, she'd seen less and less of that look. The last thing she wanted was to bring it back on her account.

"Well, if you're sure," he said slowly.

"I am."

"Then the table by the door needs a refill on their pitcher."

"Oh. Right." She was supposed to be tending bar tonight, and instead, she'd spent half the night staring into space.

For all her keeping one eye on the clock and one eye on the door, when Brendan finally did arrive, she missed him, stuck in the back room switching out a keg. The nut on top had gotten stuck, requiring several sweaty, frustrating minutes with a crescent wrench to wiggle it free.

As she came back out front, wiping her hands on a bar towel, she heard a laugh. A very familiar laugh.

There he was, with Dennis and Frank. And talking to *her father*. The two completely separate spheres of her life had just collided head-on.

Oh, Jesus, what had he said to Dad? Had he told him he knew her? Did he tell him they'd dated? All of that would be news to Dad. And while she knew he wouldn't be upset about it, he *would* ask questions…questions she still didn't want to answer.

"Hi, Dad," she said, stepping up behind them. "Keg's swapped out."

He turned to her with a grin. "Brendan here tells me you two went to high school together."

Her eyes shot to his. A small smile was playing around his mouth, but otherwise his expression gave her no clues.

"Um, yes, high school. Right. How have you been?"

The half smile turned into a full-blown one, and she was suddenly aware of all the hair that had escaped her ponytail while she was wrestling with the keg, the sheen of sweat on her upper lip, and the dust streaked across her tank top. "Since I saw you this morning?" he teased. "Fine. I've been fine."

Her mouth fell open as she stared at him. He stared back, clearly enjoying her panic. He was going to just blurt that out? Here? In her bar? In front of Frank and Dennis and *her father*?

*Yeah, Mr. Romano, this morning in your kitchen, Gemma practically climbed me like a tree.*

Then he shifted his attention to Dad. "I ran into Gemma at the market today," he explained.

Oh. That was entirely innocent. And pretty much exactly what happened. Why was she being such a basket case about this?

"Brendan says you've taken pity on him and started feeding him along with these two strays." Dad hooked a thumb at Dennis and Frank.

"Brendan's figured out it's the best meal in the neighborhood," Dennis said, clapping Brendan on the shoulder.

"Our Gemma is a wonder," Dad said with pride.

Brendan looked back at Gemma with a knowing smile. "One taste and I was hooked."

And just like that, her whole body was flooded with heat. She was nearly light-headed with it. "Um, I... I'll get your dinner." Then she turned and fled back into the back room.

For the next hour, she steered clear of him, waiting on the tables and letting Dad man the bar. He and Brendan seemed to be getting along swimmingly. Every time she looked over, they were deep in conversation or laughing it up about something.

Fourteen years ago, her heart would have soared seeing him bond with her father. Now it just added to her confusion. She couldn't very well jump into some fuck-buddy situation with Brendan when he was friends with her dad. Everything was getting too complicated. He was becoming too tangled up in the rest of her life, when she hadn't even decided yet what she wanted to do about him. Or with him.

When the last table of customers departed, she had no choice but to slip back behind the bar. Actually, most of the customers had gone. Just Dennis and Frank. And Brendan.

"Did you know Brendan's in business here in the

neighborhood now?" Dad asked, tossing his bar towel over his shoulder and leaning his elbow on the bar. "He just bought the DiPaola's building."

"Yeah, I heard that," she murmured. "I don't know what we're going to do without DiPaola's next door."

"Can't say I blame them. Running a business gets tougher every day around here."

"Well, us Romanos are a tough lot."

"Sure are. Hey, why don't you take off early tonight, Gem? I know you've got a lot of work to do for your catering job. Run on and I'll close up."

"You sure?" It was already too late to try out any new recipes tonight, but she had a couple of cookbooks she wanted to read through, and another shopping list to make.

"Sure. I think I can handle tossing these two old reprobates out in the street."

Dennis and Frank argued good-naturedly with Dad as Gemma took her time cleaning up and tidying the register area.

Brendan was still here. Would he leave when she left? Would he want to walk her home again? Would he—

With a growl of frustration, she slammed the cash register closed. She was behaving like she was sixteen again.

With forced breeziness, she called out, "Night, Dad… Guys." Lumping him in with Dennis and Frank seemed safer than singling him out by name.

As she lifted the pass-through and let herself out from behind the bar, Brendan slid off his bar stool and dropped some bills on the bar. "Think I'm gonna head out, too. Thanks for the beers and the conversation, John."

"Anytime. Nice to meet you, Brendan." *Great.* They were on a first name basis already. Then Dad turned to her, a slight smile twitching under his mustache. "Stay safe, Gem."

Ugh, he *knew*! He *knew* Brendan had been hanging around waiting for her. That's why he was chasing her out early. He was doing his best to throw her together with the only eligible male who'd walked into Romano's in years. He was worse than Kendra.

Feeling trapped and annoyed—with Dad, with Brendan, with herself…she didn't know which bugged her more—she turned and left without a word. Brendan was right on her heels. Outside, the wind had picked up and a wall of clouds hung low in the sky. A storm was brewing.

"Looks like rain," he said, falling into step beside her.

"Probably."

"You heading home?"

"Yep."

"Okay."

"You really don't need to walk me home," she said pointedly.

"My apartment is this way."

"It is?"

"Two blocks from you."

"You bought an apartment two blocks from my house?"

"I'm renting, and it's what was available when I was looking."

"You're a real estate developer but you don't own your own place?"

"Eventually I'll live in one of my buildings. When they're built."

"Right."

He was going to live in one of those sleek, expensive new condos springing up everywhere. Someplace with a doorman and an on-site gym and sweeping views of Manhattan. Just as glossy and perfect as he was now. Except…he wasn't jetting into Manhattan every night to hang out at some hip craft cocktail place like she would have expected. He was hanging out at Romano's, talking to Dennis and Frank, getting to know her *dad*. That didn't quite line up with the perfect suit and the expensive watch. Whatever. He was just trying to get into her pants. Guys would pretend to be into almost anything if they thought it would get them laid.

"I like your dad. I'm glad I finally met him."

"Fourteen years too late," she muttered. A sharp gust of wind buffeted them. The air felt charged with electricity.

"Hey, that was your idea."

"Good thing, too. I mean, why bother introducing you to my family when you weren't sticking around anyway?"

"Gem, it was complicated," he said quietly.

"Seems pretty straightforward to me. There was money to be made, and it wasn't here in Brooklyn." They were almost there. Only a few more houses to go and then she could escape. Not that she was running away or anything. She wasn't afraid of anything Brendan Flaherty could throw at her.

"You don't know the whole story."

"And I don't need to. It was fourteen years ago. Ancient history." They'd reached her house, and her hand was on the front gate to push it open when he spoke again.

"Didn't seem so ancient this morning."

She froze. Damn.

"Seemed alive and well this morning."

"Listen—" She turned to face him, but he was standing so much closer than she expected that whatever else she was about to say vaporized in her mind. It wasn't fair, the way his dark eyes turned all sleepy and enticing when he looked down at her, or the way his jawline met the hard, corded column of his neck. She was on social media. She'd seen what was beginning to happen to the other guys she'd gone to high school with. Why wasn't he morphing into some soft-faced soccer dad like the rest of them?

No, here he stood, all sexy and fit and even better than before and staring at her like he wanted to eat her up. And—she realized with grim resignation—she wanted to eat him up, too. The streetlights picked out every lingering hint of gold and red in his thick, silky hair as the sharp breeze ruffled it like loving fingers— like she wanted to ruffle it. Her mouth was practically watering for him.

"Yes, Gem?" His voice was pitched low and rumbling, and it sent an answering tremor through her body that she could feel in her stomach.

What had she planned to say? Probably something sensible about forgetting this morning ever happened. Except right now, she didn't want to forget it happened. She kinda wanted it to happen again.

Was that *such* a terrible idea? Would that open up a can of worms that had been successfully closed up tight for fourteen years? But maybe that can had already burst open. All she'd done all day was fantasize about him. So maybe Kendra was onto something. Maybe she should just sleep with him again and get it out of her system. What was stopping her? Why shouldn't she just take what she wanted from him and not worry about the rest? Didn't she deserve it after all this time? Didn't he *owe* her a little no-strings-attached fun?

He stared down into her face with those chocolate eyes of sin and smiled his sexy smile, and her uterus gave a sudden, urgent pulse, some primal hormonal scream of "I want that now!"

And then it was like her hormones locked her brain in a closet and took over the operation, because she reached for him, her hand fisting in his nice, crisp blue dress shirt. She didn't need to yank him forward this time, because he came on his own, his hands leaving his pockets and landing on her hips in the same instant.

In another instant her lips found his, his opened for her, her tongue swept in and tangled with his, a slick, delicious dance that she felt from her hair to her toes, and along every nerve in between. Brendan made a sound in his throat, a low, sexy growl that was lost in her mouth, and his fingers curled into her hips. Her hand slipped up the hard contours of his chest and over his broad, solid shoulder. Oh yeah, she wanted this. So bad she was nearly shaking with it.

Hooking her arm behind his neck, she pulled herself to her toes, aligning their bodies in some elemental way that seemed baked into her DNA. One of his hands slid up her back, his fingers tangling in her hair, wrapping around her ponytail. The gentle yet insistent tug sent a rush of molten desire through her and her teeth closed on his bottom lip in response. He nipped back in a dizzying tangle of kisses and licks and bites until all that internal debating about whether or not to fuck him had burnt down into a tiny pile of ash.

And that was before his hand landed on her breast. The pressure, the stroke of his thumb across her nipple through the thin barriers of her bra and tank top, sent a shiver rocketing through her body and she groaned into his mouth.

"Jesus, Gem," Brendan muttered against Gemma's hot, sweet, perfect mouth. He'd had no expectations tonight when he'd started walking her home. Just another chance to get her alone and hopefully chip away a little more at that wall of anger. Making out against her front fence, his hand on her breast, had not at all been on the agenda, but he wasn't complaining one bit.

She shoved herself away from him as quickly as she'd grabbed hold of him and he let her go just as fast, even though every inch of his body was screaming to hang on. This was where she was once again going to pretend this hadn't happened, but he didn't intend to let her get away with it this time.

"You kissed me again," he said.

"Well spotted, Flaherty." She was breathing hard, her breasts rising with every inhalation. Her voice was low, raspy, and just a hair unsteady. She wasn't as calm as she was trying to appear. Neither was he.

She took another deep breath. "Okay, here's how this is going to work. Sex. Just sex."

His brain skidded to an abrupt stop. "What?"

"Sex," she repeated. "You and me." That's what he thought she said, he just couldn't believe it.

"You want to have sex *now*?"

"You got other plans?"

"No," he said quickly. "No plans." And if he had,

he'd have blown off every one of them. "I just didn't think you'd want—"

"Look, it's pretty obvious we've still got a lot of unresolved sexual tension. I'm just suggesting we resolve it." Her chin was tilted up defiantly, and there was a challenge in her dark eyes.

"I am fully on board with that proposal."

"But that's all that's happening here. I'm not forgiving you, or falling for you again, or any of that other bullshit. We're just two consenting adults working off a little..."

He finished the sentence for her, taking his time with each word. "Unresolved sexual tension."

"Exactly. Are you cool with that?"

He considered it. So he was still no closer to winning her back. But he might have a better shot at that if she was naked in bed with him. He was certainly willing to try, and he couldn't deny that he'd enjoy it immensely. A rumble of thunder broke the tense silence. "I'm cool with that."

She let out a breath slowly, and so did he. He took another step closer, reaching up to run his fingertips along the edge of her jaw. "Should we go inside to finish this conversation?"

She licked her lips. "No conversation necessary. And we're not doing it here."

"Okay." He took a step back and held out his hand to her. "My place, then?"

She ignored his hand, walking past him up the sidewalk. "Your place. Keep up, Flaherty."

"Trust me," he said roughly as he fell into step beside her. "That is not going to be a problem."

## Chapter Sixteen

"It's going to rain," Gemma said as she walked quickly up the sidewalk at Brendan's side. Great, she'd been reduced to making inane comments about the *weather*. They hadn't even had sex yet and he was already scrambling her brains.

Brendan tipped his head back to look at the sky. The clouds were moving in fast, a roiling mass, glowing orange from the streetlights below. "Looks bad." He looked back at her, heat sparking in his eyes. "We'd better get inside."

She shivered, some tangle of anxiety and anticipation. "Yeah, that sounds like a good idea."

Brendan's apartment was the top floor of a three-family brownstone just a couple of blocks away from her place. It was nice enough, in its modest middle-class Brooklyn way, but she suspected it was a far cry from how he'd lived back in Chicago. But she didn't want to think about any of that. Him, her, their fraught history… she wasn't going to think about any of it tonight.

"Want a glass of wine?" he asked as he walked toward the kitchen. There wasn't much furniture, and what there was looked like it belonged to someone else altogether, all sleek and hard and modern.

"Sure," she said, wandering through the living room, running her fingers across the back of the white leather couch. Seriously, white leather? "This doesn't much look like your style," she called.

Brendan came back into the room, carrying two glasses of red wine. "It's not." He handed her a glass. "I bought the model unit of my last development and it came fully furnished. I brought it with me when I moved. I'll ditch all this when I finally move into my next development."

*Nope.* She absolutely was *not* going to think about his work. That would spoil everything. She didn't care who he was now or what he did for a living. She was only after what he was packing in his pants, what he could do with that mouth and those magic hands.

He took a sip of wine, watching her over the rim as she did the same. There was only one lamp on in the corner, so the room was more shadow than light. It cast his features in stark relief, highlighting the hollows under his cheekbones and the gorgeous, sculptural shape of his lips.

"This is good," she said.

"Glad you like it."

Gemma paused, considering her wine, considering his. Then she reached out and took his glass from him, setting both of them down on the glass coffee table.

"What's wrong?"

"We didn't come here to drink wine and discuss your furniture."

Brendan gave her a crooked smile. "I'm trying to be a gentleman here."

"Completely unnecessary. We both know why I'm here."

One golden-flecked eyebrow arched as he smirked at her. "So where does that leave us?"

She shrugged and spread her arms. "Where do you want to start?"

He let out a sharp huff of laughter. "That would require a very long answer."

"Start with the top of the list, tiger."

His tongue darted out, wetting his lips as he stared at her. It was embarrassing how aroused that tiny motion made her. All of this had her strung tight and ready to burst. He hadn't laid a hand on her and they both still had all their clothes on and she was already more turned on than she could remember being in her entire life.

"Naked," he finally said.

"Excuse me? Naked?"

"I know we have a pretty substantial…" He broke off and waved a hand between them. "Sexual history. But I never saw you naked."

"I was naked with you an awful lot, Brendan."

"Yeah, in the middle of the night, in that shitty shed in my backyard. We couldn't even turn on a flashlight for fear of being caught. My hands knew every inch of you, but my eyes… I never really got to *look*. With the lights on. And lots of time."

She considered that for a moment. "Okay. Naked. Let's start there." Grasping the hem of her T-shirt, she whipped it up and over her head. Brendan's eyes went straight to her breasts, straining against the edge of her basic beige bra. They stayed there as she toed off her shoes and unzipped her jeans, bending forward at the waist to wiggle out of them. Once she was out of them, she straightened up again, wearing nothing but a bra and panties. "Next?"

"Your hair," he rasped. "I haven't seen it down since—"

She dragged her elastic out of her ponytail and shook her hair free before he could finish his sentence. He swallowed hard. She might have just stripped nearly naked for him, but she was the one holding all the cards right now. She could feel the power coursing through her veins like electricity. Outside, another boom of thunder shook the building. It made her nipples hard.

"You know, I never got a good look at you, either."

His eyes, dark with lust, raked up to meet hers. "What?"

"I mean, my mouth knows the shape of your cock better than my eyes do."

He squeezed his eyes shut. "Damn, Gem. You can't say shit like that right now."

When he opened his eyes to look at her again, she hiked an eyebrow at him. "So?"

His hand went to his tie, dragging it loose from its perfect knot. She imagined doing something really fun with that length of silk and filed the thought away. Maybe later. Tossing his tie away, he went to work on the buttons of his dress shirt. Was there anything sexier in the world than a man unbuttoning a shirt?

Stripping out of it. That was definitely sexier. Gemma's mouth went dry as his toned, sculpted shoulders and biceps came into view. Then he reached up behind his head, grasped the back of his white tank undershirt, and whipped it off over his head in one smooth, drool-inducing move. Damn, that was hot.

The lean soccer-player's body she remembered from high school was gone. He was a little thicker, his shoulders were broader. Now the muscle definition came not from hours running back and forth on the soccer pitch, but from serious time in the gym. He was fucking gorgeous. There was a light dusting of red-gold hair across the tops of his pecs that continued in a tantalizing line down his stomach before disappearing beneath the waistband of his pants.

"Nice," she murmured.

"Same," he said, gesturing to her.

"What next?" she asked him, throwing her shoulders back in a way she knew made her breasts raise enticingly.

"Bra," he muttered.

Her hands went to the back clasp, flicking it open. She hesitated just a moment, holding it to her chest in front as his eyes practically begged her for a glimpse, before she finally tossed it away.

Brendan bit his bottom lip, watching as her dark pink nipples drew in tight and pebbled under his gaze. It was hard, holding still as he stared at her. Some tiny, destructive voice in her head reminded her that she didn't have a sixteen-year-old body anymore. But that seemed to be the last thing Brendan was thinking, so she let him stare, let the erotic weight of that stare settle into her body, ratcheting up her own desire.

"You next," she said, jerking her chin at his lower half.

Without ever looking away from her, his hands went to his belt and he began toeing off his shoes. Watching him leap to do as she asked was its own kind of hot. He slid his pants and boxer briefs off with one quick movement. When he straightened again, his cock was hard and swollen, curving up to his abdomen. She kind of remembered his size, but those memories had grown hazy, and they'd existed in the vacuum of her total lack of experience. She had plenty of experience now, though, and she was quite sure—Brendan's cock was a thing of beauty.

"Good?" he said, smirking at her.

"Very good." Slowly, she hooked her thumbs in the sides of her panties. "These next?"

He nodded mutely.

She shimmied out of them and tossed them in the direction of the rest of her clothes. Shaking her hair back over her shoulders, she held herself upright and stared back at him. "Okay, I'm naked. So are you. Now what?"

Without a word, he stepped forward, hooked an arm around her waist, hauled her body in against his, and kissed her. The force of it bent her back. The sudden invasion of his tongue stole her breath. Her body flared to life wherever his touched, nothing but skin on skin all the way down. His cock throbbed, hard and hot against her stomach. Her hands fluttered helplessly before landing on his arms to steady herself.

His kiss was relentless, devouring her, staking claim to every inch of her lips, her teeth, her tongue. While she was still clinging to him, trying to find her balance, his hand came up to her breast and rolled her nipple hard between two fingers.

She let out a harsh cry, her nails digging into the warm, smooth skin of his biceps. He did it again, this time pinching just hard enough to add a hint of pain, and she moaned again. A tremor raced through her from the roots of her hair to her toes.

His mouth never left hers, even as his fingers released her and slid between her legs. Then he was there, his fingertips sliding into her wetness, brushing against her clit, circling her opening, and then she was there, hovering right on the edge of a climax faster than it had ever happened before.

"Brendan," she gasped, tearing her mouth away from his, panting for air, desperate to find something to center herself on.

"I'm here, babe," he murmured. He ran his fingers along her jaw and pressed a kiss to her open mouth. She started to pull away from that tender touch, that gentleness in his eyes, that stupid endearment, but before she could, he let her go and dropped to his knees. "I'm right here."

"Wait…what…"

Then his hands were wrapping around her thighs, and he was urging her legs apart. All she could do was grip his shoulders to keep from falling over as his fingers parted her and his tongue snaked out to find her.

She let out another inarticulate cry as he found her clit, and another as he sucked gently on it, and then it was all over. In less than a minute, she was shaking uncontrollably, tears leaking out of the corners of her eyes as her orgasm hit her broadside like an oncoming train. He was gently relentless, working her over, drawing the pleasure out even as she thought surely she was going to collapse from it.

When she didn't think her legs could support her another minute, he stood up, took her face in his hands, and kissed her with a gentleness that left her reeling. Oh, no fair. How dare he touch her with that kind of tenderness when this was supposed to be a straightforward sexual transaction? He needed to stop blurring this line.

Before she could protest, he swept her up in his arms and, as the aftershocks were still racing up and down her limbs, he carried her out of the room to his bedroom, like he was some romantic movie hero or something. Well, he could forget what this was about all he wanted, but there was no way she would. Fisting her hand in his hair, she dragged his face down to hers and kissed him, all heat and sexy promise, and no goddamned romantic feelings.

His bedroom was dark, and the bedsheets cool and smooth under her as he laid her down. She was more than ready for him to climb on top of her and thrust in, but he sat back on his heels and stared down at her nakedness.

"Are you going to get on with it, Flaherty?"

"We had plenty of flashbangs in high school, Gemma. Tonight I want to take my time."

*No, no, no.* This was just supposed to be sex. Hard, dirty, meaningless sex. She wasn't here for tender touches and lingering looks. She was here for some bone-shattering orgasms and that was all. But he'd already given her one of those—a very good one—and her body was more than ready to see what else he could do if she gave him the chance to do it again.

"What are you going to start with?" she challenged. *Keep it physical.*

"Well, I was thinking your breasts."

"My breasts? What about them?"

"You know they're fantastic, right?"

She raised her hands to her breasts, cupping them, squeezing them together. "These?"

"Those." He didn't even try to look her in the eye, which was good. Exactly what she wanted.

"What do you want to do to them?" she asked, watching the way he watched her hands with such hunger. It was so hot. "This?" She pinched her own nipples and arched up off the bed for good measure.

"Jesus, woman." He was on her in a moment, whipping her hands away and out to her sides, pinning them there with his hands. Then he lowered his mouth and now when she arched off the bed, there wasn't an ounce of teasing in it.

"Brendan…"

"When I'm good and done," he murmured as he kissed his way in a slow circle around the outside of her left breast. Her nipple throbbed with need, but he ignored it, shifting his attention to the other breast. Again a long, slow circle of openmouthed kisses, of bites just on the edge of painful, but still, he left her nipples alone.

She writhed underneath him. His hands tightened on her wrists as he continued with his slow torture.

"Please," she begged, willing her nipple into his hot, wet mouth.

"Not until I'm ready."

"You're going to make me come again," she groaned.

"Could you really? Just from this?" he asked, before continuing his slow exploration of her breasts, leaving her nipples to throb with thwarted need.

*No*, she almost answered automatically, because she'd never even got close that way. But then she felt it, the low, heavy ache in her abdomen, the delicious tightening of her sex, even with no direct stimulation.

She was panting as he kissed his way across to her left breast again, and she twisted underneath him, squeezing her thighs together in search of some sort of relief. Then, with no warning, his mouth closed over her and he sucked hard.

She cried out, her voice echoing in his quiet bedroom, and her sex throbbed.

Not quite, dammit. She was so close she could scream, but he kept her there, hovering on the edge as he worked her tender nipples.

"Please, Brendan," she begged. "Please, please." Her voice sounded entirely too needy to her own ears. Needy and weak.

"Please?"

"Please fuck me," she said, twisting under him again.

He dropped his head against her breastbone, breathing heavily. His hands released her wrists, coming to her sides, shaping her torso. "Gemma…"

Time to remind him what this was about. She dug her fingers into his hair and hauled his head up, dragging his face to hers where she kissed him with hungry thoroughness. Lifting her legs, she wrapped her thighs around his hips until he was flush against her. His cock slid into the warm wet cleft between her legs and they both hissed in a breath.

"I need a condom," he muttered, dragging himself against her one more time, teasing them both, before rolling away to frantically dig in the bedside table.

When he rolled back, holding a foil packet, Gemma sat up, plucking it from his hands. "Let me."

"I'm on the edge of death here," he cautioned, as she ripped it open and slid it out. But he lay back, allowing her full access to his body.

She wrapped her hand around the base of him, about to roll the condom on, but she hesitated, unable to resist tormenting him just a little the way he'd tormented her. She gave him one firm stroke from base to tip, and he groaned, his head falling back, every tendon straining.

Another stroke had him muttering a stream of curses, his hands fisting in the duvet. Look at him, so helpless before her. She could drag this out forever or bring him to a shattering finish in minutes. He was all hers. She could be the one to walk away or she could be the one to stay, and this time there was nothing he could do about it one way or the other.

She lowered her head and licked him, one long slow lick along the entire length of him.

"Gemma…"

"Yes?" she murmured, before she lowered her head and took him fully into her mouth. He hissed and arched underneath her, one hand coming to tangle in her hair.

She didn't linger there long. He was too close to coming and it wasn't happening that way. Releasing him from her mouth, she went to work rolling the condom on as Brendan gasped for air underneath her.

"I can't go slow," he warned her as she finished and sat back.

"I don't want you to," she said, as he flipped her onto her back and loomed over her. Then he was there, shoving his way between her thighs, spreading her wide. The incredible pressure eased in and filled her.

"Oh," she gasped, when he'd fully seated himself.

"Good?" he ground out.

"Fuck me, Flaherty."

Her words were the last leash holding him back. He drove into her, hard, relentlessly, over and over, dragging her leg up over his shoulder when he wanted more. She let go, gave herself over to it. This…this was what she wanted, what she needed. A raw, primal fuck with him, to banish all that emotional shit from the past. It was over and done with. All they had now was this.

Except she couldn't quite forget high school, because it was rapidly becoming clear that despite how hot they'd been together then, how good he'd been, he was better now. Because they'd been horny teenagers sneaking around, most of their earlier sex had been, out of necessity, fast. Adult Brendan was a liar, because he was taking his damned time. He spent forever moving one way, then angling another way, paying attention to every sound she made and every hitch in her breathing, figuring out what she liked and what drove her wild.

It was effective, because her body was responding to him in ways it never had to anyone before. There should be no way she could come now, helpless on her back, pinned under him as he drove himself into her. But it was happening, a tightening that she couldn't hold back. This time was different, a deeper, darker release, a molten pleasure that didn't explode so much as flood her, slowly, thoroughly, endlessly. It reached parts of her that had nothing to do with skin and nerve endings, parts that felt tender and satisfied and scared all at once. Stupid pheromones.

She lost all sense of time and place as she crested endlessly on a dark wave of bliss, focusing on the sensation and blocking out every single other thing. Then she felt his hand on her face, his thumb rubbing across the top of her cheekbone. She knew that touch. He always touched her face that way when he was close to coming. When she was sixteen, it had made her feel so wanted, so cherished. Now she wrenched her head away, looking to the side as his breathing grew ragged. His hand slid into her hair instead, fisting tight as he pounded into her. Then he heaved, cried out, held still, and his orgasm took him under, too.

Afterward, she lay sated under the sweaty weight of his body. "Damn, Flaherty, I think you killed me."

"You okay? Did I hurt you?" His hand came up to stroke her cheek again. She wiggled out from underneath him.

"I'm fine. I just meant that you kind of fucked me to death just now."

He rolled to his side, propping himself on his elbow. "I'm going to take that as a compliment."

Gemma sat up, sweeping her hair over one shoulder. "You should. You've picked up a few tricks since the last time we did this."

He reached out, running a finger down the length of her spine. "One or two."

She bent over, pulling away from his touch, reaching for a T-shirt he'd abandoned on the floor. "Lucky me."

Outside, the rain had started, a hard downpour that muffled all the sounds of the streets below. Gemma surged to her feet. "I better get going."

Brendan paused for a moment before responding. "It's pouring outside. Why don't you just stay?"

*Yeah, not a chance.* She flashed a tight, forced smile over her shoulder. "You know the deal."

When she made to leave, he leaned forward, grasping her wrist and pulling her backwards until she tumbled back on the bed. "Brendan—"

In a flash, he had her pinned under the length of his body again. "Yeah, I know the deal. The deal is just sex. And I said I was going to take all night with that."

"Just sex means no sleepovers. I'm not staying."

Brendan considered that for a moment, even as his hand was sliding up the inside of her thigh. "What if I made it worth your while?"

She should get up out of this bed, put her clothes on, and leave. This was only going to work if she kept that line drawn firmly between them. But oh, then he touched her and it made her shudder and arch underneath him.

"You have one hour to make us both come again," she said. "And *then* I'm leaving."

He lowered his head and kissed the side of her neck. "Deal."

## Chapter Seventeen

She did eventually go home. After the storm had blown through, after Brendan had made her come *three* more times. He'd still pressed her to stay the night again, but she held firm, wiggling back into her clothes and slipping away into the quiet darkness to walk home alone.

She *had* let him put his number into her phone before she left. He'd said in case she wanted another go, and at the time, that sounded like an excellent idea. Except he'd already texted her once this morning, just a brief message wanting to know if she'd made it home okay. It felt a little too familiar, like she'd let him get too close, so she purposely didn't respond. And she still wasn't sure if she was going to take him up on his offer of a Round Two. It was undoubtedly a bad idea, but it was hard to say no to more of that sex.

She looked up from her grandmother's recipe book, where she'd been pretending to look for recipes for Carlos's dinner instead of replaying last night's sex marathon in her head. Tony Santini had just come back down from inspecting Mr. Mosco's apartment to give them the verdict.

"Well?" Dad asked.

Tony rubbed the back of his meaty neck. "You can

probably get away with keeping most of the wiring. Just replace the outlets and ground 'em, so that'll save you busting into the walls. But we gotta rewire the kitchen, and that means opening everything up. You plug a microwave in up there and you'll blow a fuse for sure."

Dad sighed. "Do what you gotta do, Tony."

"I got a guy who does drywall. Want me to include him in my estimate or you want to get your own guy?"

"Your guy's fine."

Tony took a pen from the pocket of his work shirt and finished writing up his estimate before sliding it across the bar to Dad. Gemma watched him for a reaction, but Dad was as poker-faced as they came.

He nodded and Tony left, heading up to Mr. Mosco's apartment to make a few more notes.

Gemma waited until he was gone to ask, "What's it going to cost us?"

Dad slid the estimate down the bar to her. She flinched. Even with the extra money from Carlos's dinner, that was going to hurt. But they had to do it, or they'd never be able to rent the place.

"Where are we going to come up with that?"

"Richie said he'd loan us the cash if we need it." Dad laughed in disbelief. "Can you believe it? Richie's loaning *me* money now."

"It's good he's doing so well."

"Yeah, but I hate to lean on him like this."

Gemma laid a hand on his shoulder. "Dad, he leaned on you when he needed it. He wouldn't have his business without you."

Dad nodded, looking around Romano's. "But maybe we wouldn't be in this bind if I hadn't bought out Richie and Marianne."

"Richie needed it, and so did Aunt Marianne, in her way."

A few years after 9/11, Aunt Marianne, their Uncle Vincent's widow, decided she wanted to move away with her kids and get a fresh start. Brooklyn held too many memories. Still being tied to her dead husband's share of a house in Brooklyn and a business she wasn't there to participate in was a burden she didn't want or need, so Dad had bought her out.

"It seemed like a smart thing to do at the time," Dad said. "Getting sole ownership. I thought it would be better to pass it on to you girls in one piece, rather than having to split it up with a bunch of cousins. That's how family feuds start."

"You did the right thing, Dad. Now I don't have to put Cousin Paul into a headlock every time we need to pay the tax bill. Romano's is all ours."

Dad gave her a small, half smile. "For better or for worse."

"Well, I've got this cooking job coming up, so that'll help some."

"You're already working full time here. You shouldn't have to work a second job just to keep us afloat."

"You do it."

He looked at her in surprise and she rolled her eyes. "Come on, Dad. You think I don't know that Uncle Richie is paying you to help him on the boats whenever you go out there for the weekend?"

He looked embarrassed that she'd caught him. "Richie needed an extra pair of hands."

"And we needed the extra money. There's no shame in that, Dad. I don't mind doing my share, too. I just hope I don't make a fool of myself trying."

"Not a chance, Gem." Sliding an arm around her shoulders, he kissed the top of her head. "What would I do without you, kid?"

"Starve, probably."

"What's this?" He indicated her recipe book.

She sighed and pushed it away. "It's Grandma Romano's recipe book. I was looking for something I could adapt for this dinner party, but I don't know."

"I didn't know you used this."

"How do you think I taught myself to cook, Dad?"

"I just figured it was all those cooking shows you watch on TV."

"Those are for inspiration. This is for knowledge."

Whipping his bar towel off his shoulder, he started wiping down the bar in preparation for opening. "Well, at least someone's getting some use out of it. Your mother couldn't be bothered."

"This was Mom's?"

He nodded. "My mother gave it to her as a wedding present."

"Really? But Mom couldn't cook." Mom had raised them on boxed macaroni and cheese and hot dogs. She barely knew how to turn on the stove. Angela Romano had been charismatic, outgoing, fun, and warm-hearted, but one thing she had not been was domestic.

A memory of her mother flared up in Gemma's mind—the clatter of a pot as Mom dropped it into the sink, the hiss as she turned the tap on and water hit the hot pot, the acrid smell of burning food, the air in the kitchen hazed with smoke. Mom had thrown her hands up in the air, muttering angrily to herself about "answering one little phone call and the dinner went to hell." Gemma had come in, taken one look at the blackened disaster in the pot, and asked her mother how on earth she'd managed to burn pasta when the pot was mostly water. In an instant, Mom's anger fled, replaced with laughter, and soon, Gemma was laughing, too. Mom's temper was quick to catch, but it burned out fast. The laughter, though—she was always laughing. It was what Gemma regretted most about losing her when they did. She'd just gotten old enough to know her mother as a person, to begin developing a new kind of relationship with her. They liked going shopping together and obsessing over *American Idol.* Jess and Livie had missed all that, and they'd never get it back.

"Your mother wasn't interested in stepping foot in the kitchen," Dad said. "A bunch of recipes from the old country were the last thing she wanted."

"But these are the best!" Gemma ran her fingers lovingly over her grandmother's recipe for Pasta e Fagioli. Okay, maybe Grandma didn't use enough salt, and Gemma's was definitely better for the addition of caramelized leeks, but the bones of the recipe…those were impeccable. It was a classic.

"Your grandma thought so, too. I'll tell you…" Dad broke off, then laughed and shook his head. "It caused a bit of a stir, that cookbook."

"Why?"

"Your grandma didn't use written recipes. Everything she knew, she'd been taught by my grandmother. It was all up here." He tapped his temple. "But Ma… she took the time to sit down and figure them all out. She knew a modern girl like your mom wasn't going to spend her life in the kitchen, memorizing her mother-in-law's recipes, so she made her a recipe book to follow. What she didn't realize was that your mom wasn't interested in the kitchen at all, recipes or no recipes. They fought like a couple of wet cats about it. Not sure Ma ever really forgave her for not learning to cook."

Usually when Dad shared a memory of their mother, his expression turned unbearably sad, like he was experiencing the tragedy of her loss all over again. But today, he looked almost…amused. He'd also never told her a story before that painted their mother in a less-than-saintly light. Maybe that meant he was finally getting over her, putting Angela Romano in her place in his past and leaving her there. And while that was bittersweet for Gemma, it was good for her father.

"Well, Mom didn't know what she was missing in here. Grandma's recipes are amazing."

"I'm glad you found it, Gem. Your grandma would be, too."

Smiling to herself, she pulled the worn notebook back to her, thumbing lovingly through the pages. It fell open to the recipe for brasato al Barolo, beef slow cooked in red wine. It was a Northern Italian dish, not from the Central Region, where the Romanos hailed from. She'd always supposed the Italian immigrants from all regions cross-pollinated each other once they were all in one neighborhood.

She'd made the Brasato before, with a tough chuck roast and a cheap red wine. But what if she classed it up? Individual portions of a good quality beef, full of marbling to add flavor? She could talk to Leo at Vinelli's about doing the cuts of meat custom for her. Then slow cook them all day in a great Brasato wine. And instead of dumping it on polenta, which is what she'd done when she'd made it for the family, she could do something nicer... Oh, whipped potatoes in individual ramekins, maybe, and piped in so they looked fancy, and then use the kitchen torch to brown the edges. Delicious comfort food, but with a modern take and elegantly presented. Maybe it wasn't flavored sea foam and slivers of things placed with tweezers, but it felt like her, for better or for worse. She could only hope that was good enough.

Fishing a notepad out from under the counter, she started a shopping list. It would be too late to shop for it tonight, but maybe tomorrow first thing. Excitement buzzed through her veins at the possibility. She couldn't wait to see how it turned out.

"Here comes your sister," Dad said, glancing out the front window. "And she looks like she's on fire."

Gemma glanced up to catch a glimpse of Jess hurrying down the sidewalk, her hair whipping behind her. The next moment, she came charging into the bar.

"Mariel said yes," she announced.

"What, to Dan? They're really getting married?" Mariel was secretly a hopeless romantic. Who'd have guessed?

Jess nodded as she came to take a seat on a bar stool, wiggling her way up the same way she'd been doing since she was twelve, because she'd never gotten any taller.

"Yep."

"Well, that's great news," Dad said. "I like Dan. He's alright."

It amused Gemma no end that because of Jess's relationship with Alex, the billionaire media mogul Dan Drake had actually been a guest in the Romano house, and that he and her father were now friendly. Dad could probably call up Dan today and Dan would write him a check to cover the bar's debts, but Dad was as proud as Jess about those things. A loan from Richie was one thing. He was family, and he owed her father. But Dan's money—Dad would die before asking, and Gemma didn't blame him.

"Here's the best part, though," Jess said. "Mariel was all for having a small ceremony with a Justice of the Peace or something and a little dinner afterward. She even wanted to ask you to cater it."

"Me?"

"Well, that was before Dan got involved. Because he doesn't want some quickie ceremony with a couple dozen friends and family. Dan wants a freaking blow-out wedding."

"*Dan* wants a big wedding?"

"He's such a big sentimental softie when you get underneath the suits and the swagger. He pulled in a few favors and got the Plaza Hotel next month."

"They're throwing together a big society wedding in a *month*?"

"Yep. For three hundred guests. When you've got Dan's money, anything is possible."

"Well, I guess I'm not catering that one for her."

"You couldn't cater it anyway, because you're going."

"What?"

"She's inviting you. She's inviting all of us."

"She's inviting our whole family?"

"Well," Jess said. "We're kind of *her* family too, don't you think?"

"You're right, Jess." He flipped his bar towel back over his shoulder. "There's always room for more in the Romano family."

Gemma folded Tony Santini's estimate into ever smaller squares. Seemed like a big family welcome was about all the Romanos could offer anyone these days.

## Chapter Eighteen

Kendra burst through the swinging door of Carlos's kitchen. "We have an emergency."

Gemma stopped, her hands frozen over the entrees she was furiously plating. "Oh, God. Someone's throwing up. I knew it. I knew I shouldn't have gone with the tuna carpaccio."

"No." Kendra waved her hands in annoyance. "They're practically licking their plates out there. One woman moaned. Like, legit sex noises."

"Oh. Well, that's good." She didn't tell Kendra the same thing had happened to Brendan when he'd tried it. Because she wasn't thinking about him, or the fact that she'd shown up at his place two more times this week after closing the bar. She wasn't thinking about all the mind-blowing sex they'd had, and she *definitely* wasn't trying to figure out when they could do it again.

"So what's the emergency?" Gemma turned back to her plating again, painstakingly arranging sprigs of fresh chives on a tiny bed of Parmesan shavings with a little spiral of prosciutto. She'd gotten the idea from *Top Chef*, but hers was better, because her decorative flourish was actually meant to be eaten with the meal, a perfect bite full of salty and savory, with a fragrant, grassy finish.

"One of the guests is a pescatarian. I have no idea what that is, but you'd think if she was following some weird religious diet she could have let me know when she RSVPed—"

"Kendra, it's fine. It just means she eats fish but no meat."

"But your entree is beef!"

"I prepped a few vegetarian entrees just to be on the safe side. One's in the oven now."

"For real? Gem, you're a genius."

"Nah, I just figured someone would have an issue. It's gluten free, too, in case she decides she's that."

"The servers are clearing the starter plates now. Are you okay on time?"

Gemma straightened, ignoring the twinge in her lower back. She was going to hurt for a week when this was done. As she surveyed the entree plates, lined up in rows on the counter, prepped and ready, the whipped potatoes, fresh out of the oven in their individual ramekins, their piped swirls artfully bronzed and crisp, the beef, simmering in its sinfully rich wine sauce on the burner, she nodded, slightly amazed at herself.

"Yes. Incredibly, I'm ready. I'm going to start plating. The servers need to be in here in five minutes, ready to take two plates at a time. We need to have all the entrees on the table in the next ten minutes or the sauce will start cooling."

Kendra nodded with a brisk efficiency that surprised her. Kendra was a solid friend, but hadn't always been the most responsible adult. Gemma had to admit, though,

Kendra knew what she was doing on the job, and she ran a tight ship. She'd really hit her stride working for Carlos.

When she'd gone, Gemma took a deep breath and reached for a fresh serving spoon. Time to get the main event onto the plates and out to the table.

Ten minutes later, she ran after the server, sprinkling a final dusting of chopped parsley over the last two plates before she let him disappear out into the dining room.

It was done. Her dinner was out there being cut into and eaten. The guests were tasting what she'd created and deciding what they thought about it. But she had no time for nerves. There was still cream to whip and chocolate curls to arrange before she could plate dessert, and the coffee still needed to be started.

She was piping whipped cream onto the cups of chocolate mousse with essence of orange when the first servers returned with entree plates. There didn't *seem* to be much left on them. That had to be a good sign, right? If they ate it, that must have meant they liked it.

When the last of the plates were returned to the kitchen, Gemma was just setting the final two dessert plates on a serving tray.

She passed off to a server. "Here you go. These are the last ones. The coffee's out there in a carafe already, but offer espresso or cappuccino, if anybody wants one. I can make them in here."

The server nodded and disappeared with the last of the desserts. Gemma took what felt like her first full breath all day. It was done. She'd made it. For better or for worse, all three courses had been prepared and served, with no major mishaps or kitchen disasters. All her careful planning, practice runs, and Excel spreadsheet schedules had paid off, at least in that regard. From an execution standpoint, she'd succeeded, and was proud of herself. As for the rest—how it had all been received—well, that remained to be seen.

She slumped against the counter of Carlos's beautiful, spacious, spotless kitchen and rolled her stiff shoulders. Just then, Kendra swept into the kitchen. Gemma looked up cautiously, not sure if she was ready to hear. Maybe she should just go home, flush with the success of cooking and plating a three-course meal for twenty without anything catching on fire, and hear the reviews tomorrow.

"Do I want to know?" she asked wearily.

Kendra hurried toward her, barely holding in an ecstatic grin. "Girl, you are a *hit*!"

"Really?" She felt nearly weak with the flood of relief. "They liked it?"

"Carlos is annoyed because nobody wanted to talk about his new investment plan. They were too busy talking about the food."

"You're exaggerating."

"No way! Cross my heart." She swept one long glossy red fingernail in an X over her heart. "I heard Bebe Kavanaugh tell Carlos that dinner was *divine*." Kendra rolled her eyes, her voice taking on an annoying nasal drawl, which Gemma supposed was what Bebe Kavanaugh sounded like. "Trust me, she's a judgmental bitch who finds fault with *everything*."

"I can't believe it. They really liked it?" Her exhaustion was momentarily forgotten in a rush of glee. Sure, she'd heard compliments about her cooking for years, but that was family. They had to tell you it was good. Or Dennis and Frank, who'd eat a chunk of the bar if she poured gravy on it. These people knew what they were talking about and they liked it!

"Trust me, by tomorrow, they're going to be telling all their friends about this fabulous new caterer they discovered at a little dinner party. These people love to be first to find stuff. They're going to be crawling all over themselves to book you."

"But Kendra, they can't book me. I don't have a business."

"Okay, let's talk about that—"

The kitchen door swung open, cutting Kendra off, and they both turned to see who'd come in. The woman was in her seventies, although her face was eerily line-free and elegantly made up. Her black hair, which was more dye than hair, was scraped back into a severe French twist. Her whippet-thin body was encased in a sleek black designer dress.

"Mrs. Simonsen, is there something I can help you with?"

Gemma suppressed a smile hearing Kendra slip into her work voice.

"Is this her?" Mrs. Simonsen's voice was deep and resonant, and she lifted one thin finger, with a glossy burgundy nail, to point at Gemma. The diamond ring she wore looked heavy enough to snap her wrist.

"Her?"

Mrs. Simonsen advanced into the kitchen, holding out her hand to Gemma. "Are you the chef?"

Gemma awkwardly clasped her fingertips, which was the closest she could come to shaking her hand when she was holding it that way. "I cooked dinner tonight, so, um, yes? I guess I'm the chef."

"My dear, it was *sublime*. I must have you."

"Have me?"

"I'm having a little dinner next month. Just a few friends celebrating the ambassador's birthday—"

"The *ambassador*?"

"—and you simply *must* say you'll do it. If I might get your card, I could call on Monday to discuss all the details."

"I don't have a—"

Kendra swept in, tucking her hand around Mrs. Simonsen's arm. "I'll call you with her contact info, Mrs. Simonsen. She's wonderful, isn't she? Carlos found her. Isn't he smart about these things?"

"A *genius*! It was *superb*, my girl. You really *must* do my little party. I look forward to speaking with you this week!"

Gemma waved weakly as Kendra ushered Mrs. Simonsen back out of the kitchen. Then Kendra turned, flattening herself against the door and looking at Gemma. "We need to talk about your catering business."

# Chapter Nineteen

As soon as she'd started the last load of dishes in the dishwasher, Gemma escaped Carlos's kitchen, leaving Kendra to ride herd on the rest of the evening and deal with the servers. The house was quiet and dark when she got home, which she expected. Dad and Clyde were covering the bar until closing tonight, so she could work her catering gig. The thought of that nice fat check sitting in her wallet, more than enough to cover Clyde's paycheck and the beer distributor invoice, with some left over to put towards Tony Santini's electrical work, left her glowing with happiness, despite her exhaustion.

Maybe, she thought, as she hung up her jacket in the entryway, she could figure out how to do a few more of these. Then they'd be able to do some serious renovations to Mr. Mosco's apartment, and charge more for it. But that was a puzzle for tomorrow. Tonight, all she wanted was a hot shower and a soft bed.

It took several minutes for her to sense something wasn't right in the house. Usually a floorboard creaking where it didn't ordinarily creak was enough to catch her attention, but her tired brain was still buzzing with all of tonight's new experiences, so her spidey sense didn't start tingling until she was getting a glass of water at the kitchen tap.

She froze, listening for anything that sounded out of place. After a moment, she heard it—a groan, almost too soft to hear, followed by an eerie, irregular scuffling, like something flailing around.

That's when she realized what was missing when she'd come in—Spudge. He wasn't by the front door to greet her.

"Spudge?" Her voice sounded sharp and echoey in the empty, silent house.

There was no response. Frantically, she began searching all his favorite sleeping spots—on the rug by the back door, under the dining room table, in front of the sofa—he wasn't in any of them.

"Spudge? Where are you, buddy?"

There was no answering click of his toenails as he lumbered in to greet her, no thump of his tail against the floor, no happy doggy groan of greeting.

She raced to the stairs, and had gotten three steps up when she heard that eerie rustling sound again, this time much closer. There was only one room on this floor she hadn't checked, the half bath under the stairs. When she flipped on the overhead light, she found him. He was sprawled across the white-and-black tiled floor, his eyes closed, his mouth open and tongue lolling as he panted heavily. His ribs heaved with each labored breath. Tremors were racing through him, causing his paws to scrabble ineffectually against the tile floor.

"Spudge!" She dropped to her knees, ignoring the pain as her knees collided with the tiles. When she touched his head, he made no response. He didn't even seem aware of her presence. Another seizure racked his big body and panic gripped Gemma's heart.

Who could she call? It was Saturday. Dad couldn't leave the bar. Livie…in Colorado. Jess…out of town with Alex for the weekend. Kendra…still at Carlos's.

Spudge let out another groan, but not his usual delighted doggy groan. This sound was just…wrong. It sent chills down her spine. Oh, God, Spudge was dying and she was helpless here on the floor with him.

Why his name suddenly popped into her head, she had no idea. But in seconds, she was on her feet, scrambling back to the entry hall, digging through her discarded shoulder bag for her phone. With trembling fingers, she scrolled through her contacts and pressed Brendan's name as she hurried back to Spudge.

"Hey," Brendan answered, his voice smooth and full of sexy innuendo. "You know you don't have to call first. Just come on over and—"

"Please help me."

In an instant, he sobered. "Gem? What is it? Where are you? What's wrong?"

"It's Spudge. I don't know… I think he's dying." Her voice broke on the last word and when she spoke again, it was through sobs. "Please come help me. I don't know what to do."

"Hang on, I'll be right there."

It felt like forever, as she sat wedged into the tiny half bath, Spudge's heavy head in her lap, holding onto his body, whispering soothing words every time another one of those horrible seizures ripped through him. She'd never felt so alone in her life.

When her phone buzzed with Brendan's text, though, it had been less than five minutes.

"Pulling up out front."

Carefully, she eased Spudge's head back down on the floor. "I'll be right back, sweetie. Just hang on, okay? Don't go yet."

She hurried to the front door, flipped the dead bolt and threw it open just as Brendan mounted the front stoop, taking the steps two at a time. He paused just long enough to clasp her hand.

"It's going to be okay. Where is he?"

She led him to the bathroom, where Brendan sidled in next to Spudge's bulk.

"Hey, buddy. Let's get you some help, huh?" His voice was low and soothing as he quickly and efficiently slid his arms under Spudge and hefted him into his arms. With a jerk of his head, he indicated that she should go ahead of him. "I looked it up on the way over. There's a twenty-four-hour emergency vet near Atlantic Terminal. Just get the doors for me."

Gemma hurried to open the front door and stood to the side as Brendan sidled past her with Spudge in his arms.

"It's okay, buddy," he whispered. "You're going to be okay. Everything's okay."

He was talking to Spudge, but his quiet, reassuring words, the low, steady timbre of his voice, his solid, sure presence, burrowed down into Gemma's heart, too. For the first time since she'd found Spudge lying on the floor, she could breathe. She wasn't alone.

It was nearly one a.m., but the bright overhead fluorescents made all sense of day and night disappear. Gemma sat in one of the uncomfortable waiting room chairs, elbows on her knees, staring at the white linoleum floor. Brendan sat next to her, his knee bouncing slightly as they waited.

Two vet techs had rushed to greet them as soon as Brendan had shouldered his way through the door with Spudge. They'd swept him away into the back for emergency care, and now there was nothing to do but wait. She'd texted Dad, who was coming over as soon as he closed the bar at one, so he'd be here soon, but for now, it was just her and Brendan.

"Maybe they'll let me go back now," Gemma said, sitting up and gripping the arms of her chair.

"They said they'd come get you when you can see him."

"But what if he's dying back there? I can't let him die alone—"

Brendan's hand came down over hers and squeezed. "He's not going to die."

"How do you know? He's old and overweight. Oh, God, I knew we shouldn't let him keep eating that crappy dry food he loves. It's terrible for him. And Dad is always sneaking him table scraps—"

"Gem, stop. You made that dog happy. There's no crime in that."

Abruptly her eyes, already puffy and burning from crying, welled with tears once more. "I don't know what I'll do if he dies," she whispered. "He's just…" In a flash, she knew why this was hitting her so hard, why she was so scared. "He's all I have left."

"What the hell are you talking about?" Brendan half turned in his chair to face her. "Spudge is *not* all you have left."

Now that she'd started giving voice to her innermost fears, she couldn't seem to stop. "Livie and Jess are both gone. Dad's going to marry Teresa and I'll lose him, too. And then what? It's just me and Spudge."

"Gem, stop." He reached across her to take her by the shoulders. "Livie and Jess haven't gone anywhere. They're still your sisters, just like John is still your father. You have a huge family who loves you. You have a bar full of customers who think of you as family."

It was terrible, succumbing to all her fears now, in front of Brendan, of all people, but she couldn't seem to help it. She felt ice cold down to her bones. Her hands were even shaking with it. "Then why do I feel so left behind?" she whispered.

Brendan's expression softened and he pulled her into his embrace, wrapping his arms around her. His body had become familiar to her over the past couple of weeks, but not like this. There was no heat and lust now, just warmth and solidity. Her arms slipped around him and her hands fisted in his shirt. "Hey," he murmured into her hair as she squeezed her eyes shut and tried to hold back her tears. "Can't you see it, Gemma? You haven't been left behind. You've been set free."

"Free of what?" she muttered into his shoulder. Because she felt the exact opposite of free.

"You've had to be the grown-up who takes care of everyone else since you were a kid. You took care of them and look at your sisters. Look how successful they are. *You* did that. But now it's done. Now it's your turn."

She pulled back, swiping at her wet cheeks with her palms. "What are you talking about?"

He reached up, gently swiping his thumbs under her eyes, drying her cheeks. The gesture was so painfully tender that her heart twisted. She probably should have pulled away, but right now, she couldn't bear to. "You've got the rest of your life in front of you, Gemma. What do you want to do with it?"

She let out a little huff of laughter, because what kind of question was that? She'd had her life figured out since she was old enough to understand the concept of a future. Her life was Romano's bar. Her place was there, like her father before her and his father before him, all the way back to her great-grandfather, Angelo Romano, in 1934. That was her past and it would be her future.

"Brendan, I know what I'm doing. What I want."

He looked at her like he'd just stripped her bare and peeked inside to the depths of her soul. "Really? Where were you earlier tonight?"

"At Carlos's, cooking dinner. Why?"

"And how did that go?"

"Um, it went well, actually. Everybody seemed really pleased."

"And how did you feel while you were doing it?"

There was the question she hadn't let herself dwell on. Tonight had felt amazing. Stressful, yes, and most of the time, she'd been absolutely terrified, but once it was all done, when she'd seen all her careful planning and skill come to fruition...that was the best feeling in the world.

She was saved from confessing that uncomfortable truth to Brendan, though, by the arrival of one of the vet techs from in back.

"Mr. and Mrs. Romano?"

Gemma shot to her feet. "Oh, we're not...he's not... it's just me, Gemma Romano." Although for the past hour, she hadn't been alone. Brendan had been beside her. She'd consider how she felt about that later. "How's Spudge?"

"He's still sedated, but you can come back and see him now."

"He's not going to...die?"

The tech, a young woman with a sweet face and a wide, comforting smile, shook her head. "No, he's not going to die. The vet will come talk to you in a few minutes."

The relief left her nearly weak kneed. "Oh, thank you." She pressed a hand to her chest. "I was so scared."

"He's going to be okay," the tech told her reassuringly. "Come on, he's just back here."

Gemma was halfway to the door when she remembered Brendan and turned back. He was standing where she'd left him, hands in his pockets. "Go on. I'll be right here."

"It's okay. Dad will be here any minute. You don't need to wait."

"Are you sure?"

"I'm sure."

"Okay. Let me know how he's doing, okay?" He turned to go but stopped when Gemma called out to him.

"Thank you. I don't know what I would have done if you hadn't come."

"Of course I came," he said simply. "Take care, Gem."

Then he was gone.

## Chapter Twenty

The vet's diagnosis was canine diabetes. After a couple
of days at the vet, Spudge came home none the worse
for wear, although he was deeply unhappy about his
new diet dog food and the complete ban on table scraps.
There were daily insulin injections to deal with, too,
but Gemma didn't mind. It was a small price to pay to
have Spudge back home and good as new.

She hadn't seen Brendan since that night. She wasn't
sure what to say to him, after she'd sobbed into his
shoulder and confessed all her deepest insecurities.
He'd been so…supportive, kind… Frankly, he'd been
the Brendan she'd fallen in love with, that sensitive, gentle boy who'd taken the time to reach out to her in her
grief when no one else had. She'd thought that boy had
died when Brendan left for Chicago, or that maybe he'd
never really existed at all. But he was still in there—
that boy she'd fallen in love with—hiding under Brendan's glossy new surface, and she didn't know what to
do with that information.

So she hadn't called him when she probably should
have, and she hadn't shown up for any more late-night
booty calls. She'd texted to let him know Spudge was
okay, and they'd had a brief exchange, all about the

dog. That was cowardly on Gemma's part, she knew, but she felt like she was picking her way through a field of landmines where Brendan was concerned and rushing headlong into it seemed like a recipe to get herself blown to bits.

He hadn't been into the bar either. Maybe her weepy breakdown over a dog had scared him off. He was into her, but maybe not *that* into her.

Whatever. She had too many other things to worry about. Like how they were going to pay for the renovations to the apartment upstairs. Tony Santini had found a few more things that needed to be done, and the estimate had steadily climbed northward, until once again, she had no idea how they were going to come up with the money.

It was a Tuesday night, and the bar was dead—again—so Dad had sent her home early. She didn't argue. At least at home she could cook something to distract herself. She was absolutely *not* going over to Brendan's.

She was mounting the steps to the house, fishing her keys out of her bag, when her phone buzzed. Brendan. *Calling* her. She thought about ignoring it. Chatting on the phone was one more intimacy she shouldn't be allowing. But she was still feeling guilty over ghosting him after he'd been so nice about Spudge, so after another moment's hesitation, she took the call.

"Hey," he said.

"Hey. Spudge is fine," she said hurriedly. "He hates his new dog food, but—"

"Glad to hear it, but I didn't call about Spudge."

Her stomach tightened with desire. She could *hear* the lust in his voice. "What are you calling for?"

"You. Me. Here."

She had to lean against the door, pressing her thighs together against the rush of heat. "Um… I'm cooking." Lame excuse. She hadn't even made it inside yet, never mind started prepping anything.

"Come cook it here. Just come."

She shouldn't. She really, really shouldn't…

"Okay."

He probably shouldn't have called her.

The sex had definitely been going well, and then there'd been the emergency with Spudge, when she'd actually leaned on him, accepted his help. He'd thought maybe things would be different after that, but instead, she'd pulled further away than ever. All that intimacy and sharing had scared the hell out of her. He probably should have let her be and waited until desire brought her back to his door on her own.

But it had been a long, shitty day. First another prickly visit to his mother, and then some colossally bad news from the attorney making the offer on what was supposed to be his next property acquisition. He'd been summarily outbid, the deal done with cash before he could even come back with a counteroffer, and he had a sneaking suspicion who was behind it all. Fucking Jimmy Walsh.

He'd prowled around for a couple of hours, drinking scotch and generally being miserable, until he'd broken down and called Gemma. If this was just sex, then fine. Tonight he wanted sex. He wanted her. However he could have her.

And now she was here, coming when he'd called. After he buzzed her in downstairs, he went to open the front door for her and found her climbing the last steps weighed down with shopping bags.

He hurried to relieve her of the bags. "What's all this?"

"I didn't know what you had in your kitchen so I brought everything."

"Smart move, because I have nothing in my kitchen."

"I kinda figured."

"I'm glad you came. This is the only good thing that's happened to me today."

"I expect you to pay me back with orgasms," she said, slipping past him into the kitchen.

"Whatever, Romano. You know I'm good for it." He heard the snap in his voice, but he was hours past trying to rein it in.

Gemma stopped unpacking her bags and raised an eyebrow at him. "You seem pissed tonight."

There was no way to explain without going into a whole lot of backstory she didn't know yet. And tonight didn't seem like the right time. She wasn't ready for that kind of sharing from him. "Just a shit day. A deal gone bad. That's all."

She shrugged and started browning meat in a heavy pot she must have brought in with her, because he'd never seen it before.

"Plenty of those to go around," she said.

Brendan opened a bottle of wine, poured two glasses, and joined her in the kitchen. He handed her a glass of wine and moved to lean on the counter, far enough to be out of her way but close enough to watch her while she worked. He watched her work, wondering if he should press her to explain. But she was here, and they had their clothes on, so maybe this was a chance to push a little further. "Anything specific?"

She shrugged, keeping her eyes down as she transferred browned beef out of the pot and added some vegetables. "We need to renovate Mr. Mosco's apartment before we put it back on the market and it's going to cost a lot."

"Was Mr. Mosco your tenant?"

"Yeah. He'd lived there for decades, so we didn't really upgrade anything. It needs so much. New kitchen wiring at a minimum, but really it needs new windows, new floors… It's just a lot."

"Well, if there's anything I can do to help…"

She flashed a grim smile at him. "Nope. I got it under control."

"Okay. Just know…you can talk to me about, well… anything. I'm happy to listen."

She nodded, keeping her eyes on the pot. Her jaw was tight with tension and her eyebrows furrowed. It was weighing on her more than she'd admit, but the fact that she'd shared it with him at all had to count as progress, so he'd leave it alone for now.

Setting his wine down on the counter, he moved forward until he could settle his hands on her hips. She didn't want to share yet, but he knew exactly what to do to relax her again.

"Tell me about this magic you're making in my kitchen. It smells amazing."

"Just beef bourguignon."

"That sounds French, Miss Romano."

"My skills extend beyond pasta and red sauce, you know."

"Oh, yes, I'm well aware of just how far your skills

extend." He slid an arm around her waist and with his other hand, moved her hair aside so he could kiss the side of her neck. "You're extremely talented in many ways."

"It's just food," she protested, stiffening slightly.

Any hint of affection that didn't involve taking her clothes off made her start for the door. But he persisted, pulling her back against his chest. "Tell me what you're doing now," he murmured against the silky skin behind her ear.

He felt her soften, arousal warring with her fear. He kissed her behind her ear, flicking her slightly with his tongue. She let out a low sigh, her head tipping to the side in surrender. "Um…sautéing the vegetables."

"It smells fantastic. So do you."

"That's just the beef." She emptied a small bowl of minced garlic into the pot, her hands less steady than they'd been a moment ago, and the fragrance blossomed around them. "And the garlic."

"Mmm, this spot right here is all you." He nipped at her and her breath hitched.

She reached for a bottle of cognac that must have come in with her and poured a healthy splash into the pan, which sizzled and hissed, steam swirling around her.

"What are you doing now?"

"Building the sauce. The liquid deglazes the pan—"

"Deglazes?" His hand slid under the hem of her T-shirt, coming to rest on the warm smooth skin of her stomach. "What's that?"

Her voice went soft and a little unsteady. "When you add alcohol or another liquid to pull up all this browned stuff from the bottom of the pan. It's called the fond. That's where the flavor is."

He kissed her neck again, tracing a line down to the edge of her T-shirt with his tongue. "If you say so." She shivered under him then pulled away enough to retrieve the bottle of wine he'd opened.

"Wine too?"

"The cognac was just for deglazing. It'll simmer in the wine."

She added the meat back to the pot, then poured the rest of the bottle over it.

"That's a lot of wine."

"It'll thicken up."

Something else was about to start thickening up, but he didn't want to distract her while she worked. Well, any more than he already had.

She dropped a few more things in—a spoonful of sugar, a few pinches of salt, a couple of twists of the pepper grinder, some sprigs of herbs, and beef broth—then stirred, staring down into the pot.

He couldn't see anything past the sexy slope of her neck, the shadow between her breasts as he peered over her shoulder. She dipped a finger in and tasted it. His groin tightened as he watched her suck on her finger in contemplation.

"Looks fantastic."

She reached for a spoon, dipped it into the pot, then twisted in his arms, holding it up to his mouth. "Here, taste. More salt?"

Eyes on hers, he opened his mouth for her and let her slide the spoon inside. It wasn't even done yet and it tasted perfect, rich and meaty and velvety. She was perfect, staring up at him with her dark, expectant gaze, lips parted as she waited for his verdict.

"It's good." Swallowing, he licked his lips. "Will it keep?"

"What?"

"If it sits here while I take your clothes off, drag you to bed, and fuck you, will it be ruined?"

She blinked then turned back to the stove, turning down the heat and dropping a lid on the pot. "Lucky for you, it's got to simmer for at least an hour."

"Thank God," he muttered, working her shirt up over her head before she'd even turned around. She lifted her arms, letting him whip it up and off, and her long dark hair tumbled back down the smooth expanse of her back. She started to turn, but he crowded her in from behind, pinning her to the counter, sweeping his hands up her rib cage to cup her breasts.

She groaned, throwing her head back against his shoulder and pushing her hips back into his. He ground his dick against her, reveling in the perfect friction, the burst of mind-numbing pleasure, and he did his best to convince himself that this was exactly what he'd wanted when he called her—that it was *all* he wanted.

Gemma succeeded in twisting around to face him, her arms twining around his neck and one leg coming up to hook over his hip. Their lips crashed together inelegantly, hungry to taste. Her tongue plunged into his mouth and her teeth nipped at his bottom lip as her fingers fisted in his hair hard enough to hurt.

Hooking an arm around her waist, he swung her away from the counter and they staggered ungracefully through the kitchen and out into the living room. When Gemma slid a hand between their bodies and cupped him through his jeans, he had to stop moving, dropping his forehead on her shoulder.

"I hope you have a condom in your wallet," she said into his ear. "Because we're not gonna make it to the bed."

As if he needed another reminder that she was only here for one reason. Still, that reason was better than nothing, and if it was the only part of her he could have, he'd take it. For now.

He tightened his grip on her, walking her backwards until she collided with the back of his couch. "I do."

Gemma sucked in a breath. "You get that while I get this." She began to unbutton the fly of his jeans, and with clumsy hands, he retrieved the condom from his wallet in his back pocket.

"Give me this," she whispered, swiping it from his hands and tearing the foil packet open with her teeth. While she rolled it onto his dick, he unzipped her jeans and started working them down her hips. But they were tight and she was wearing fucking boots and there was no way he'd survive long enough to strip her out of all these clothes.

"I need you inside of me," she hissed in frustration.

So he spun her around and bent her over the back of the couch. Gemma gasped, her hands splaying across the pristine white leather as he tugged her jeans down over her ass. "I hope you meant that," he muttered, lining himself up.

"I did."

"Good." And he rammed home, sheathing himself in her to the hilt. She gasped again. He groaned. It was so tight and hot and perfect. "God, Gemma." He wanted this feeling to last forever. But he was greedy enough to want more. He wanted all of her, and he wasn't sure he'd ever have it.

"Hard," she murmured, fingers curling into the back of the couch.

It was pressing in on him from all sides—the long, frustrating day, this maddening woman who would only give him crumbs of herself—until he felt like he was drowning in it.

"Don't think I can do it any other way right now," he muttered as he drew almost all the way out before ramming home again.

She made a soft sound, somewhere between a gasp and a moan, that trickled down his spine like electricity, and it was the last coherent thought he had. His hands gripped her hips hard enough to leave marks as he pounded himself into her, letting everything out.

Gemma took it, bowing her head and hanging on as he satisfied himself with her body. But as he could feel his release start to tingle in the base of his spine and his balls, he needed more from her. He wanted to feel her shake to pieces around him, helpless and trembling. He wanted her to need him as much as he needed her.

Sliding a hand around her hip, he slid his fingers into the tight cleft between her thighs, still bound together by her jeans. When he found her clit, she let out a low moan.

"Come on, baby," he said, working her over as he pounded himself nearer and nearer to release. He needed this, needed to feel her fall apart as he did.

"Brendan," she said, her voice little more than a whimper.

"Give it to me, Gem."

And then she did, letting out a cry that was nearly

a scream, almost as cathartic for him as it was for her. Her thighs began to shake around him, her hips bucking back against his as much as they could in her restricted position. The added pressure was all that it took to send him over the edge. His entire world whited out with pleasure. There was only Gemma's body under his, sheathing him in unimaginable bliss.

He came slowly back to himself as the last tremors of his release eased through his body. He was curled over Gemma, his chest pressed to her back, his forehead resting between her shoulder blades. His hand was still between her thighs, cupping her. She was shaking underneath him, her breath coming in soft pants.

"Holy shit," she rasped. "I take it back. I fucking love this couch."

"That was good."

She chuckled and he could feel it through his entire body, a warm aftershock that left him tingling. "You always were the master of understatement, Flaherty."

He pressed a weary kiss to the soft skin of her shoulder.

"You're going to have to help me out here because I'm not sure my legs work anymore."

With a pat to her hip, he eased himself out of her body. "Hang on. I'll be right back."

After quickly disposing of the condom, he hurried back to her. She was just pushing herself upright, hands braced against the back of the couch. Turning her around, he lifted her until she was sitting on it. Then he went to his knees, unzipping first one tall suede boot then the other. When he'd worked those off, he peeled her jeans the rest of the way down her legs, getting her naked at last. Usually at this point, she'd be pushing him away, uncomfortable with any show of tenderness or caring on his part. But tonight she let him undress her, and made no protest as he ran his hands gently down her thighs, up her back, through her hair.

Standing, he moved between her knees, hands bracing her hips to balance her. "How's dinner?"

She glanced at the clock on the wall behind him as she worked his T-shirt up his rib cage. "Another thirty minutes, at least."

"That'll work." He bent his head to capture her mouth with his. Amazingly, after that orgasm that shook him to his bones, he felt his cock begin to stir again. Gemma hooked one long arm around his shoulders as she slipped her other hand between their bodies, her fingers curling around his rapidly swelling cock.

"Mmm, perfect," she mumbled against his mouth.

Sliding his hands underneath her ass, he lifted her until she could wrap her legs around his hips.

*Yes*, he thought as he carried her through the living room toward his bedroom. *Yes, you are most definitely perfect, Gemma Romano.* She'd always been perfect. Now it was on him to prove himself worthy of all that perfection—if he could.

## Chapter Twenty-One

Gemma had just finished locking the security gate after closing when she spotted Brendan halfway down the block. At first she'd thought he'd come to meet her, but he was on his phone, facing the other way, and he looked mad, so she didn't think he was here for her.

The other night at his place, he'd mentioned having a terrible day, some deal gone bad. When they'd fucked, so hard and fast, she'd sensed his bad mood, like a black cloud hanging over him, and she'd been curious, despite herself. She hadn't asked, though. That night had already gotten intimate enough, cooking for him, eating dinner together later, naked and wrapped in sheets. She hadn't been about to start asking personal questions about his life and sharing feelings.

But now here he was again, frustrated and angry about something. She hesitated, watching him fist one hand in his hair as he talked. She couldn't hear his words, but she caught the tone—clipped and furious. He'd never so much as raised his voice to her.

Before she'd entirely thought it through, she hefted her bag on her shoulder and walked toward him. He was half turned away from her, so he didn't see her approach, which meant she heard the tail-end of his conversation.

"Come on, it's too small to be of any interest to you. You did this for one reason, and one reason only… Yeah, I see how it is. But don't think you've won. This isn't over."

Tearing the phone away from his ear, he pressed the screen to end the call, muttering an oath under his breath.

"Brendan?"

He startled and swung around to face her. "Gemma. What are you doing out here?"

She hooked a thumb over her shoulder. "Just closed the bar and heading home. Something up with the sale?"

"No, the deal on the DiPaolas' building is done." He blew out a frustrated breath and pointed to the building next to DiPaola's. There used to be a Chinese takeout place in there, and before that, a hardware store, but the storefront had been unoccupied for a few months. "I was trying to buy this one, too, to double the parcel, but someone scooped me on it."

With their recent tumble back into bed, it had been easy to forget what had brought Brendan back to the neighborhood after all this time. Now it came crashing back into her mind like a wrecking ball, which is just what he was planning to do to her neighborhood. He'd come here with one goal—to develop the neighborhood. And dumb her, she'd been worried that he was *upset*.

Gemma frowned in false sympathy. "Too bad. You'll have to build your empire someplace else I guess."

He narrowed his eyes as he looked at her, and Gemma felt a twinge of guilt, which was stupid. A real estate developer, even the one who'd helped save her dog and was currently sexing her up on the regular, didn't deserve her sympathy. Developers were rapidly devouring her beloved borough. She'd do well to remember that before she started having more warm, fuzzy ideas about how much she *liked* him.

"You don't even know what my plans for the property are."

"I'm sure they're just like all the others who've come through here and bulldozed buildings." She waved a hand up the street, where many older buildings had recently been leveled to make way for shoddily constructed apartment buildings that stood out like a sore thumb from their surroundings. "Nothing but slapped-together luxury rentals that nobody can afford except trust-fund kids and foreign billionaires who never even step foot in them. Nothing that contributes to this neighborhood."

"Give me a little credit, Gem."

"I haven't seen a developer yet who improved things. You guys are just out to make a buck, and never mind what it does to the rest of the neighborhood."

Anger flared in his eyes, but she really didn't care. Let him be mad at her. That was for the best, really. She might have momentarily forgotten who he was now and what he was here for, but that was a dangerous thing to do. Right now, she was kind of mad at him, too. How dare he rescue her dog and be all tender and sweet after sex and be the same kind Brendan she remembered, when the whole time he was planning to bulldoze her neighborhood? How could such an otherwise good guy make such a nakedly greedy choice?

"So you think that's all anybody's capable of…rampant greed and destruction?"

"That's all I've seen. Not one of those new buildings has done a damned thing for Carroll Gardens except drive up rents and drive out working-class families like mine. But those developers sure cleaned up."

He stared at her, his jaw twitching as he ground his teeth, and Gemma forced herself to stand her ground. His money didn't intimidate her.

"Do you have a minute?"

"What? *Now?*" He really wanted her to come home with him and have *sex*?

"Yeah, now. I want to show you something. Just come take a ride with me."

Oh. Not his place for sex. "Where to?"

"I promise we won't leave Brooklyn. Come on, you might think I'm a soulless capitalist, but I know you don't think I'm an ax murderer."

Curiosity finally won out. "Okay."

"My car's around the corner." He motioned for her to walk beside him, and after a moment's hesitation, she did. Maybe this was yet another stupid move where Brendan was concerned, but she seemed incapable of avoiding them at this point.

The adrenaline was still coursing through his veins as Brendan walked Gemma to his car. He was not in the right place for this conversation tonight, not after that infuriating phone call. But he also wasn't in the mood to stand there and take it as she accused him of being some heartless carpetbagger. There was still so much she didn't know, and if they were ever going to move beyond meaningless sex, they needed to address their past.

When they reached his car, he leaned down to unlock

it. Gemma lowered herself into the passenger seat and he shut the door behind her. Well, here went nothing.

"So where are we going?" she asked after the first few minutes of the ride had passed in silence.

"Bensonhurst."

"Wow, Bensonhurst at midnight. You really know how to show a girl a good time, Flaherty."

He smiled tiredly. "Laugh it up, Romano, but I'm about to share my life's work with you. Show a little respect."

She laughed, too, and his lingering anger from their argument in front of DiPaola's dissipated. Brendan felt the tension slowly leaving his shoulders as he drove through the dark Brooklyn streets. Under different circumstances, in that other life he'd had to leave behind, he could imagine them driving home together like this. Maybe with a couple of kids asleep in the back seat…

Well. Life had had other plans for both of them.

He turned onto Eighteenth Avenue and pulled up to the curb across the street from his building. "We're here."

Gemma peered through the windshield. "Where?"

"Hop out. I'll show you."

When they were standing side by side on the sidewalk, he nodded to his building across the street. "That's it."

"What is?"

"The first project of my new company."

Gemma looked at the brick building with new eyes. "You built that?"

"Well, I arranged for it to be built. Bought the lots, hired the architects, had it constructed. They're finishing up the interiors now. Hopefully we'll have people in there in the next couple of months."

It was a fairly simple four-story red-brick build-ing, with storefronts on the street level and apartments above. It was a little bigger than the buildings on the rest of the block—most of those were two- and three-story, but it wasn't an eyesore. She had to admit, the tasteful brickwork was actually an improvement over the vinyl siding sported by most of the other buildings on the block.

There were thoughtful touches, too, like the large, multi-pane windows that gave the place a faintly old-fashioned look, and the carved stone entryway, nestled between the two storefronts. French doors and black wrought iron railings on the balconies made the build-ing almost look European. She could imagine that, with warm light pouring out of the windows, and potted plants and cafe tables on the balconies, the building would look very inviting. Someplace you'd like to live.

"Okay, it's not a total architectural atrocity," she con-ceded. "It's pretty."

"It's meant to be more than that. Look at the apart-ments above these other storefronts. One unit, with two tiny windows up front and two in back that look out on the building behind it. Those apartments are dark, dank floor-throughs, with tiny, outdated kitchens and baths. I wanted to build something different, something bet-ter. Big windows that let in plenty of light, good layouts that let you live in a little peace and comfort, and every unit has a balcony, so every family gets some outdoor space of their own."

"Assuming there are families that can afford these."

"See, that's part of what I'm doing. I kept construction costs as low as possible. Screw granite counter-tops and Sub-Zero kitchen appliances. I wanted to build apartments real families can afford. There are plenty of places with all kinds of high-tech amenities and every luxury bell and whistle. Your average middle-class family doesn't care about an on-site gym and concierge service. They just want a couple of decent-size bedrooms for the kids and a kitchen you can cook a meal in.

"Gemma, I know you're mad that places that have been here a long time are getting torn down, but that's going to happen no matter what. If Brooklyn is changing, if the old has to go, then I want to have a hand in what's new. Yes, families have lived in some of these places for a hundred years. I want to build the homes families live in for the next hundred years. *That's* what I'm doing here. *That's* why I came back to Brooklyn."

Gemma blinked at him, feeling suddenly off kilter. Whatever she thought he'd brought her here to see, it was not this.

"Wow," she finally said, looking at her feet, which seemed safer. "You sound like George Bailey in *It's a Wonderful Life*."

He shoved his hands into his pockets, shoulders hunched forward. "Maybe. George Bailey had the right idea."

"Um, Brendan, George Bailey never made any money. You caught that part, right?"

"No, he didn't. And I'm not going to make a lot on these either."

"I don't understand."

"It's kind of a long story. There's a little park on the next block. Are you up for a walk?"

"Sure."

Then he held his hand out to her, watching her steadily, almost a challenge. Brendan Flaherty was still largely a mystery to her. But right now, he was a mystery she desperately wanted to unravel. So she took his hand.

## Chapter Twenty-Two

The park in the next block was indeed very tiny. Just a strip of blacktop with some benches on one end and a cluster of worn-out playground equipment on the other. If this was the only public outdoor space around here, then Brendan's apartments, with their little balconies and big windows, seemed even more appealing.

Brendan led her to one of the park benches. The streetlight was halfway down the block, so it was dark where they sat, the scraggly tree overhead casting a pattern of dancing shadows on the ground in front of them.

"So tell me why you've embarked on this fool's errand."

"First," he said, "I should point out that I can afford to. These places aren't going to turn a huge profit, but they'll pay for themselves, with a little extra, and I've got enough money personally to front the expenses."

"Right," she said, gripping the park bench on either side of her thighs. "Because you've been raking it in all these years."

"I have," he acknowledged. "But it came at a cost."

"What kind of cost?"

Brendan inhaled deeply, and a tremor of unease raced down her spine. He was about to tell her something serious, something important. She had the feeling it was the key to unwrapping who he'd become during the fourteen years he'd been gone, and maybe why he'd left. "First I have to tell you about my uncle. Do you remember him?"

"Jimmy Walsh." How could she forget the glitzy, polished businessman who showed up in Brooklyn throwing his money around, and then left town with her boyfriend in tow?

"He's in real estate development, but on a much larger scale than what I'm doing here. Not these six-and eight-unit buildings you're getting in Carroll Gardens. The last project I worked on with him was thirty-one floors, forty-seven units. The cheapest one sold for two point five million."

"Jesus…" The thought of that kind of money left her weak kneed.

Brendan smiled ruefully. "That's what we did. We put together those deals. Found the properties, made the purchases, put together the funding, and brought in the architects."

Listening to him talk about that life was like listening to a stranger. It was hard to believe that the Brendan she'd loved in high school had willingly chosen that kind of life, money or not. "And you made a lot of money."

He turned his head to look at her fully, still smiling. "I made a *stupid* amount of money. Seriously, it's obscene."

"You can quit bragging anytime, you know."

"Sorry, couldn't help it. It's all just an explanation, anyway."

"It's not explaining why you walked away from all that to build middle-class apartments in Bensonhurst."

\* \* \*

"I owe that to Mrs. Lopez," Brendan said, speaking her name out loud for the first time in six months.

"Who is she?"

He took a deep breath, preparing to fill Gemma in on his fourteen years of morally dubious success.

"My last project with Walsh Construction was called the Triangle Tower. Jimmy had been working on the deal for years, buying up lots on the edge of Old Town. That's in the north part of Chicago. Back in the day, Old Town was full of hippies, but now it's gentrified like you wouldn't believe. Anyway, the Triangle was set to be a big payout for us.

"When I first came into the business, Jimmy had me doing a little of everything, but the part I liked best was the concept and design stuff. I liked coming up with a vision, talking to the architects, all that. Jimmy hated talking to architects, so he was happy to put me there and eventually, I took it over."

He paused, because this was his chance to explain it all to her, but he didn't want to sugarcoat his own motivations and actions.

"Maybe I hadn't planned that for my life, but once I got into it, I liked it. It felt creative, like I was really *building* something. I liked figuring out what the buyers were looking for, planning the amenities we could offer, imagining what the building would look like. I glad-handed investors, loan officers at the banks, potential buyers. I sold them all on the lifestyle as much as the real estate. I got really good at it."

Gemma said nothing, frowning down at her feet in clear disapproval. He didn't blame her. After all the plans they'd made together, she was probably furious, listening to the life he was describing.

"The land deals, getting the plans approved by the city, the permits, that was all Jimmy's deal. He had an army of lawyers and paper pushers, and his team worked like a well-oiled machine. When we hit a snag on the Triangle, he flipped out."

"What kind of snag?"

"A holdout. Jimmy would scope out a parcel he wanted to develop and send his team in there to purchase properties he needed to put the deal together. If anybody said they didn't want to sell, Jimmy would sail in with a fat offer." Brendan shook his head, half in wonder, half in disgust. "I never saw anyone tell him no."

"Just like the DiPaolas didn't tell you no."

The two were *not* the same. The DiPaolas had welcomed his offer, and he wasn't going to feel guilty for being the one to make it. "Hey, they wanted out. I just walked in with the right offer at the right time."

She ducked her head and nodded reluctantly. "No, I know. I get it. But losing them hurts."

He touched her arm. "I'm sorry, Gem. I know how hard it is for you."

She shook her head briskly, sitting up until his hand fell away. "It's business. I know that. So tell me the rest of the story about your tower."

"The holdout was the corner lot, the last parcel we needed to lock down the entire block. The woman who lived there was in her eighties. Mrs. Lopez. Her grandfather built the house." When he closed his eyes and thought back to that big, ramshackle house on the corner, he could almost see that woman's tired, lined face as she glared at him from her front porch. "Anyway, she wouldn't budge. She was going to die in that house, and then pass it on to her kids and her grandkids, like it had been passed on to her. When someone's committed like that, it's not about money. Nothing Jimmy could have offered her was going to change her mind. So I started drawing up new plans with the architects. We'd move the main entrance to the opposite side, make the backside, abutting her property, the service entrance."

"That sounds fine."

"It would have been. We could have sold those fucking units for exactly the same price, no matter which road we fronted on to."

"So what happened?"

"Jimmy doesn't like to be told no. He sicced his lawyers on this woman, determined to get her house."

"I don't understand. What could the lawyers do to a woman who owned her own house?"

His blood chilled as he remembered all the answers to that question. "You'd be horrified to see what a pack of highly trained, ruthless lawyers can do to someone, especially if there's plenty of money to back them up. Jimmy didn't even have to have a suit he could win. He just had to drag it into court and keep it there as long as possible. The expense of fighting back was enough to ruin an ordinary person. Of course, for him, it was nothing. Just the cost of doing business. And then there were the bribes."

"What? Who did he bribe?"

"City commissioners, city planners, whoever it took to regulate Mrs. Lopez right out of her house." Maybe he'd been willfully naive, but he'd never fully understood until then exactly how dirty the whole thing was, how stacked the deck was against ordinary people.

"How is that legal?"

He scoffed. "It's not. You think that matters? Or that anyone cares? It's all about the money. I always knew Jimmy was hard-nosed. He's a self-made man, and incredibly successful. That doesn't happen by accident. But I'd never seen that ruthlessness up close. He just *buried* this poor woman under lawsuits. His lawyers hounded her relentlessly. She wound up having a stroke and landed in the hospital. Jimmy was crowing. Now that he'd gotten her out of the house, he knew he could win. That's all he saw."

"I hate him." Gemma had always been ready to fight for those who couldn't fight for themselves.

"I'm not his biggest fan these days, either. Honestly, he was probably always that way. But I was off in another division, getting lulled by architects' renderings and heated floors and Italian marble tiles. I never saw this side of Jimmy's business." He paused and blew out a breath. No sense in baring his soul if he didn't bare all of it, even the ugly, shameful parts. "Maybe I didn't want to. Maybe I didn't ask too many questions because I knew I wouldn't be able to stomach what I found out. I've been thinking about that a lot lately. The life I was living out there, the money we'd made together… I got used to it. I *liked* it. Maybe I got lured in by it and quit looking as closely as I should have."

When he felt Gemma's hand slide into his, he looked up at her in surprise. "Just the fact that you questioned it means you're not the same as him."

He looked down at their clasped hands. "I hope you're right about that."

"I am. So what did you do?"

He ran a hand through his hair, staring off across the dark little patch of park. "I owed Jimmy a lot. He brought me into the business, taught me everything I knew, gave me a chance to succeed when I really needed it. The money I'd earned with him—" He broke off, although he was going to have to tell her everything before the night was through, if he was serious about this. "Let's just say it made a lot of things possible. I was in his debt."

"But…" Gemma said slowly. "He's a monster."

"I wasn't convinced of that at first. I thought he'd just lost sight of the point. Maybe if I talked to him, as family, I could get him to calm down, and see that there was still money to be made for us, and a little old lady could keep her family home."

"What happened?"

He paused, remembering back to that night. He'd waited until almost all the office staff had gone, so no one would see him calling Jimmy out. He'd wanted to give his uncle space to back down and admit he was wrong without losing face in front of everyone working for him.

"He said I was too soft. He called me a weak-willed coward. There was a lot more. It got pretty ugly. But he summed it up by saying it took guts to make money, and maybe I didn't have what it took."

Gemma was gripping his hand with hers like a vise. "And?"

Brendan shook his head. "It was like in church when we were kids, those stories about the saints having a revelation and seeing the truth. Standing there in Jimmy's office, listening to him rant and rave, knowing he felt entirely justified—no, *entitled*—to ruin the life of this harmless woman—a woman who didn't have the power to fight back on any level... I just asked myself what the hell I was doing there? How long would it be until I was the guy behind the desk, acting like crushing a helpless person into the ground was just some unavoidable cost of doing business? I felt sick. Like, *physically* sick. So I told Jimmy I quit and I walked out."

"That's it?"

"Well, I went straight to the bathroom and threw up. But then, yeah, I cleaned out my office that night and I walked away."

"You did the right thing."

"Oh, I know. I just hope I did it soon enough."

"What do you mean?"

He swallowed hard, focusing on their joined hands for strength. "I feel like, if I died tomorrow and my life was put on a scale, weighing the good I've done against the bad, the bad would still win."

"I'm not so sure about that," she said quietly.

"I'm not either. That's what Flaherty Developments is about. Tipping that balance back."

"So you're just going to spend all your money out of guilt?"

He looked up and gave her a small smile. "It's not a charity, Gem. I'm running it like a business, and it'll turn a profit. Just a modest profit. No more than I need to live on. More than that..." He paused and shook his head. "For me, to reach for more than that is a trap I can't fall into again. I *won't*."

"You walked away from it all. That's something he'd never be able to do. You're not going to turn into Jimmy."

He squeezed her hand. "I know. But it's also about making up for my time there. How many lives did he ruin while I was looking the other way? How many people did he crush to earn the money I lived on?"

"You can't hold yourself responsible for what Jimmy has done. He's the one who has to answer for that, not you."

He looked down at their joined hands again, his thumb taking a slow swipe across her knuckles. "It's not just about Jimmy," he said carefully. "It's about you, too."

## Chapter Twenty-Three

"Me?" Gemma asked.

When Brendan looked up, his eyes were filled with such forthright honesty that she felt the bottom fall out of her stomach. She hadn't realized that they were at the precipice of this—a reckoning of what had happened between them—until suddenly she was staring down over the edge.

"And my mother."

"I don't understand."

"You know all about my dad."

"That he died on the job? Of course."

"When Dad died, Mom didn't handle it so well. I mean, nobody would, but Mom took it harder than some people might have. It took me a long time to figure this out, but my mother…she's not like other people. She's fragile. And she's always relied on the men in her life. First her father, then when he died, her older brother—"

"Jimmy."

"Yes. And then when she got married, she relied on my dad."

"That's what you're supposed to do in marriage. Rely on each other." At least, that's what her parents had done. Personally, Gemma didn't have a clue how they worked. The only man she'd ever imagined being able to rely on in that way had ditched her in high school. But she was starting to get the feeling there had been much more happening back then than she realized.

"Mom's different, though. You never met her, but she's helpless in a lot of ways. She's terrified of being alone, she doesn't think she has what it takes to make it in the world on her own. And she doesn't, really. Being left to manage everything after Dad died, paying the bills, taking care of us…she was overwhelmed. She was just this shell. Some days, she didn't even get off the couch. She cried all the time. Every damned day. She stopped cooking, stopped cleaning, stopped taking care of us. I was twelve when Dad died. Tim was just eight. So it all fell to me. I fed us sandwiches and pasta and rustled up a pizza now and then. I cleaned, I did our laundry. I figured out how to fill out her checkbook and forge her signature so that I could keep the bills paid."

"Brendan, I had no idea."

"Because I didn't tell anybody. It wasn't her fault. Her husband had died."

Gemma wanted to protest that a dead husband didn't cancel out her two live boys who needed her, but she knew better than anyone that everyone handled grief differently. She supposed she had to cut Claire Flaherty some slack.

"She was just so—" He broke off again, seemingly unwilling to say it out loud.

"It's okay." She squeezed his hand again. "You can tell me. I won't judge you for whatever you were feeling."

He turned his head just enough to give her a small smile. "I think that's my line."

Back when they first met, when she was still deep in her grief, that's what he always told her. *There are no wrong emotions. It's okay to feel how you feel.*

"It's the truth. Just say it."

"She was just so *needy*," he said at last. "Emotionally. Every fear and anxiety she had she dumped on me. Every night, I held her while she cried and worried about not being able to take care of us, about running out of money, about losing our house, about dying…"

"Jesus, Brendan. No little kid should have to handle that."

"There was nobody else. Tim needed to feel like his mom was there for him, so I kept him away from that as much as I could."

"How long did this go on?"

"A couple of years? Three? She met Harry Murphy when I was fifteen, and things changed after that."

"Who's Harry Murphy?"

"He said he was a firefighter from Philly. Said he'd moved to Long Island to help his sister with her kids after she lost her husband in nine-eleven."

"You say that like it wasn't the truth."

Brendan released her hand, leaning forward, elbows on his knees. "It wasn't. I have no idea what his real story was. Was there a sister and two nephews on Long Island? Was there a brother-in-law who died in the Towers? Was he even a fucking firefighter? I have no idea. I have my suspicions, but nothing I can prove."

"What suspicions? What happened?"

"So they met at this charity thing for nine-eleven families. We weren't one…the fire Dad died in was just some warehouse fire six months before that. But Dad was a firefighter, and Mom was a widow. His old firehouse invited her to all that stuff. She never went. She didn't go anywhere, really. But I talked her into going to this. I thought it would be good for her to get back out there and talk to people…people who weren't me. Jesus, that sounds terrible." He dropped his head into his hands, fingers gripping his hair.

Gemma placed her hands on his shoulders, leaning over the curve of his back. "Brendan, no. You were a kid who was being asked to handle way too much."

Almost like he couldn't bear her sympathy, he sat back, shaking her hands off. "So she went. And she met Harry there. Within a couple of weeks, they started dating. She changed overnight. She was so happy, so excited. She got her hair cut, she bought new clothes. She started cooking again, like she used to, back when Dad was still alive. It was like we had our mom back again. And best of all, not once did she come to my room and cry herself to sleep in my bed. I was fucking thrilled. In my opinion, Harry Murphy was the best thing that had ever happened to us."

"Did you like him?"

"I didn't care if I did or not. He was an adult, a man, and he was doing everything for Mom I hadn't been able to do. He moved in after a few weeks and for a while, everything was good. He took Tim to softball practice and fixed stuff around the house. All I had to worry about was school and soccer, just like before. Then Mom came to me and said they were thinking about getting married and how would I feel about that?"

"What did you say?"

Brendan turned to look at her, that old bitterness back in his eyes—the eyes of someone who'd seen too much and grown up too fast. She knew because those were her eyes, too. "What do you think I said? I was so fucking happy to be free of the burden of my mother that I practically shoved her into his arms."

"Hey, no—"

"Don't worry. Fate taught me a lesson pretty quick. He was a fraud. Harry Murphy wasn't even his real name. I don't know what his real name was. He was a con man."

"But…what could he have possibly conned out of a widow and two kids?"

"My dad's death benefits. Mom got almost ninety thousand dollars, plus half his salary. That was the only reason we'd survived until then, because it's not like Mom could hold down a job. We'd spent some, but there was still plenty left. Plus, Harry convinced Mom to take out a mortgage on the house. He had all these big plans for renovations. They'd pay for themselves, he told her. Well, as soon as Harry got Mom to put him on her bank account, he cleaned out every dime and disappeared."

"That son of a bitch."

"Yeah. I have this theory that he'd come to New York sniffing around for a nine-eleven widow. They got huge payouts. Millions. But there was too much public attention on them. It would have been too obvious. Mom had a lot less money, but she was easy pickings. As you can imagine, she didn't handle his vanishing act very well."

"Brendan, you never told me any of this."

"Because by the time we met, it was over. He was gone, and she seemed to have gotten over it. She felt terrible about having brought Harry into our lives, and she promised everything would be fine now that he was gone. She was taking care of the house, managing the bills. We still had Dad's half salary and social security payments for me and Tim, and I figured that was enough to cover everything. I thought it was all under control. I was wrong."

He shifted, turning on the bench until he was half facing her. Then he reached out for her hands, his expression serious and purposeful.

"Gem, this is the explanation you deserved fourteen years ago. I'm sorry I didn't tell you everything then. I was still trying to protect her, I guess. And…well, I felt guilty because it was my fault."

"What are you talking about? What was?"

"A few months before I graduated, I found a bunch of statements. Credit card statements, another mortgage on the house…it turned out things hadn't been okay. She hadn't been making ends meet on Dad's half salary. We were nearly a hundred thousand dollars in debt."

"What? How is that *possible*?"

"She was paying the first mortgage and the car payment with credit cards. We were living on the second, but she wasn't making payments. Month after month. Everything was already in collections by the time I found out."

"Jesus."

"When I confronted her, she fell apart, of course. She didn't know what to do, how to fix it. Neither did I. I was supposed to start college classes in the fall, but fuck, how was I supposed to do that?"

"I remember," she murmured. It had all been part of their plan. While she'd been scribbling Brendan's name in the margins of her notebooks, dreaming about decorating their first apartment, he'd been dealing with his entire life melting down. She felt a stab of anger, this time not because he'd left her, but because he hadn't trusted her. "You should have told me. I deserved to know."

"I know. You deserved the truth. But I guess I kept it from you because I felt like a failure. I was the one who'd slipped up, who let my guard down and let Harry Murphy into our lives. And after… She couldn't handle anything before Harry, so why the hell did I think she'd be able to handle things after? I should have asked more questions after he left. I should have stepped up. Instead I buried my head in the sand for two years, hanging out with my friends and playing soccer, pretending I was a normal high school kid. If there was trouble at home, I didn't want to know about it."

"You were in high school. Taking care of your family wasn't your responsibility."

"That's rich, coming from you."

"My situation was different. My mom died. I had to help take care of everybody."

"And my dad died," he snapped, his anger breaking through in a rare flash of raw honesty. "I was supposed to take care of them and I *failed*."

She still thought he was being too hard on himself, but she didn't press it. She knew better than anyone the sense of obligation.

Brendan inhaled deeply, reining in his emotions again. "Yes, I should have told you what was going on. I'm sorry. But telling you the truth wasn't going to keep the inevitable from happening."

"Which was?"

"Mom was a wreck. Because of Dad, I had scholarship money from the city for college, but it wasn't like I could still go. I couldn't spend two years taking classes and studying for the firefighters' exam just to get a firefighter's starting salary, not when we had all this debt hanging over our heads. And what about Tim? In four years, *he* was graduating. He'd qualify for a scholarship, too, but just tuition at a state school. Nothing else. Do you know what it really costs to send a kid to college?"

Having sent two sisters through Ivy League colleges, yes, she knew. Even with scholarships, it had cost a fortune. Every week there was some new thing that cost money, some new thing that wasn't covered.

"We needed money. A lot of it. I didn't know how to get us out of the hole, so I called Mom's brother."

"Jimmy."

"Jimmy. He and Dad had had a fight years before, when they got married. Jimmy thought Mom could do better than some Brooklyn firefighter. They hadn't spoken since. I'd never even met him. But I was desperate, so I called. And he came. He got the creditors off Mom's back with a phone call."

"Why didn't he just pay off her debts? Sounds like he could have afforded it."

"This is the guy who celebrated an eighty-year-old woman's stroke because he stood to gain something from it. Jimmy doesn't believe in charity. But he does believe in providing people with opportunities."

Gemma could see all the pieces falling into place, the mysterious forces that had suddenly driven Brendan away from her all those years ago. She untangled her hands from his. "And that's what he did for you. He made you an offer you couldn't refuse."

"He was offering me a chance to earn more money in a year than I would have earned in five if I stayed here. Gemma, I didn't want to leave you, but I had no choice."

"Why didn't you tell me the truth? You just ended

things and said you were leaving. No explanations. Like you and I…like what we had…was nothing."

Up until the moment the words had come out of his mouth, her trust in him had been absolute, her belief in their future together unshakable. In one shocking moment, her whole world had crumbled, and the boy she'd loved so completely had become a stranger. The pain of it still had the power to leave her breathless.

"What would you have done if you'd known?"

She threw up her hands. "I don't know. Fight—"

"Fight who? Jimmy? My mother? Fight what? The debt we owed? There was no one to fight. No way to win."

"So you just left. I deserved to know the whole story. It was my life, too, Brendan. I'm not like your mother. I don't need to be protected from the world. Jesus, I spent *years* wondering what happened, what I might have done to drive you away—"

Brendan winced as if she'd struck him. "Gem, you were perfect. You were everything I'd ever wanted, and I had to let you go, and I didn't know how to do it. I was eighteen and stupid and overwhelmed."

"So *you* decided how it was going to end. We'd been talking about spending the rest of our lives together and you figured you'd handle this on your own."

"I'd been handling shit alone since I was twelve. I didn't know how to do it any other way. Gem, I couldn't see a way out that ended with us together. More than anything, I wanted to take you with me, but I knew it was impossible. I thought a clean break might be easier. I thought—I *hoped*—that we'd both get over it and move on. I know now that I was very wrong about that, because I never got over you. I am so sorry."

She blinked against the sudden burning in her eyes. "There was no way I could leave Brooklyn. I had my family."

His eyes were full of regret. "I know. You had to stay for your family. And I had to leave for mine."

Her throat felt tight. Goddamn him. Damn him for using the one example sure to evoke her sympathy. Who knew, better than her, what you sometimes had to sacrifice for family? If the situation had been reversed, if she'd had to give up Brendan for her family, wouldn't she have done the same?

In her heart, she still felt bruised and angry, frustrated at having had no control over something so devastating. But in her head, she understood his point. Nothing she could have said or done would have changed anything. The girl she was at sixteen wouldn't have accepted that. She'd have fought losing him until her last breath, and then she'd have lost him anyway. Because leaving hadn't been possible for her. What she hadn't understood at the time was that staying hadn't been possible for Brendan.

If she'd loved him a little less, he might have been right. She'd have nursed her broken heart for a while, then met someone else and moved on. But she had to finally admit it to herself—she'd never really gotten over him, either. They wouldn't be sitting here in a dark park having this conversation if she had.

So what was she supposed to do with all of this? His mistakes, her anger, a love that had never quite died for either one of them? Damned if she knew the answer.

"You're making it really hard for me to hate you right now," she whispered.

She felt his hand on the side of her face, his palm cupping her cheek. "I really hope you don't hate me.

In the end, I can't regret leaving. I didn't have a choice. But I never stopped being sorry for it. And I'm so sorry for what I did to you. I'm sorry I ever made you doubt yourself. I'm sorry I let you believe I didn't want you. That was never the case."

When she opened her eyes again, he was right there. Not the Brendan from fourteen years ago. That boy and the mistakes he'd made had been lost forever. There was no getting that boy back or undoing his choices. He'd been replaced by this man. This man who had all of that boy's innate goodness inside, this man who'd done his best in impossible circumstances. Yes, he'd made mistakes that had hurt her deeply, but not out of spite. Not because he didn't care. If anything, he cared too much, about everybody in his life.

"I don't hate you," she said. She'd tried that for fourteen years, but it just wouldn't take.

His eyes were still sorrowful, but the corner of his mouth tugged with a smile. "I'm glad."

"But fourteen years is a long time to be mad at you."

"I know I can't fix it overnight, but I'd like to try. I knew I was coming back to Brooklyn to build and make amends, but what I didn't realize until I saw you again was that I'd come back for you, too. I want another chance with you, Gem, if you'll give me one."

And because she didn't know what to do with what he was feeling, any more than she knew what to do with what *she* was feeling, she did what she couldn't seem to help but do when she was around Brendan—she kissed him. But this time, it wasn't a violent clash of lust and hormones. She leaned in and pressed her lips against his, long and lingering. Her lips said what she didn't have the words for yet.

*I'm sorry you had to grow up too soon. I'm sorry for everything we had to give up. I'm sorry for thinking the worst of you all these years and forgetting the best of you.*

It didn't fix anything, but for the first time, she felt like she could set down the burden of her anger. What might replace it was still unknown.

His fingers slid back into her hair, pulling her closer, as his lips urged hers apart. This kiss, unlike the ones that had come before, felt like a longed-for homecoming. It felt like his apology, his reassurance that she'd always been enough, always been the one he'd wanted.

But as right as this homecoming felt, the fourteen years were still there, and that was a lot to bridge. Those teenagers, dreaming of a happily ever after together, were gone. And happily ever afters in the real world were hard to come by.

Tonight, though, Gemma didn't care about the ever after. Tonight was enough, all on its own. She'd worry about the ever after when the sun came up.

## Chapter Twenty-Four

When Brendan realized he'd been staring at the same email for ten minutes without reading a word of it, he decided his day was pretty much shot. Considering he'd spent much of the night before having lots of very enthusiastic sex with Gemma, he felt he could hardly be blamed for his lack of focus.

Things were…better. They were…something. She still hadn't spent the night with him or gone public about their relationship, but she'd stopped pretending all they had was sex. This was a relationship now. Fragile and new, but real. He was hoping with time and patience, he could earn her trust. Maybe eventually her love.

His phone rang and he scrambled for it, hoping, pathetically, that it was Gem. The sight of *Mom* flashing on the screen did a lot to throw a bucket of cold water on his filthy thoughts.

"Hi, Mom, is everything okay?"

"Well, this morning there was some water on the floor upstairs and something's hanging off the front of the house. I was going to call that man whose number you gave me—"

"No, never mind, Mom." He sighed. "I'll be right over to take a look."

\* \* \*

The problem was apparent right away. The front gutter had come loose from the edge of the roof. It hung perilously from one end, banging against the brick wall in the breeze. Inside, his mother followed him upstairs to the bedroom that fronted the house, twisting her hands together anxiously. She hadn't made a move to clean up the puddle of water that had leaked in.

"Okay, your homeowner's insurance probably covers this. I'm going to go dig out the policy and make a call. Why don't you grab an old towel and mop up the water?"

"Oh," she said, blinking in consternation. "Yes. An old towel. I can do that."

While he left her busy digging through the linen closet, he went downstairs to the desk in the corner of the dining room, where all her official papers were stacked haphazardly. He should just take over her bills, instead of sending her money to pay for them, he thought, flipping through junk mail four years out of date. Even with the funds in her account, she'd undoubtedly missed a dozen deadlines in this mess.

In one overstuffed drawer, he found the folder that looked like her official papers related to the house. It did not, he noticed, contain the letters from the banks notifying her that he'd paid off the loans against the house. Who knew where she'd squirreled those away? At some point, he'd have to track those down, but not today.

Near the back of the folder, he found the deed and the title to the house, which was useful. As he flipped them over, he noticed another document paper-clipped to the back. It was a photocopy of something. Unfolding it, he scanned it. Then he went back and read it through again. Slowly. His blood ran cold as its meaning sank in.

It was a document transferring ownership of the house—his mother's house, left to her by his father, handed down by his grandfather—to Jimmy Walsh, dated from the same month he'd graduated high school, when they were in the middle of that crisis. When Jimmy had swept in to save the day.

Jimmy owned this house. All these years, as he'd worked his ass off in Chicago, scrimping and saving, paying off first one, then the second mortgage she'd taken against the property, thinking he was doing it to save his mother's house, he'd been saving fucking Jimmy's house.

"I got the water up, but the floor looks a little warped in that corner—"

He spun around, holding the letter aloft. "Mom, why did you sign this?"

She squinted at it, puzzled. "What is that?"

"It's a transfer of the deed into Uncle Jimmy's name. You signed it fourteen years ago."

She laughed nervously. "No, I didn't. Why would I do something like that?"

"I don't know, Mom. That's what I'm asking. Why did you sign this?"

"There were so many papers back then." Her hands fluttered helplessly in front of her. "Just legal stuff. Jimmy said he'd take care of everything. He just needed my signature on the paperwork so he could take care of all those awful creditors."

No, Brendan had done that, paying out over half his paycheck every month to keep the debt collectors off her back and the house out of foreclosure. "But this…"

Shaking her head, she squeezed her eyes closed, as if turning away from the unpleasant memory. "We had all those money troubles, and Jimmy sorted it out for us. That's all."

"I know what I'm looking at!" He couldn't help shouting as the enormity of what had happened sank in. "This paper you signed turned the house over to Jimmy. He owns it now. He has for fourteen years."

"No, I'm sure you're wrong. It's just the paperwork from when he took care of all that financial trouble for us."

"No, Mom, I did that. Jimmy didn't spend a dime to get us out of trouble. I did. I've spent the last fourteen years of my life working my ass off to pay off that debt so you'd still have this damned house…so that one day Tim and I would have it…and the whole time, that bastard had stolen it from you right from the start."

"Don't you talk about Jimmy that way!" Her eyes sparked with the heat that only an attack on her beloved big brother could generate. "He's my brother. He'd never do something like that to me. He took care of us when things were bad."

"No, Mom, that was me. It's always been me." He felt the fire go out of him. Gone. The house was gone. The money to pay off Tim's med school loans, to pay for his mother's upcoming care…all gone. Stolen by Jimmy fucking Walsh, just because he was an opportunistic bastard and he knew he could. And there she stood, defending him to her dying breath. He understood it, but he didn't have to fucking accept it.

He thrust the evil document in her face. "He stole this house from you, Mom. Which means he stole it from me and Tim, too. It was our legacy from Dad, and he took it from us."

"Don't you say such terrible things about him—"

He held up his hands to cut her off. "Mom, I'm going. I'll call the insurance people in the morning to sort out the gutter, but I can't stay here right now."

Storming out when she looked so fragile and upset was a dick move, but he couldn't help it. He'd spent his whole life wrapping his mother in cotton, doing his best to make sure nothing could hurt her. And here she'd dealt her sons an irreparable blow out of blind loyalty to some asshole who hadn't done a tenth of what he had for her.

He had to get out of there before he said things he couldn't take back, so he just left. And left his mother alone to shut out what she'd done to her sons for the sake of her worthless brother.

## Chapter Twenty-Five

Elin Lang Catering wasn't just fancier than the places Gemma had visited for Kendra, it was like an entirely different class of business. Kendra had been up against a wall, and there had been few options available so last minute. In theory, Dan and Mariel, getting married in less than a month, should have been in the same situation. But as Gemma was learning, Dan's name and money opened all kinds of doors. Places that would have laughed Kendra and her deadline off the phone were scrambling to have tastings prepared for Gemma the very next day.

When Gemma had offered to vet the caterers and help choose a menu for Mariel, she'd just been doing her a favor, trying to help her out when she was overwhelmed. She hadn't expected it to be such an enjoyable and eye-opening experience. Elin Lang Catering, headquartered in a fancy new building in far west Chelsea, was turning out to be the best one so far, and she hadn't even tasted the food yet.

A woman in a crisp sky-blue suit met her at the door and introduced herself as Tara. If they went with Elin Lang, Tara would be their point person for the entire event. Next, Tara ushered her into a meeting room that felt like a fancy dining room in someone's home. It was small and comfortable, with soft green and gold striped wallpaper, a plush patterned rug on the glossy hardwood floor, and a dining table in the middle of the room set for six. Through the wall of windows on one side lay a sweeping view of the Hudson River.

"Have a seat," Tara said, motioning to a chair. "Let's talk about your event."

"Oh, it's not my event. I'm just helping out the bride and groom, because they're so short on time."

Tara glanced at her clipboard. "Ah yes, Daniel Drake and Mariel Kemper. Yes, a month isn't much time at all."

"Will that be a problem?"

Tara smiled in a way that told Gemma nothing would be a problem when Dan Drake was the client. "Not at all. We've worked extensively with the Plaza, so the event should be fairly seamless to put together. Now tell us what the bride and groom are looking for."

"It'll be a sit-down dinner for three hundred. Beyond that, they've kind of left it up to me." Gemma laughed softly to herself, looking around at the opulent little room. God, she hoped she didn't make a hash of this.

"Well, let's taste a few hors d'oeuvres and see if we can't make a start there."

"Sounds great."

The first thing they brought out, served by one of the chefs in a white jacket and everything, was a tray of appetizers. But these were nothing like the antipasti platters Gemma threw together to keep the wolves at bay until her big family dinners were ready. There were tiny crisp spring rolls with a rich, dark dipping sauce, and succulent pieces of what looked like duck, wrapped in paper-thin slivers of radish, glistening pink pearls of caviar and crème fraîche nestled in perfect little puff pastry shells, green apple and brie, stacked on a thin wafer of lavash and sprinkled with toasted pistachios... It was all so perfect, so elegant, so utterly delicious.

"Usually for an event this size, we'd choose six to eight of these to pass during the cocktail hour before dinner."

"The only problem I'm going to have is narrowing it down. They're all so good. Is that kaffir lime I taste?"

Tara's eyebrows shot up. "Yes...in the gingered salmon bites, I believe."

"We have to have this one. And the duck. And those shishito pepper shrimp."

"I believe we have another tray of options still for you to try," Tara said with a smile.

"This is going to be really hard. And I haven't even gotten to the entrees yet."

Tara leaned in, voice lowered conspiratorially. "Just wait until dessert."

Hours later, she finally left Elin Lang's beautiful offices, her stomach full and her head buzzing with everything she'd seen and tasted. She couldn't wait to tell Brendan all about it. Her phone rang as she waited for the crosstown bus, and she thought she'd get her chance now, while it was all still fresh in her head, but it wasn't him.

"Hey, Kendra."

"Tell me you can do Mrs. Simonsen's party. The woman is calling me twice a day."

"Ugh, Kendra, why does she even want me? I'm a total fraud."

"What are you talking about?"

"I just came from this place I booked for Dan and Mariel's wedding—"

"I can't believe you can't sneak me on to that guest list, girl. Do you have any idea who Dan Drake is friends with?"

"Sorry. When Mariel Kemper writes a Pulitzer Prize winning exposé about your mother's death, I'm sure she'll invite you. Anyway, you would not believe this caterer. This isn't food, it's art. Every little hors d'oeuvre's so pretty you don't even want to touch it, never mind eat it. But then when you *do* eat it…like, every flavor is perfectly balanced. And the entrees!"

"It's a wedding dinner," Kendra said flatly. "We've been to enough of them. 'Do you want the chicken or the beef?' and then it doesn't matter which one you picked, because they taste the same."

"Uh-uh. Not this chicken or beef. Chicken with tender porcini mushrooms and this beurre blanc that made me want to weep. And the beef! A bordelaise like I've never tasted in my life, with this fine dusting of horseradish shavings…just enough to add the perfect bite, but not enough to overpower."

"Okay," Kendra cut her off. "In addition to rubbing elbows with freaking *Oprah*, or whatever, you're also going to get to eat the most amazing food that's ever been cooked. Quit rubbing it in and tell me you'll cook for Mrs. Simonsen."

Gemma let out a sigh, certain that anything she produced would pale in comparison to what she'd just experienced.

"She upped her offer, by the way." Kendra named the new per-plate figure.

Well. That decided it. Whether she was up to scratch or not, Mrs. Simonsen was willing to pay her handsomely to cook, and Gemma desperately needed the money.

"Okay, I'll do it."

"Good. Now we should talk about Mrs. Baxter—"

"Kendra!"

## Chapter Twenty-Six

"He won't budge?"

Brendan listened to the answer he knew was coming while he rubbed his eyes with his free hand. Screw this day.

His lawyer said a few more things that amounted to "you're fucked, change your plans" before he ended the call. Brendan sat back with a weary sigh.

Flory, his administrative assistant, gave him a sympathetic smile. "No go?"

"Not a chance. Not that I thought there was one."

Flory pushed back from her desk. "I'm meeting my boyfriend for lunch. Want me to bring you something back?"

"Nah, I'll order in. Thanks, though. Enjoy it. Tell Matteo I said hello."

As Flory was shrugging into her jacket and gathering up her bag, the buzzer for the door downstairs rang. "I'll let them in on my way out. Hang in there, boss man."

Well, sitting there fuming wasn't going to fix anything, and apparently he had a lunch meeting he'd forgotten about because someone was on the way upstairs to his tiny office. Was it the plumbing fixtures guy? Was that today or tomorrow? Brendan pushed back from his desk, ran his hands through his hair quickly, and stood to greet whoever he was supposed to be meeting with.

A frisson of electricity shot through his body as Gemma came through the door.

Her smile was uncertain. "The woman downstairs told me to just come up?"

"Flory. She's my assistant. What brings you here?"

"You said you had an office in the neighborhood and I was curious. Have you eaten lunch yet? I brought food."

His heart swelled to a ridiculous degree. "No, I haven't." Laying his hand against the back of her neck, he pulled her face to his and pressed a brief, hard kiss to her lips. "You're a goddess. Here, let me make space." He lifted a stack of tile catalogs off the corner of his desk and pulled the spare chair up.

"It's smaller than I expected," she said, looking around the office. "And a lot less fancy."

It was two cramped rooms, up a flight of narrow, dark stairs, over a falafel place. Small and not fancy was putting it mildly. "Yep, it is. But it gets the job done and keeps expenses low."

"At least you're upstairs from King Falafel."

"Is it good? I haven't tried it yet."

"Best falafel in Brooklyn. I've been trying to get Amen to give me the recipe for his tahini sauce for years, but he guards it with his life." Gemma unpacked her bag, opening a plastic container of pasta and sauce and handing it across to him with a fork. "This isn't much. Nowhere as good as a falafel from Amen. Just a bolognese and pasta."

"Never ever describe your cooking as nothing much," he said around a mouthful. "This is delicious."

"Flory said you'd just gotten some bad news. What's up?"

"Flory is a blabbermouth. It's just a rough morning." Then he stopped, squeezing his eyes closed. He was so used to shouldering the hard stuff on his own that keeping it to himself was automatic. But he and Gemma wouldn't be here, edging tentatively into a relationship, if he hadn't finally told her the truth about what he was dealing with. Bearing his difficulties in silence wasn't going to help this thing to grow. And he really wanted it to grow.

"I found something out yesterday. Something pretty shitty that has to do with today's bad news."

"What was it? The thing you found out yesterday?"

"Fourteen years ago, when Jimmy swept in to save the day?"

Gemma let out a low growl of annoyance. "Seems to me like you were the one to do all the saving."

"Yeah. Well in addition to not really helping, he seems to have stolen Mom's house."

Gemma dropped her fork into her pasta. "What?"

He explained, as briefly and dispassionately as possible, what he'd discovered and how his mother had reacted.

"Brendan." She huffed. "I can't believe this. That absolute bastard. Isn't there something you can do legally?"

"Mom signed willingly."

"But she had no idea what she was signing!"

"And how do I prove that? That would require her

admitting her brother swindled her, and she'll never do that."

"I can't believe you're so calm about this. If it were me, I'd be on a plane to Chicago right now to go take out Jimmy's kneecaps with a baseball bat."

"Believe me, the impulse is there. But it wouldn't solve anything, and we're not going to perish without the house. I can manage Mom on my own."

"But you shouldn't have to. You've been doing that all your life."

"And I'll keep doing it, Gem." She needed to understand this about him and his life. His mother was a responsibility he would always have, fair or not. That was just how it was.

Her jaw worked as she stared at him. The Gemma he knew in high school would have kept fighting, certain she could win. Now, even though the injustice of it was still eating at her, she held her tongue, although he could almost hear the wheels turning in her mind. "Remember in high school, when you told me that it was okay to feel however I felt?" she finally said.

"Yeah?"

"You told me that because you could tell I'd been holding it all in…all those messy feelings you get in grief that aren't sadness. The anger, the selfishness. You told me it was okay to feel that way, that it didn't make me a bad person or mean that I missed my mother any less."

"I remember." He remembered listening patiently the first time Gemma let her anger out, let herself rage at the unfairness of it all, let herself bitterly recount all she'd personally lost, the petty shit you were never supposed to acknowledge out loud. And then he remembered holding her in his arms when all that anger finally morphed into heart-wrenching sobs.

"You're allowed to be angry, too."

"I know that."

"I'm not always sure you do. You just keep swallowing it down so you can be strong and do the right thing."

"Well, somebody has to—"

"Yeah, I know. I know that better than anyone. I'm just saying…" She looked down. "I'm giving you permission to get mad with me. The same way you gave me permission when I needed it."

He felt an almost unbearable pang of tenderness for her. That had not been easy for her to say. She'd opened herself up to him, and Gemma Romano had never liked being vulnerable. Doing it now, after all that had passed between them, had to have cost her a lot.

"Come here." Leaning forward, he slid his hand around the back of her neck and drew her forward, kissing her. "Thank you."

"So what was today's bad news?"

"I got the final no on the property next to the DiPaolas. I was attempting to reason with them and convince them to sell to me. It didn't work. Actually, let's cut to the chase. 'Someone' is Jimmy Walsh."

"Your *uncle* bought the building next to the DiPaolas? Why?"

"To fuck with me, that's why. He doesn't have a single holding in this market. He can't do a goddamned thing with a lot that small and he knows it."

"You really think he would be that petty?"

"I know he would. He fucking hates to lose. It's all about power with him. He steals Mom's house just because he can, and then spends more than it's worth buying a commercial property he can't use just to keep me from making a deal. That night you saw me in front of DiPaola's? I'd been on the phone with him listening to him gloat."

"What an asshole."

"I agree completely. But in this game, he's Goliath and I'm David. All I can do is work around him until he gets bored and goes to ruin someone else's life."

"Could he really ruin your life?"

"Nah. He can be a total pain in my ass, but he can't ruin me, and that's what's pissing him off. He can't control me anymore and he knows it." Saying it out loud was calming. Jimmy had no power over him. He knew that, but giving voice to it made it feel real in a different way.

"He's a monster," Gemma said, reaching out to squeeze his knee. "I'm sorry."

He felt better, he realized, having unburdened himself that way. He'd never done it before, always feeling he had to handle it all alone. But he wasn't asking Gemma to handle anything for him, he was just telling her what was on his mind. And she was there for him, supporting him, on his side in a way no one had ever been before. That felt...well, the sensation was so new he wasn't sure how it felt. Good. It felt good.

He set his empty container aside and reached for her hand. "Yeah, he is, but he's already gotten enough stage time today. I'd rather think about you."

"Me?" Her saucy grin was one he hadn't seen from her since he'd returned, at least not meant for him. "What are you thinking about me?"

"Would you like a list? It's been running through my head all morning."

"I wouldn't mind hearing a few highlights."

"Well." He reached for her hands, tugging until she slid out of her chair and straddled his lap. "You're gorgeous, for starters."

She hooked her hands behind his neck. "Go on."

"And sexy." He kissed the corner of her mouth. "And great in bed." Sliding a hand under her ponytail, he brought her mouth to his, kissing her softly.

"That's a good list," she said breathlessly when he released her.

He reached up and stroked his fingertips along her cheek. "You're also kind. Thank you for listening to me today. Nobody's ever done that for me before."

Her eyes went soft and a little glassy. "You're welcome."

"Now about that sexy part." He kissed her again, this time long and thorough, and soon it was nowhere near enough. Her hands started on his knees, but soon slid to his thighs, and then up into his hair. The hand he'd had on her waist quickly found its way under the hem of her shirt.

Pulling back, she muttered, "When's your assistant getting back?"

"Not until one."

"Good." Fingers gripping his hair, she brought her mouth back to his, her tongue plunging in to taste him.

He groaned and slid his hands up her firm thighs and around to grip her ass, tugging her forward until she was pressed against his rapidly swelling cock. She rocked against him, her breaths now coming in pants. Wrapping her ponytail around his hand, he urged her head back, running his lips and teeth down the arch of her neck, nipping at her collarbone, kissing his way openmouthed down her chest to the deep V of her cleavage. Closing a hand over her breast, he squeezed and she shuddered in his arms. He swept his thumb over the hardening peak of her nipple, which he could just feel through her layers of clothes.

"Fuck," she whispered, pressing herself closer to him.

Yeah, that's exactly what he wanted to do, but they didn't have quite enough time for that, unfortunately.

"We should probably stop," he murmured against the swell of her breast, squeezing again.

"Yeah, we probably should." She rolled her hips against his, eliciting another pained groan from both of them. Jesus, she was going to make him blow his load right here with all their clothes on.

"Gemma…" His voice was hoarse with frustrated lust.

"I know." She kissed him again, hard and deep, before pushing herself off his lap. She turned away, panting and tugging her shirt back in place. Brendan leaned back in his chair and rubbed his hands down his face, desperately trying to cool his boiling blood.

"Can you come over tonight?"

"Maybe? I'm not sure. Dad and I are closing together, and—"

"Got it." They still weren't there yet. He forced himself to his feet, ignoring the discomfort in his groin. It would pass. Eventually.

She took a step closer and laid her hand on his chest. "I'm sorry. I'm not ready for everybody to know about us yet."

He held up a hand to silence her. "It's fine. Really. Take your time. And sneak over whenever you can."

She laughed, pushing up to her toes to kiss him. The sound of the front door downstairs opening sent her scurrying back from him, hurriedly turning away to pack up the empty lunch containers.

Brendan ducked behind his desk. "Thanks for lunch," he said.

She glanced up and smiled, a warm, sexy smile that he felt in his chest, and he knew he'd happily give her all the time she needed as long as he still got that smile from her. "You're welcome. I'll walk myself out."

"See you around?"

"Yes, you will."

## Chapter Twenty-Seven

"Do I hear a car?" Jess called from the top of the stairs.

Gemma whipped the front curtains open so she could see the street. "Just a FedEx delivery next door."

The weekend of Dan Drake and Mariel Kemper's wedding had finally arrived, and Livie was coming home for it. She hadn't been home since Christmas. It was hard to say which of them was more excited for it.

"Ugh, when are they going to get here?" Jess said.

Teresa came in from the kitchen with a vase full of daisies that she'd picked up at the Kims' green grocery. "Their plane landed at LaGuardia at four. The traffic is going to be horrible." She set the vase down on the side table by the staircase, nudging it first one way, then the other. "What do you think, Gemma?"

"I think fresh flowers are the fanciest thing the Romano house has seen since our grandmother died."

Teresa laughed. "I just wanted it to look a little festive for Livie. It's been months since she's been home."

John Romano came in from the dining room holding two beers, one of which he passed to Teresa before dropping a kiss on her cheek. "It looks great, honey."

Although the moments of PDA between them were still a little bit surprising, it was adorable, seeing her father so smitten and affectionate after all these years. And Teresa was a gem. She'd been over all morning, helping to clean in preparation for Livie's arrival, almost as excited to see her as the family was.

"The flowers are beautiful, Teresa," Gemma said with as much sincerity as she could manage. "I love the vase you picked."

Teresa's smile was sweet and profoundly thankful, which just made Gemma like her more. She was trying *so* hard.

Gemma turned back to the charcuterie plate she'd set on the dining room table. Spudge, sitting at her feet—actually, sitting *on* her feet—stared up at her longingly, his tail thumping against her calf.

"Nice try, buddy. You're not getting a bite of this. You're finally starting to lose some weight and we're not backsliding now."

Spudge groaned in despair and dropped to the floor, resting his head on his paws.

In her back pocket, her phone buzzed with a text. Thinking it might be Livie, she scrambled to get it out. It was Brendan.

Are you free tonight?

Since that night at the park she'd slipped away to see him whenever she could manage. She hadn't told anyone about him yet. It was obviously way more than just sex now. But were they going to last? They had a lot of baggage between them. They'd agreed to try, but she had no idea if they'd be successful. Maybe they'd implode under the weight of their history.

It had been fourteen years. It would be naive to think

they could pick up where they left off like everything was fine. Telling people about Brendan would bring a whole lot of scrutiny she wasn't ready for just yet. She'd have to explain that they'd dated in high school, too, and then there'd be a lot of questions about why she'd kept *that* a secret and well…what was the point of dredging all that up with her family until she was sure they were going to make a solid go of it?

It didn't escape her notice that she'd been in exactly this position with him once before. She hadn't shared him with her family because he'd left before she could. Part of her was still holding her breath out of some irrational fear that it would happen again.

Quickly, she typed out a reply.

Livie's on her way from the airport.

Right. I forgot that was today. Have fun tomorrow.

And now she felt guilty.

"Gem?" She looked up to find Jess eyeing her speculatively. "Was that Clyde? Is everything okay at the bar?"

"It wasn't Clyde. I'm sure it's fine. It's a Thursday. We're always dead on Thursdays." *And most other days*…

Jess gave another pointed look at Gemma's phone, and she was about to start scrambling for some believable lie about Kendra when Spudge lifted his head and let out a happy "Wuff."

Outside, a yellow cab was pulling to a stop at the curb.

"She's here!"

Suddenly the entry hall was filled to capacity as Gemma, Jess, Dad, Teresa, and Spudge all squeezed in to be at the front door to greet Livie. Dad opened the door just as Livie reached the top step.

"There she is!"

"Dad!" Livie threw herself into Dad's arms and he swept her up in a bear hug. Gemma had to fight down an unexpected lump in her throat. She didn't care if Livie was a grown adult. Her moving away had felt like losing a limb.

Jess was next in line to hug Livie. Although their personalities were completely different, less than a year separated them, so Livie and Jess had always shared a unique closeness. In her mind, Gemma sometimes still saw them as little girls—Jess, always the fearless one despite being younger, taking Livie by the hand as they toddled into preschool together. And now here they were, all grown up. Jess, engaged and living with Alex, Livie all the way out in Colorado on her own.

Well, not on her own. She had Nick, and here he came now, maneuvering up the walk with both of their suitcases and overloaded backpacks slung over each shoulder. Okay, it was nice of him to manage the luggage so Livie didn't have to.

Jess finally let go of her and Livie turned to Gemma.

"You look so great," Gemma said through her tears. Livie looked better than good. She'd finally cut off her thick curtain of dark wavy hair, and now it swung around her shoulders, pretty and stylish. She'd started dressing as if she had a body under her clothes, instead of shrouding herself in her father's hand-me-down flannel shirts. And most importantly, she looked happy. Her dark eyes were bright with laughter, and her smile was wide and genuine. It was like the light Gemma had always known was inside of her had finally been turned on for the rest of the world to see.

As she pulled her sister into a tight hug, reveling in her familiar smell, Nick struggled up the steps with the bags.

"Hey, felon. Hack anybody interesting lately?" Gemma said to him over Livie's shoulder.

"Hey," Nick protested, dropping the bags inside the door. "I'm gainfully employed by the federal government now, thank you very much."

Livie drew back. "Nick hasn't hacked anybody in ages."

"Only because he'll go to prison if he does."

"Truth," Nick said. "And when this gorgeous girl is on the outside, prison looks pretty grim." He slung an arm around Livie's shoulders and kissed her cheek. She blushed. Seriously, they'd been together for months now and he could still make her blush. It was kind of cute. "It's nice to see you, too, Gem," Nick said to her, hiking one eyebrow.

"Ah come on. You know I love to give you grief."

"Yeah, I know it. Most of the time, I deserve it."

Livie moved on to hug Teresa while Gemma relented and hugged Nick, too. She really did like him, but it was good to keep him on his toes.

"You guys must be starving," she said, when the hugs and greetings had been completed. "Come on in. Dinner's almost ready."

"So then this kid turns up in my office telling me he missed the midterm because his grandmother died," Livie said as she pushed her empty plate away.

"So?" Jess asked. "I know it's a cliché, but sometimes grandmothers do die."

"Sure, but his has died no less than nine times," Livie said.

"What?"

"One of the TAs in the English department had started a thread on the graduate student message boards, asking if he'd used the excuse with anybody else. By the time I saw it, nine people had chimed in. So I got to be the one to issue my condolences for his tenth dead grandmother. And then I flunked him in my class."

Everybody around the table laughed as Gemma marveled at the changes in Livie. She was so much more confident now. She chatted easily about her life in Colorado, her research at the university, and her plans for the future. She was going to Chile this summer! Apparently, they had some massive telescope down there, and if her school could work out the logistics, they were sending her down to work for a month.

Transferring to McArthur University to finish her PhD had been the best thing to ever happen to her. Gemma was unbearably proud of her, even if living without her was hard.

Livie shifted her attention to Jess and Alex, who'd come over after work to join them for dinner. "So, Jess, how is Mariel holding up with all this last-minute wedding planning?"

"Losing her mind. Thank god Gemma volunteered to deal with the caterers, or I really do think she'd have called the whole thing off."

"No way Dad would have let that happen," Alex said. "He's counting the minutes."

"Well, I think it's great you pitched in to help her out, Gemma."

"It was just a few tastings. No big deal." It was hardly a trial. Choosing the menus for the wedding, with no budget restrictions, hadn't been a burden at all. It had been the most fun she'd had in ages. Outside of Brendan's bed, anyway.

"It's a big deal to Mariel," Jess said. "She doesn't really have any family to help out."

"Well, she's going to get plenty of family with us all there," John said.

"Everybody's invited?" Livie asked.

"Sure," Jess replied. "Me and Alex, of course, and you and Nick, and Dad and Teresa, and Gemma."

Gemma's stomach sank as the realization hit her. Oh, God, every member of her family was bringing a plus-one to this thing except her. Maybe she should have invited Brendan. But bringing him to this wedding, introducing him to her entire family and all their partners…nope. There was no way she'd subject him to the Romano Family Inquisition right out of the gate. Not until she was sure about him.

Soon, she promised herself. She'd introduce him soon. Just not now, not like this.

# Chapter Twenty-Eight

The next day, Alex and Jess arrived early to pick up Livie and Nick for the wedding. Jess wanted to be there to give Mariel a hand if she needed anything. Once they'd gone and the house quieted down, Gemma shut herself in her room to examine herself in the speckled mirror over her dresser. The glass was hazy and spotted, because it dated back to her great-grandmother's day, but she'd found a little haze on the mirror could be flattering.

Twisting to the side, she examined the back of her dress, a simple black knit sheath. A few years back, it seemed someone she'd grown up with or gone to high school with was getting married every other month. She'd bought the dress for the first wedding, not realizing just how many she'd be attending in the next few years. She didn't have a lot of call for cocktail dresses in her ordinary life—like, none at all—so she wasn't going out buying a new dress every time another heavy, white, calligraphied envelope dropped through the mail slot. The dress, which she'd ironically nicknamed her wedding dress, had gotten quite a workout. At least no one at Dan and Mariel's wedding would have seen it before.

She looked okay, she decided. The dress did a decent

job of showing off her curves. Her eyes were smoky and dark, and she'd worn her hair down, loose and straight. She kept hearing Brendan's voice in her head as she brushed it out. He loved it when she wore it loose. For about the hundredth time, she wondered if she'd made a mistake not inviting him. Well, it was too late now. They were leaving for the city any minute. She just hoped being the lone singleton in her family wouldn't feel as awkward as she feared.

Her father bellowed up the stairs, putting an end to her last-minute primping. "We need to get going if we're gonna beat that Midtown Tunnel traffic!"

She swiped on a little more deep red lipstick, grabbed her tiny black purse, and hurried downstairs where her father and Teresa were waiting.

The whole evening was beginning to feel surreal, and the wedding hadn't even started yet. Gemma had never stepped foot inside the Plaza Hotel, or anywhere nearly as swanky. The closest she'd come was her high school graduation dinner at Gargiulo's Catering Hall in Coney Island. One quick glance around the other guests in the lobby told her the price tag on her dress needed about three more zeroes on it to fit in. Her fingers traced her neckline, making sure those little hanging loops were tucked in all the way and that her bra straps were staying put. Dad, looking uncomfortable in his black suit and tie, tugged at his shirt collar.

"Stop tugging on your tie, John," Teresa scolded gently, surreptitiously smoothing a hand over her blond French twist. "You'll mess up the knot."

"Damned thing's about to strangle me."

Upstairs in the entrance hall off the elevator, they

wound their way through Dan and Mariel's impressive guest list. Gemma recognized more than a few famous faces, a reminder of just how rich and powerful Dan Drake was. It was a good thing she often forgot that in his presence, or else she might feel embarrassed about that time last Thanksgiving when she argued with him about a cooking show that had been canceled on one of his networks.

At the entrance to the high-ceilinged Terrace Room, Gemma gasped and stopped in her tracks.

"It's…so *pretty*," she breathed.

"Oh, it's just lovely," Teresa sighed beside her.

Rows of gilded chairs faced away from them, each tied with a sheer cream ribbon on the back. The sides of the room were lined with tall, arching branches, scattered with little white blossoms. Suspended among the branches were thousands of little flickering tea lights in hanging glass holders. More candles floated in large glass vases, half-filled with water, on every available horizontal surface. At the front of the room, an arch had been fashioned from more flowering branches, and a carpet of candles illuminated it softly from below.

"Dan sure knows how to do it up right," John said. "Wonder what all this set him back?"

Gemma knew how much the catering bill was and the answer was…a lot.

A woman in a black dress stepped forward to greet them and offer a wedding program. With a flare of panic, Gemma realized the hostess's black dress was probably nicer than her black dress. "Bride or groom?" the woman asked.

"Um, both?" Mariel was Jess's boss and mentor. Dan was her future father-in-law.

"Then feel free to sit where you like." She gestured toward the white silk runner that ran the length of the room between the two banks of chairs. They'd just picked out a row near the back—right behind a well-known cable news anchor—when Gemma's phone buzzed in her purse.

When she fished it out, there was a text from Jess.

You here yet?

Just got here. What's up?

Mariel's a little freaked out. I could use a hand.

Freaked out? About what?

What could she possibly be freaked out about? Everything was beautiful.

Jess texted again.

Getting married.

Oh. Oh, dear.

I'll be right there. Where are you?

She stood up quickly. "I have to go. Jess needs me." Dad looked up at her. "Everything okay?"

"Sure," she answered uneasily. "It'll be fine."

Gemma made her way to the suite that had been reserved for the bride. She tapped lightly on the door and moments later, Jess swung it open.

"What's going on?"

"Um, an attack of nerves, I think."

Just then, Mariel paced past behind Jess, muttering to herself. "I don't know *what* I'm thinking. I mean, I must be out of my *mind*. I have two Pulitzers! How can I be this stupid?"

Jess turned to Gemma with wide, panicked eyes. *"That."*

Gemma sidled in and shut the door behind her. "Hey, Mariel, what's up?"

Mariel stopped pacing and swung around to face her. If Gemma looked half as good as Mariel Kemper when she hit fifty, she'd count herself blessed. The woman had some amazing genes—flawless, unlined, creamy skin, gorgeous cheekbones, and stunning green eyes. Her thick chestnut hair fell in satiny waves around her shoulders, held back on one side by a spray of phalaenopsis orchids. Her dress, a long-sleeved, bias cut, cream charmeuse sheath, cut straight and high across the front but draping dramatically in back, baring her back to her waist, made her look like a thirties film star.

Mariel was also scary smart and a total badass. She had no time for bullshit, which is why it was a wonder that slick, charming Dan Drake had managed to get under her skin. If it had been just about scratching an itch, she'd have tossed him aside months ago. But here she was, wearing the white dress and an enormous piece of ice on her left hand, because the guy had gotten into her heart, too, even if she was currently too freaked out to remember that part.

Mariel's hands twisted around each other. "I'm about to make a terrible mistake."

"Why do you say that?" Gemma asked cautiously.

"I'm about to marry *Dan Drake*! Anyone in America could tell you that's a disaster waiting to happen. Hell, most of our *guests* would tell you that."

Mariel spun around and stormed over to one of the plush white leather sofas in the living area, dropping on it in an ungraceful heap of shimmering fabric.

"Why do you think this is a mistake?" Gemma asked.

"Because I've done this before, and it was an absolute disaster."

"You've been married before?" Jess asked in surprise.

"I was twenty-two, right out of college, and absolutely clueless. I thought it was true love." Mariel snorted dismissively. "It didn't last a year."

Gemma crossed the room and perched on the edge of the coffee table, so she was eye level with Mariel. "What happened?"

"I got my first byline before he did, that's what happened. Men can't handle a successful woman. I learned that early."

"*Some* men can't handle a successful woman," Jess conceded, sitting on the arm of the sofa. "But Dan's no ordinary man."

"No, he's ten times worse!" Mariel said, spearing a finger in the air for emphasis. "He's spent his whole life chasing twenty-year-old bimbos. You know why? Because twenty-year-old bimbos don't challenge him. They make it easy, and he likes it easy. Leopards don't change their spots, and *I* am not easy."

"Maybe," Gemma said, "he's marrying you because you *do* challenge him. Maybe he likes that you're not easy."

Mariel was silent for a moment, staring into the middle distance, her expression bleak. "But will that be enough?" she whispered. "How long is he going to be intrigued by me? How do you know, when you say 'I do,' that it'll last forever? That he won't get bored? That *I* won't get bored? That you won't end up hating each other?"

Wow, wasn't that a question for the ages? Gemma had thought she'd had it all figured out at sixteen. She'd been ready to promise the rest of her life to Brendan, when, in retrospect, there was so much she hadn't known about him, so much she hadn't understood. And sure, he'd known her situation, but he hadn't even met her family. They'd both had such complicated lives. Had they been equipped in any way to weather the inevitable storms? Maybe, under those pressures, they'd have imploded after a year, too. What did teenagers know about true love anyway?

"You don't know," Jess acknowledged. "You don't know who he'll become, or who you'll become, or what those two future people are going to think of each other. I guess you just have to ask yourself this: Do you trust him? Do you believe that he respects you? Enough to do right by you, no matter what happens, no matter who you both become?"

Mariel looked down at her hands as she thought about that. Before she could answer, a knock came at the door to the suite.

"I'll get it." Gemma hurried to the door. When she opened it, Alex was standing there, with Dan right behind him. Gemma looked back over her shoulder. "I'm not sure this is a good time."

"He insisted." Alex sighed.

"You're not supposed to see the bride before the wedding," Gemma told Dan desperately.

"Bullshit," Dan barked. "I want to see her and she wants to see me, too, whether the stubborn woman will admit it or not."

"Oh, hell." Gemma stepped aside and let them in.

Dan crossed the room in a few strides, his natural confidence and star power radiating off him. Mariel was on her feet before he reached her, ready to go toe-to-toe with him even now.

"Tell me you're not afraid," he said.

"I'm not afraid of anything! I'm just being rational. Dan, this is crazy."

Dan scoffed dismissively. "Of course you're afraid."

"You arrogant, pompous, presumptuous—"

He cut her off, his voice utterly calm. "Mariel, why do you think I'm here right now?"

"Alex told you—"

"Nobody told me anything. I'm here because I knew you would do this. I *knew* you'd panic and get cold feet." He took a step closer to her, until the toes of his shiny black dress shoes bumped into the toes of her open-toed satin pumps. "Because, you maddening, sexy, brilliant woman, I know *you*. I know how strong you are, and I know what you're afraid of, and I'm here for all of it. The good, the bad, and everything in between. *That's* why I want to marry you."

"I've done this before and it was a mistake."

"That boy you married out of college doesn't count. I've done this before, too. Look." He gestured to Alex. "I got this amazing kid out of it. I also screwed up. A lot."

"So—"

"Let me finish. So I know what it takes to make it work. And I know what I did wrong. I know how hard it is to go the distance. That's why I haven't gotten married again until now. Because I never met anyone who seemed worth it to me. And I never met anyone who was up to that challenge. Until you."

Mariel rolled her eyes. "Ugh, do you have to be so goddamned romantic?"

Dan grinned his trademark megawatt grin. "Did it work? Are you going to get your ass out there and walk down that aisle?"

"You stupid, charming asshole."

He snagged her fingertips with his. "You love this stupid, charming asshole."

"God help me, yes I do. Now get out of here." Mariel slapped lightly at his chest. "I have to fix my lipstick."

Dan backed away, grinning ear to ear. "There's this altar out there and I'm going to go stand in front of it. I expect you to show up, woman."

"I said go!" she said, but it was without heat, and there was a smile tugging at her lips as she turned toward the mirror over the vanity.

"Get him out of here," Jess said, pushing Alex toward the door.

"So it's okay?"

Jess shook her head in mystification. "I guess so? They confuse me."

Gemma patted Alex on the arm. "They're fine. She'll be out there."

Alex snagged Dan's elbow and hauled him toward the door. "Okay, see you guys out there. Dad, let's go."

When he opened the door, Livie was on the other side, hand raised about to knock.

"Is everything okay?"

"It is now," Gemma said, pulling her inside and pushing the Drake boys out. "See you, Dan." She shut the door in his smiling face.

"What happened?"

"Nerves. But they're good."

As Mariel touched up her makeup, and Jess and Livie fluttered around her retrieving her bouquet and finding her earrings, Gemma thought about what Mariel had said. On the surface, she agreed with Mariel's freak-out. Dan Drake was a terrible bet, by anyone's estimation. He had a history and it wasn't good. Mariel had a history and it was painful. There was no logical reason Mariel should trust that it would be different this time.

But something had happened when Dan came to talk to her. He'd seen right through her brave front to the insecurity underneath, to the fear. And then he'd said exactly the right thing to blow that fear away, because, in some crazy way, Dan Drake was the perfect match for Mariel Kemper. He knew what made her tick and he loved her for it.

If you were lucky enough to find that person—well, you'd be a fool to turn them away and screw it all up just because you were afraid, right? Choosing to love, choosing to believe, was the biggest leap of faith a person could make.

Jess was right about trust. Nobody knew what the future held. When you made that promise, there were never any guarantees. All you could do was trust in the person you'd chosen, trust that, no matter what came at you, they'd have your back, they'd be on your side.

Dan's shady past be damned, Gemma fully believed in

this moment, that he would always be Mariel's staunchest ally. The rest? Well, the rest was up to fate.

"Thanks for that," Mariel said quietly, adjusting her earring.

"It's no problem," Jess said.

Mariel's eyes dropped to her hands. "There's no one else I could have said all that to. I don't have family around anymore."

"Well," Gemma said briskly. "Lucky for you you're part of the Romano family, and once you're in, there's no shaking us off. Stick with us and you'll have more family than you know what to do with."

Mariel gave her a grateful smile through the mirror. "Thank you."

"No problem. Now where's your bouquet?"

"I've got it," Livie said.

"Well, then," Mariel said, getting to her feet. "I guess I should go get married."

As Mariel, Jess, and Livie bustled around the suite making last-minute preparations, Gemma took out her phone and scrolled to Brendan's name. She hadn't asked him to come today, because it seemed like what she *should* do. After so many years, they should take it slow, proceed with caution. But the truth was she wanted him here with her. There was no guarantee she wouldn't get hurt again, but deep down, she trusted Brendan. She trusted the man he'd become. He'd never purposely hurt her again. And that was enough to go on.

Out in the hall, she reached out and grabbed Livie. "Tell Dad I'll be out in a couple of minutes, okay?"

"Sure. What are you doing?"

"I have a phone call to make."

She waited until they'd disappeared into the elevator

to make the call. Brendan picked up after just two rings. "Hey, what's up, beautiful? Aren't you busy today?"

She took a deep breath and made her leap of faith. "So I'm at this super fancy wedding right now, and it's suddenly occurring to me that it's a real shame that I don't have a date."

Brendan paused for a beat. "It is, huh?"

"I should have asked you," she said quietly.

"It's okay. I understand why you didn't."

"Okay, here's the thing. If you've got a suit handy and you leave now, you can be here in time for the reception."

Another long pause, and Gemma's stomach clenched. Damn, she'd screwed this up already.

"Is that what you want?"

"Yes," she said firmly. "That's what I want."

"Then I'll be there in time for the reception."

# Chapter Twenty-Nine

The ceremony was lovely, in the end. Dan and Mariel couldn't take their eyes off each other as they spoke their vows, and by the end, everyone was crying—even Oprah, who was indeed a guest, and sitting across the aisle from Gemma.

As her family gathered together and prepared to move to the reception hall, Gemma hung back, keeping one eye on the door.

"Gem?" her father asked, when she stayed behind the rest of them. "You coming?"

"In a minute. I just have to go downstairs and check on something."

She was down in the lobby of the Plaza when Brendan strolled through the glass and brass doors looking like something out of a James Bond movie. *He came.* Until the relief hit her, she hadn't realized she'd been a little worried he might not. But he'd come. He was here.

Gemma couldn't draw in a breath as she watched him look around for her. He was wearing a black suit, closely tailored to his long, slim body, with a crisp white shirt and a silver tie. His golden-red hair looked darker tonight, the gorgeous waves tamed and controlled. He looked delicious and utterly climbable.

His eyes finally landed on her and she felt it like a shock down her spine. As his long legs ate up the marble lobby floor, she was frozen in place, getting more turned on with every step closer. He stopped in front of her and smiled. She smiled back. This was it. After fourteen years and a very long detour, they were back together and going public at last.

"Okay," she said shakily. "You ready for this?"

"Dan Drake's wedding reception? Absolutely. Let's go." He reached for her hand and started for the elevators.

She hauled him to a stop. "No, not just Dan Drake's wedding reception. My whole family is in there."

"So?"

"So, like…my dad. My sisters. Their partners. *Everybody.* Are you ready for *that*?"

Brendan grinned, all bright white teeth and slashing dimples, the high school Brendan who had charmed the wimple off every nun at Sacred Heart High School. "Gem, it's gonna be fine. Trust me. Did I tell you how gorgeous you look? You look gorgeous."

"It's old." She tugged at the hem of her dress, feeling small and self-conscious all over again.

"Old or not, it's hot."

"Thanks," she conceded. "You look pretty nice yourself."

He ran a hand down his lapel. "Lucky for me, I keep suits handy for emergency wedding reception dates."

"I'm sorry I didn't ask you."

"You *did* ask me. I'm here, aren't I?"

He really was so damned sweet and charming.

He leaned in, his voice dropping to a whisper. "Am I allowed to kiss you in public?"

She fought down a last flare of nerves. She'd asked him here because she was ready to bring him into her life, and that meant no more hiding. "Yes. Yes, you can kiss me."

"Good."

He stepped in close, sweeping an arm around her waist and pulling her up tight against his body. His head dipped and his lips found hers in a hard, hot kiss. An elderly couple passing by smiled and whispered.

"Okay," he said when he released her. "Are *you* ready for this?"

No more time for hiding. Fear and self-protection weren't going to get her anywhere. They certainly weren't going to get her a future with this man. And that was something she wanted…so very much.

So she took his hand, and she decided to trust him, and she let him lead her to the reception.

Upstairs, the grand ballroom was overflowing with well-heeled guests. Nothing Brendan hadn't seen before, but Gemma was hanging on to his hand with a viselike grip as they made their way through the crowd looking for their table.

"How about we sit there?" Brendan gestured to a table to her right, trying to lighten the mood.

"We can't sit next to Nancy Pelosi!" she hissed.

"Why not? She seems nice."

"Yeah, she probably is. Which means she'll make small talk to the people next to her, except I'll get all flustered and say something dumb."

"I'm pretty sure she hears dumber stuff every day at work. But don't sweat it. There are seats free at George and Amal Clooney's table, anyway. Let's sit there."

She took a swipe at his arm. "Will you *stop*? We're sitting at the table we've been *assigned* to, which is with my whole family, Mr. Smartass."

"I told you, Gem, it's going to be fine."

"Let's see what you have to say at the end of the night. You'll be wishing you'd sat with Nancy Pelosi."

As they approached the Romano family table, every face turned his direction. John Romano looked surprised—but maybe also just a little bit pleased—as they appeared hand in hand.

"Everybody," Gemma announced. "This is Brendan Flaherty. He's, well…" She turned to him, eyes wide with low-key panic. "He's my boyfriend. I guess."

It felt wonderful and a little surreal to hear her call him that after all these years, and he squeezed her hand in reassurance. Gemma's announcement was met by the table with a beat of stunned silence. John Romano was the first to break it, slowly getting to his feet and extending his hand. "Nice to see you again, Brendan."

"Good to see you, too, John."

John looked briefly at Gemma. "Gemma didn't mention you'd be here."

"It was last minute," Gemma said. "Brendan, this is Dad's friend, Teresa. Teresa, Brendan. We…"

"Gemma and I went to high school together." Brendan leaned past Gemma to shake Teresa's hand.

"Um, Brendan, this is my sister Livie, and her boyfriend Nick, and this is Jessica and her fiancé Alex. Dan is Alex's dad."

Brendan made his greetings to the table, paying extra attention to Livie and Jess. He felt like he already knew them so well, listening to Gemma talk about them, but of course he was a complete mystery to them, and the last thing he wanted to do at this point was screw this up. He really wanted her sisters to like him.

"Have we met before?" Livie Romano asked, her dark eyes wide and guileless.

He shook his head. "Don't think so." But it was entirely possible she'd seen him lurking around the neighborhood when she was younger. There had been one or two close calls with the girls as he slipped out of their house following an after-school assignation with Gemma.

"Huh. You look so familiar."

"Well, it's nice to meet you," Jessica interjected. "We didn't know Gemma was seeing someone." She shot her sister a pointed look.

He looked at Gemma. She looked back. "Well, it's…"

"New," Gemma said brightly. "Very new."

And top secret for Gemma. But they were here now and that was good enough.

"Well, have a seat, you two," John said.

"So," Teresa said brightly when they were all settled again. "You said you guys went to high school together?"

"Gemma was two years behind me, but yes."

"John and I went to high school together, too," Teresa said. "Of course, we weren't involved back then. He was dating Angela and I was with Dave."

"You headed to Chicago right after graduation, didn't you, Brendan?" John asked, something speculative in his eyes.

"Before that, actually. Skipped graduation. Went right to work for my uncle." He'd missed all those senior year celebrations—prom, the parties, the senior trip, graduation… At the time, it had seemed easier, once his finals were done, to just get it over with and go.

"Huh." John nodded, as if figuring something out for himself. Then he turned to Teresa. "Brendan's just moved back to Brooklyn to start a business. He bought the DiPaolas' building."

"You did? What are you going to put in there?"

"Ah, I'm going to put an apartment building on the lot, actually." He braced himself for the chill he was sure was coming. To Gemma and the Romanos, he must seem very much the enemy.

But Teresa just nodded with polite interest. "One of those tall ones, like up the street?"

"No, this will only be three units." He'd intended it to be six, but then fucking Jimmy Walsh had to come sweeping in to fuck with him. "I like to design developments that are in keeping with the existing neighborhood. Anything above four stories wouldn't fit in with the rest of the block."

"That's nice," Teresa said, casting a glance at John. "Usually nobody thinks about the neighborhood like that."

"Brendan's got some interesting ideas," John said. He'd given John the short version of his business plan the night he'd met him at the bar, leaving out his personal mission and the impassioned George Bailey bits. It was hard to get a read on John Romano, but he'd seemed quietly impressed. That was before he was dating the guy's daughter, though. Who knew what he thought of him now?

"What were you doing in Chicago all these years?" Teresa asked.

"Working for my uncle. He runs Walsh Construction."

"Oh." Teresa's eyes went wide. "Dave…that's my ex-husband…he worked in building construction in Jersey. I've heard of Walsh. That's a big outfit."

"It is."

"And you left all that to come back to Brooklyn?"

"Well, it's home. I wanted to build something of my own, and I wanted to do it here."

Servers arrived, silently setting dinner plates in front of them, but that didn't divert anyone's attention. "So, Brendan," Jessica said, leaning forward on her elbows. "You've known Gemma for fourteen years?"

"Ah…not exactly. We knew each other in high school, but we, um, lost touch after that."

"Lost touch," Jess echoed, glancing pointedly at Livie. "Huh. And you just moved back to Brooklyn?"

He chewed and swallowed. "Yes. A couple of months ago."

"For good?" Livie asked.

Brendan glanced at Gemma, who was keeping her eyes glued to her plate. He couldn't quite tell, but he was pretty sure she was fighting back a smile. Well, she *had* warned him. He didn't mind, though. It was sweet, seeing how protective they were of Gemma. He'd seen plenty of Gemma's love and concern for her family. So much that he'd never even dared ask her to follow him to Chicago. It was nice to see they felt the same about her. These were the people who'd loved and supported Gemma when he wasn't here to do it. He'd never feel resentful of them.

"For good." He took a bite of his chicken, hoping that might dissuade more questions. No such luck.

"You still have family here?" John asked. John was prodding, too, in his own, subtle way, feeling him out, getting the measure of him.

"My mother lives in Carroll Gardens. My brother is doing his residency in Buffalo."

"A doctor?" John nodded in approval. "Your dad was a firefighter, wasn't he?"

"Yes, sir. Engine 233, Bushwick."

"He died on the job, didn't he?"

"Oh, in nine-eleven?" Jessica asked, her eyes full of sympathy.

"No, a warehouse fire a few months before that." He glanced at Gemma again. Nope, she wasn't going to step in to derail them. She wasn't kidding about an inquisition. The Romanos were relentless, in their kind, gentle way. Alex and Nick were utterly silent, keeping their eyes fixed on their food, seemingly relieved not to be in the hot seat.

"Have you ever been married?" Livie asked.

"Livie—" Jessica interjected.

"What? At his age, it's a valid question."

"Okay, I'm getting Jess another drink," Alex said, pushing to his feet.

She looked up at him. "But I don't need—"

"I'll join you," Nick said, standing too.

Brendan finally sensed an escape. "Me, too. Gem, another champagne?"

She finally looked up at him, the corner of her mouth twitching with a smile. "Sure. Thanks."

He squeezed her shoulder briefly before following Alex and Nick to the bar.

"Sorry about that, man," Nick said. "We've been there."

"At least you didn't have to declare your favorite sports team in front of a room full of Romano men," Alex said, shaking his head. "I didn't think I was getting out of there alive when I said I didn't like football. At least I like the right baseball team."

"Who's your team?" Brendan asked cautiously.

Alex scoffed. "The Mets. Are you kidding?"

Brendan let out a breath. "Well, that's one hurdle passed."

Nick laughed and clapped him on the shoulder. "See? You'll be fine. Welcome to the Romanos."

# Chapter Thirty

"So he's cute," Jess said when the men had departed and Teresa had dragged Dad off to look at the spectacular floral display at the front of the ballroom.

"Glad you think so."

"You've known him since high school, huh?"

"That's what we said." She should have known they'd jump all over Brendan. Well, she *had* known, she just hadn't quite imagined how relentless her sisters would be with their inquisition.

"And you guys just ran into each other again after all these years?" Livie asked.

"He came into the bar."

"Is it serious?" she pressed.

"Oh my God! Listen to the two of you!"

"Hey, you grilled me about Alex."

"And you lectured me about Nick."

"That's because I'm the big sister. It's my job." She was used to looking out for her sisters, sizing up anyone they got close to. It felt strange when they did the same. Strange, but also kind of nice, if she was being honest.

"When we're all adults, you don't get to pull the big sister card anymore," Jess said. "We're just sisters."

"So is it serious?" Livie asked again.

"It just started. I don't know yet." But she hoped. Oh, how she was hoping.

"He seems pretty serious about you," Livie commented.

Jess turned away from Gemma. "I know. Did you see the way he looks at her? Hot."

"Very. Do you think they've—"

Gemma pushed to her feet. "That's enough speculation from the two of you." No way was she sticking around to get grilled about her sex life, and that seemed like where this was headed. "I'm going to the ladies' room."

As she walked away from the table, Jess and Livie erupted in laughter. "Fine, laugh it up, you two!" she called back over her shoulder.

Gemma visited the ladies' room long enough to touch up her makeup, but decided she needed a break from being the center of attention at the Romano table. A towering floral arrangement in one corner of the ballroom provided cover where she could check out the glittering guests eating the two-hundred-dollar-a-plate dinner she'd chosen for Mariel. She'd checked in with Tara early on, and she knew it was all in good hands, but she still wanted to see people's faces as they tasted the food.

Everybody seemed to be enjoying it, remarking over one dish or another. At a smaller table at the head of the room, Dan and Mariel sat with their heads together, talking and laughing, dinner forgotten, as it should be.

"Here you are."

Gemma startled as her father leaned on the other side of the giant urn full of flowers, hands in his pockets. "Just looking around. It's beautiful, huh?"

"It's quite a party, that's for sure. Food's delicious."

"These guys are in another class altogether than those outfits Kendra sent me to. They're real *chefs*. This food is like art."

Dad smiled at her. "You sound excited."

She shrugged. "It was kind of fun, seeing how they put it together. It doesn't come cheap, though. You wouldn't believe what this is costing."

"Dan can afford it."

"Ten times over."

They fell into a comfortable silence, just watching the elegant, well-dressed guests laughing and mingling as dinner wrapped up and people got to their feet.

Dad drew in a deep breath. "Was it him?"

"Was what who?"

"The summer after your mom died. Something happened to you. Was it Brendan leaving?"

Gemma turned to him in shock, feeling her blood turn cold. "What are you talking about, Dad?"

"Come on, Gem. I know I was a mess back then, but I didn't miss everything. That spring, you'd been doing okay. Better than the rest of us. You seemed…alive again. I figured you were just better at coping, maybe you'd bounced back faster than your sisters. Then school ended and you just weren't yourself. It was like the light had gone out in you."

She opened her mouth to respond but nothing would come. Her throat felt too tight for words. She'd tried so hard to hide her devastation when Brendan left. She was so sure she had. But Dad had seen right through her.

"I asked you if you were okay a few times, and you always insisted you were fine. I could see that you weren't, but I didn't know what to do for you." He shrugged helplessly. "I figured you were just dealing with your mom in your own way. But it was Brendan, wasn't it?"

"Dad, I..."

"Why didn't you tell me about him?"

She sighed and dropped her head. "How could I? We'd just lost Mom. Jess and Livie were still crying themselves to sleep at night." *You were, too,* she silently amended. "You were half dead but still working your ass off to keep the bar going. And I was going to drag Brendan home and tell you all I was in *love*? That I'd met the guy I was going to marry? How could I do that? It would have been so selfish."

Dad's eyes widened. "You were gonna *marry* him?"

She closed her eyes and shook her head. "We were kids. We didn't know what the hell we were talking about. Things got complicated. And then he had to leave."

Dad inhaled deeply, rubbing a hand over his face. "There's nothing selfish about being happy, Gemma."

"But not then. Not when everybody needed—"

"Dammit, for once in your life, quit worrying about what everybody else in this family needs and think about what *you* want."

Her mouth snapped shut. She wasn't sure she'd ever heard Dad speak with such heat, especially not directed at her. He pushed off the side of the urn and took a step closer, reaching for her and gripping her by the shoulders. "You deserve to be happy, sweetheart. I don't ever want to stand between you and your happiness again."

"You didn't, Dad."

He didn't reply, but his expression said he didn't fully believe her. He leaned in, pressing a kiss to her forehead. "I won't," he said quietly, almost to himself. Then he released her and backed away. "Go find Brendan and enjoy yourself tonight. You deserve it, kid."

"You deserve it, too, Dad. Go show Teresa a good time."

He smiled awkwardly and waved over his shoulder as he walked away. Her heart ached with love for him. He tried so hard. He'd been trying all his life, and most of the time, barely managing. She wanted him to be happy, more than she even wanted happiness for herself. If anyone deserved it, Dad did.

"Found you."

Brendan stepped around the urn and held out a glass of champagne. "Nobody at the table knew where you'd gotten off to."

"Just seeing how the dinner is going." She left out that unsettling conversation with her dad. She wasn't sure yet what to make of it. Taking the glass Brendan offered, she took a sip.

Brendan looked back over his shoulder across the ballroom. "Looks like dinner's over. The dancing's started. You ready?"

"What, to dance?"

"You're acting like I just asked if you're ready for dental surgery."

"I'm not much of a dancer." Another one of those phases of her youth that seemed to have passed her by.

"Don't worry, it's a big band at a wedding, not a rave. Just follow my lead."

He ditched their champagne flutes on the tray of a passing server and took her by the hand, leading her down the length of the lavishly decorated ballroom to where the parquet dance floor began. Several couples were already there, swaying as the band played something slow and jazzy and old-fashioned.

Brendan turned and pulled her into his arms in another smooth-as-silk James Bond move.

"Okay, smart guy, I'm here. Now show me what to do."

"One hand here," he said, settling her hand on his shoulder. "The other here." He curled his palm around hers.

"Now what?"

"Now we dance."

He was right; it wasn't so hard gently swaying in his arms as he moved them easily in a small circle. The only problem she was having was keeping her head on straight when Brendan was holding her so close, staring down at her with those sexy brown eyes, smiling at her like they shared some intimate secret—it was almost enough to make her swoon. And add to it the lush music, the low golden lights, the glittering couples swaying all around them, and she felt like she'd fallen into a dream.

"We never got to do this," Brendan said.

"What, dance together?"

"I was going to take you to senior prom."

"You were?"

"Of course. But then…" He shrugged. "I wasn't even here for it."

For a moment, all those old feelings surged again—the hurt, the anger, the betrayal. But letting herself succumb to them was just going to sabotage whatever she and Brendan were trying to do here. It was hard, but she had to push away those knee-jerk emotions.

She let herself imagine it, for once free of her bitterness, and the image was lovely. Brendan in a tux, her in some terrible prom dress, questionable hairstyles and corsages, all of it preserved for posterity forever by their families.

"Yeah," she finally replied. "That would have been nice. Going to prom with you." She hadn't gone to hers, either. After Brendan left, there hadn't seemed much point to any of that stuff.

He pulled her closer, until his cheek rested against hers, just like in the old song. "Tonight's pretty good, too," he murmured, right next to her ear. His breath tickled her earlobe, and her fingers clutched at his shoulders.

The ballroom, the band, the other couples, seemed to fade away. There was just the two of them, pressed together, caught up between the past and the present.

Finally, she drew back and looked at him. "Tonight is better than any prom could have been."

One of Brendan's dimples made an appearance as the corner of his mouth tugged up in a smile. "Why's that?"

"After prom, you'd have had to bring me home by midnight."

Brendan's eyes lit up with sexy mischief. "Are you saying tonight I get you for the whole night?"

She hadn't spent an entire night with him yet. It felt too intimate, too big. But now there was nothing else she'd rather do. Sex, yes, absolutely. *Lots* of sex. But also, everything that might come after sex. She wanted to lose herself in Brendan's tenderness, she wanted to fall asleep in his arms, let him hold her all night, and she wanted to wake up to his face in the morning.

"You get me for as long as you want me," she whispered.

The look he gave her left her weak in the knees. "Are you really in the mood for cake and coffee?"

She shook her head, then fished her phone out of her little sparkly purse and typed out a message to Jess and Livie.

Leaving early.

Jess texted back right away.

Enjoy it.

Livie texted back, too.

Nick and I are going to see Jess's new place after the reception. Won't be home tonight. Dad's going to Teresa's tonight. Just so you know.

So Livie was now her sexual wingman. That was new.
"Everything okay?"
"Everything's great."

A slow grin curled his lips and he slid a hand down her arm until he could grasp her hand. "Good. Let's go."

They were mostly silent on the drive back to Brooklyn. The air in the car absolutely hummed with sexual awareness. All Gemma wanted to do was to climb over the gearshift, straddle Brendan's lap, take him by that pretty silver tie, and kiss him senseless. The look he shot her as he shifted gears told her he was imagining the same thing. He finally tore his gaze away, staring straight ahead through the windshield and exhaling heavily.

As he navigated the streets of Lower Manhattan, shifting gears as he made his way toward the Battery Tunnel, the muscles of his thighs shifted in the most distracting way underneath those thin black wool pants. And watching his hand wrap around the gearshift was nearly an erotic experience.

"Nice car," she murmured. Jesus, where did that whiskey-rasp sex voice come from?

"That's what you said the other times you were in it."

Ugh. Her brain had gone to absolute mush, decimated by lust.

Brendan angled a smile at her, reaching out and resting a hand on her knee, his fingertips brushing lightly against the inside of her thigh. A shudder of longing raced through her, and she swallowed hard to control it.

As Brendan crossed into Brooklyn, he looked over at her. "Your place or mine?"

She *could* take him home, if she wanted. Nobody was there. And even if someone were, for the first time, they all knew about Brendan. He was officially her boyfriend. She could bring him home, take him upstairs, and make love to him in her own bed. They'd never done that, not even in high school.

But while that felt symbolic and significant and all, her bed was just a double with a saggy spot in the middle, and Brendan's was a gloriously comfortable king size. She'd bring him home and christen her bed with him some other time.

"Yours."

Her nerves flared bright when Brendan shut the apartment door behind her. Ridiculous. How many times had they had sex since he'd come back? Even since that night in the park when they started toeing tentatively into a relationship? Lots. So why did tonight feel different?

Because they were real. No matter what they'd done behind closed doors, bringing him into her family made it real in a way nothing else would. Which made this, oddly, feel like the first time.

"Is it weird that I'm nervous?" Brendan said, breaking the silence.

She let out a huff of laughter, turning to face him. "Me too."

He reached up to rub a hand across the back of his neck. "Maybe we should have a glass of wine? We could watch a movie?"

His suggestion was adorable, but unnecessary. She might be nervous, but she knew what she wanted, and that was Brendan. Crossing to him, she laid her hands on his chest. "I think we can figure it out as we go."

Then she leaned up and kissed him, sliding one hand up around the back of his neck to bring his face to hers. Brendan's hands found her hips, tugging her closer. They kissed until her knees felt wobbly and her nipples felt tender. Then she gently pushed away and turned her back to him. Dragging her hair over her shoulder, she looked back over her shoulder at him. "I think you'd better help me with this zipper."

The air thrummed between them as he reached for the top of her zipper. She held her breath, fighting back a tremor as he eased it down and the cool air hit her skin. When he'd lowered it all the way, she turned around to face him again.

She reached for the shoulders, but Brendan stopped her hands. "Let me." There was a low, ragged hint of command in his voice that went straight to her sex. She dropped her hands and held still.

Slowly, he reached out and grasped the shoulders of her dress, and just as slowly, he dragged them down her arms, over the edge of her black lace bra, down over her hips, and down her thighs. When it lay in a pool around her feet, he reached a hand up for hers, steadying her as she stepped out of it.

He took his time straightening back up, running his palms up the outsides of her calves and thighs, over her hips, and up her torso as he rose. By the time he was standing in front of her again, she was wet. And practically shaking. How did he *do* that to her?

"Turn around." Another gruff command. She did as she was told.

His fingertips brushed against her back as he undid the hooks of her bra and tossed it away. Before she could turn back, his hands slid around to the front, cupping her breasts, rolling her nipples. She moaned and fell back against his chest. He toyed with her until she was squirming, and then he slid his palm down her stomach and slipped a hand between her thighs, cupping her over her panties.

All she wanted to do was grind herself against his hand until she came, but he was still fully dressed in a suit and tie behind her and that seemed criminal.

"My turn," she murmured, turning in his arms.

Brendan smiled, holding his arms out to the sides. "I'm entirely yours. Do what you want."

"Hmm." She began working the knot of his tie loose. "That gives me all kinds of interesting ideas." As the tie slithered out from under his shirt collar, she wrapped it once around her hand and tugged. "Let's keep this for later."

His eyes lit up with interest. "By all means."

Next she pushed his suit jacket off, smoothing her palms over the hard curves of his shoulders and down his sculpted, toned arms. Then she went to work on his shirt buttons, leaning forward to kiss and lick at his chest as it was exposed inch by glorious inch.

"You're so gorgeous," she murmured as she flicked her tongue across his nipple.

Brendan's breathing grew deep and a little ragged, and he raised a hand to tangle it in her hair.

"And you," he growled, fisting his hand in her hair and pulling her face up to his. "Are fucking stunning." Then he kissed her, hard and deep, banding an arm around her waist to hold her steady.

"I didn't finish with you," she gasped when he finally broke away.

"There's no rush. We have all night," he said, before sweeping her up in his arms. "And we're going to use every second of it."

In his bedroom, he laid her on the bed and straightened up to shed the rest of his clothes. She watched him hungrily as he unbuckled his belt and shed his pants and boxers.

"You forgot your shoes." He tsked, reaching for her and easing off first one high heel then the other. He slid his hands up the length of her legs, coming to kneel on the bed between her knees. "And these." His fingers hooked in the sides of her panties and slid them off her body, too.

She was aching for him, so wet and ready she could barely stand it. Still, he took his time, tracing his way back up her legs, pausing to kiss her knees, to lick the insides of her thighs.

"You're so pretty," he said, sinking his teeth lightly into the side of her hip. "Pretty everywhere."

Then he shifted his weight, lowered his head, and put his mouth on her. Gemma groaned, arching up off the bed, but Brendan pinned her hips down with one hand as he slid the fingers of the other inside her.

"Brendan," she gasped.

He was gentle and relentless, not letting up until her orgasm had washed over her and she was shaking with the aftermath. She was panting and spent as he crawled up the length of her body.

"There's the first," he murmured, reaching for the bedside table to retrieve a condom. It made her wonder how many times he planned to make her come tonight. Whatever goal he'd set for himself, she had no doubt he'd achieve it.

"I need you," she said, tugging at his shoulders to bring his body over hers. She was pretty sure she'd never said that to a man in her life. And yeah, right at this second, she meant she needed his cock inside her, but they both knew it meant more than that.

"You have me, sweetheart," he murmured, kissing her gently as he lifted her thigh and nudged in slowly.

"Please," she gasped.

"Shh." He stroked the sweaty hair back from her face as he moved deeper in tiny increments, teasing her with it.

"Brendan…"

"Look at me, Gemma."

She hadn't realized her eyes were closed. When she opened them, his face was looming over hers, those chocolate eyes pinning her in place. Eyes wide open, he leaned in and kissed her even as he slid a little deeper. Then he eased out again and she moaned, but she didn't look away. She couldn't.

"Stay with me," he whispered, easing in again. Her back arched but there was nowhere for her body to go. He was everywhere, over her, pinning her down, his hand on her face, his thumb on her bottom lip, his cock pushing into her. She'd never felt so overwhelmed in her life. Blinking, she realized tears had begun to slide down her temples.

"I've got you, Gemma," he said. "Don't be afraid." Then he buried himself deep, forcing muffled moans from both of them, but she still kept her eyes on his.

He began to move again, deep, slow strokes. Another orgasm was bearing down on her. Instinct told her to look away, close her eyes, grip the sheets, let her body take over. But Brendan wouldn't let her, his hand on her face holding her still in the moment. "Don't look away," he commanded.

"I won't."

And she didn't. Not when her climax broke over her, not when she cried out with it, clinging to him like a life raft in a storm, and not when he gritted his teeth, every tendon flexing, growling as he came, too.

*Oh, God, I love him*, she thought wildly, as he collapsed down on top of her. *I'm totally, out of my head in love with him*.

She finally closed her eyes when he rolled off her and pulled her into his chest. It had been, without a doubt, the most intense sexual experience of her life. And she was in love with him. She should have been terrified, but right now, all she felt was safe, cherished. Brendan's hand made long, slow passes down the length of her hair as she breathed in the warm, salty smell of his skin, the scattering of chest hairs prickling her cheek as she rested her head against him.

For the first time since he'd come back into her life, she wasn't rushing on to the next sexual experience with him. Right now, being held in his arms felt like more than enough. It felt like the only place on earth she ever wanted to be. And what she wanted, more than she'd ever wanted anything, was to never let him go again.

# Chapter Thirty-One

Her father said nothing when Gemma rolled into the bar half an hour after her scheduled start time the next day. He just glanced up from the glasses he was wiping down, raised one eyebrow at her, and wordlessly went back to work.

Ugh. No doubt she looked like a walking ad for debauchery and dumbstruck infatuation. She'd stopped by the house for a shower and a change of clothes, but she was quite sure the stupid amount of sex she and Brendan had was written all over her face.

It sure felt written on every inch of her body. Her skin felt flushed and tingly, and every place that had known his touch during their night together seemed to throb, as if waiting for more. And every time she let herself imagine his face, a slow, sappy grin spread across her lips against her will. She was totally *gone* for him. Luckily it was a slow day, because she was a shit bartender in her current state.

"So is he coming by tonight?" Dad finally asked, after refilling Dennis's beer when Gemma wandered off and forgot to.

"Who?"

Dad gave her a bored look. "Come on. Your old man's not that clueless."

"Oh. I don't know," she said. "We didn't discuss it."

"You should tell him to come on over. I like him."

"You do?"

John gave a brusque nod as he rang someone up on the register. "Smart guy. Hardworking. Good head on his shoulders."

That was a glowing testimonial as far as the undemonstrative John Romano was concerned.

"And he treats you right. That's the most important thing."

Gemma smiled to herself. She'd thought the same thing about Teresa when she first started coming around. The most important thing was that she treated her father right.

She'd just picked up her phone and typed out a text to Brendan, asking him if he wanted to come hang at the bar as she finished her shift, when the door opened and he walked in. At the sight of him, her body flooded with arousal and her heart started to pound. Maybe this was a bad idea. She was having a hard enough time focusing when he was just in her head. Having the flesh and blood Brendan sitting just feet away from her was going to wreck whatever was left of her concentration.

He strode across the bar, looking positively edible in a pair of faded, worn jeans, a white t-shirt, and a leather jacket. She thought the suits were deadly, but Brendan in jeans was lethal.

"Hi there." He grinned, sliding onto a bar stool and shrugging out of his jacket.

"Hi." Some part of her realized that she was just standing there, smiling at him like a fool, but she couldn't seem to help it. It was like he had her hypnotized.

"Hey, John."

Dad nodded his head in Brendan's direction. "Evening, Brendan. Can I get you a beer?"

That startled her out of her trance. "I got it, Dad."

When she set his beer in front of him, he reached out to trail his fingertips across the back of her hand. "Is it okay that I came by?"

She flipped her hand over and briefly squeezed his fingers. "I was about to text you and ask you to."

Brendan hid his grin behind his glass as he lifted it and took a sip, while Gemma desperately tried to focus on customers who *weren't* Brendan.

It was nearly eight p.m. when the door opened and a grinning Frank strolled in. That was odd. In her distracted state, she hadn't even registered that Dennis had been here on his own for two hours. She couldn't remember the last time the two of them hadn't come in together.

Feeling bad for neglecting Dennis, she poured him another refill as she got Frank's beer and set them both down as Frank took a seat.

"Sorry, guys. I didn't get a chance to cook anything this morning." She'd been far too busy having wake-up sex with Brendan.

"That's okay," Frank said. "I've already eaten."

"You have?"

"With Veronica."

"Veronica? That's still going okay, then?" Frank had mentioned Veronica once or twice, but he'd had yet to spend the evening with her instead of Dennis, so she hadn't thought it was progressing very far. The grin on Frank's face told a different story, though.

"Better than okay." Frank beamed. "We're getting married."

Silence fell over the bar. Dennis gaped at his best friend. Gemma froze. Dad turned back from what he was doing as if he couldn't believe his ears.

"Married?" Dennis was the one to say what they were all thinking.

"Yep. Popped the question tonight and Veronica said yes."

Brendan was the first one to snap out of it, reaching over to shake Frank's hand. "Wow. Congratulations, Frank. That's great news, man."

Dad came next. "Yeah, that's great, Frank. Veronica is a lucky woman."

"You'll have to bring her in to meet us all," Gemma finally managed.

"There's more," Frank said.

"More than you getting married again?" Dennis asked. His bushy white eyebrows had hiked nearly to his hairline.

"We're moving to Florida."

"What?" Gemma couldn't hold back her shock. "Florida?"

"Veronica's got a little condo down there in Vero Beach. So we're selling up and moving down there."

"But… Florida?" Dennis said. "It's a little sudden, isn't it?"

Frank shrugged. "How many good years do we have left? Veronica and I got to talking and we decided why not? Let's go for it."

"So…you're going for it," Gemma said. "Getting married and moving to Florida."

"Isn't that what us old retirees are supposed to do? Go spend our golden years on a beach?"

"Um…"

Dad stepped into the breach. "I think this calls for a toast. Gem, we got another bottle of that prosecco hiding someplace?"

"Uh, yeah, I think we do. Hang on."

Gemma headed toward the back room to find the prosecco, but she caught a glimpse of Dennis as she passed. He looked lost, adrift, like his world had just been shaken to pieces. In a flash, she knew they'd lose him, too. With Frank gone to Florida with Veronica, what was there to keep Dennis here in Brooklyn? He'd move down to Toms River to be near his daughter and then that was it. The two last Romano's regulars would be no more.

It wasn't as if Frank and Dennis spent enough here to keep the doors open. Romano's wouldn't be much worse off financially with the loss of those two, holding down their end of the bar. No, it wasn't money that made Gemma feel like someone had just walked over her grave.

Frank and Dennis were more than customers. They were part of the extended family that had kept this place anchored in the neighborhood for nearly ninety years. She honestly hadn't ever imagined the bar without them. But now that she had—imagined the unthinkable, Romano's without Dennis and Frank—it became sickeningly easy to imagine much worse. No Romano's left at all.

# Chapter Thirty-Two

A shaft of weak early spring sunlight fought its way to Brendan's bedroom window, hitting him square in the face and waking him up. With the bedroom facing the back of the building and another building just ten feet away, the light only managed to reach that window for about twenty minutes a day, and those twenty minutes had to come at seven a.m. on a Saturday.

Groaning, he rolled over to bury his face in the pillow, but found himself instead facedown in a tangle of long, dark brown hair. He cracked one eye open to see the sublime landscape of Gemma's bare back—the sharp angle of her shoulder blade, the gentle bumps of her spine curving down her back, the shallow dip of her waist.

Sleep could wait.

Reaching out, he laid his palm in that hollow above her hip and she sighed, a low, sexy little sound that went straight to his already half-hard cock. He just couldn't get enough of her. Last night was a blur of lips and skin and heat and orgasms.

He'd thought his memories of the two of them in high school had been overblown. That almost obsessive need, that explosive chemistry he remembered—it had to be a product of their situation. It was first love for both of them, with all the heightened emotions that came with it. Add to that the sneaking around, every sexual encounter a desperate, furtive act…well, yeah, to his eighteen-year-old self, it had all seemed hotter than hell.

But it was no trick of his memory, no glow of nostalgia making it seem better than it had been. Every time they came together, it was just as hot—hotter—than it had been in high school.

The emotions were bigger, too. He'd thought he'd loved her in high school. And he *had*, as much as that idiot kid understood love. But it was nothing to how he felt now. He'd had relationships in the intervening years in Chicago, but he'd never been able to envision a long-term future with any of them, and consequently, none had lasted more than a few months. With Gemma, almost from the first time he'd kissed her again, a future was unfolding in his mind with alarming specificity. He saw all the forevers with her he'd never been able to imagine with anyone else. None of those other relationships had lasted, he realized, because he'd remained more than a little in love with Gemma for all these years.

Gemma shifted under his hand, letting out another sexy little groan, and his half-hard cock finished the job. She rolled to her back and turned her head, blinking at him with those sleepy, half-lidded, dark eyes.

"Morning," he murmured, his eyes darting down her body. The sheet remained wrapped around her waist, exposing her breasts. As he stared, her nipples hardened. He slid his hand up from her waist to cover one. She sighed, arching up slightly.

"Good morning," she said, reaching for him.

He came, rolling over and sliding between her long,

slim thighs. "You okay with this this morning? We were kind of rough last night."

She wiggled underneath him until his cock brushed against her wetness, forcing a grunt of pleasure from him. "I want you to be rough this morning, too. Let's be rough all day."

Rolling his hips against her, he watched her eyes slide closed and her head arch back. "I'll be as rough as you want this morning," he said, imagining all the depraved shit he still wanted to do with her. "But you have to work this afternoon."

"Screw work," she groaned, rubbing herself against the length of his cock.

"And I have lunch plans."

Underneath him, she stilled, her eyes opening. "You have a lunch date?"

He chuckled at her wide-eyed question. "With my mother."

"Oh."

He hesitated, then just sucked it up and said it. "Come with me?"

"To lunch?"

"To meet my mother." He'd met her family; it was time she met his, especially in light of all these forever feelings he was having.

"Um…"

He could see the uncertainty in her eyes, and he remembered how angry she'd been on his behalf the night he'd explained his leaving. She still blamed his mother. Maybe meeting her would change that. Maybe then she'd understand.

"I promise, it'll be a lot easier for you than it was for me."

She laughed at that. "Okay, I'll come. I suppose I owe you one. Meeting the whole family *and* a wedding. That was a trial by fire."

He dropped a kiss on her mouth. "I'd do it again in a heartbeat."

Her legs wrapped around his hips, drawing him closer. "But please tell me we still have time to get rough."

He slid his hands up her arms until he could close them around her wrists and pin them to the bed over her head. "Plenty rough."

## Chapter Thirty-Three

As they stood on the front stoop of his mother's house a few hours later, Gemma fiddled with the zipper of her jacket.

"Don't worry, she's harmless." Beyond harmless. His mother was like an egg walking around in the world without its shell—fragile and vulnerable.

"She nearly ruined your life," Gemma muttered under her breath.

"Not on purpose, I promise you. You'll see."

The door opened and his mother blinked in the sudden bright sunlight. "Brendan!" He could tell from the way she said his name that she'd forgotten he was coming. "Oh." She smiled tremulously at Gemma. "Who's this?"

"Mom, this is Gemma, my girlfriend." It was the first time he'd said it out loud, and he liked it. A lot.

"Oh, your girlfriend," Mom said, startled. "I didn't realize... How nice."

They exchanged polite greetings, and a handshake, Gemma clearly swallowing down her lingering resentment.

"I thought we'd go out today, Mom, if that's okay with you?"

Her hands fluttered up to her hair, which was pulled back in a clip. "Oh…out?" She spent far too much of each day rattling around alone inside that house, slipping further and further away from the world. Getting her out would be good for her.

"You look great. Let's get your jacket and we'll go."

"Where to?" Gemma asked him a few minutes later when they were out on the sidewalk together.

"I don't know. I've been gone a long time and you're the food expert. What's good around here?"

Gemma shrugged. "Well, there are all those new places a few blocks up. Or…"

"Yeah?"

"I mean, there's Sal's. It's not fancy, but they make the best subs in the neighborhood."

He grinned at her. "Sounds perfect."

Sal's was another of the old holdout Italian-owned businesses. The original owners, Sal and Lydia Caruso, had long since retired, Gemma explained as they walked over, and now their son, Joe, ran the place for them. It was straight out of a fifties mafia movie, with neon in the plate glass windows advertising Italian Food and Pizza Pies. Inside, the black and white checkered linoleum floor looked like it dated from the restaurant's origins, as did the red vinyl booths.

Gemma raised her hand to greet the man behind the cash register, a beefy middle-aged guy in a straining navy blue polo shirt. "Hey, Joe."

"Hey, Gemma. Have a seat wherever you want. It's early still."

Brendan helped his mother slide into a booth then took a seat next to Gemma, across from her.

"How long have you known each other?"

Gemma glanced at him briefly, then away. "Um, since high school?"

Under the table, he reached for her hand. "We reconnected when I came back to town. Mom, Gemma's family owns Romano's. The bar up the street?"

"Oh. Yes. Romano's. I remember that place. Your father would go there sometimes with his friends from the firehouse." She looked to Gemma. "Did you know Brendan's father was a firefighter?"

"Yes, he told me that."

"We lost him," his mother said, her expression going soft and sad. Jesus, it had been nearly twenty years and she was still on the verge of tears every time she spoke about him.

"Yeah, I know," Gemma said. "My uncle was a firefighter. We lost him on the job, too."

"You're never the same, you know. You just never get over it."

"I know," Gemma said, casting him a quick glance. But her resentment seemed to have fled, replaced by sympathy.

"Okay," he interrupted, before Mom could start crying again. "What's good here?"

"Everything," Gemma said. "But Sal's Italian sub will change your life. He does a mean chicken parm, too."

"Chicken parm sounds great," Brendan said. "Mom, what about you?"

Mom spent a minute skimming the menu then looked up at him with lost eyes. "I don't know; what do you think I should get?"

"How about the chef's salad, Mom? You love those."

"Oh, yes, that does sound good. That's what I'll have. What do you think? Should I have iced tea, too?"

"Sure, Mom. Iced tea sounds great."

Under the table, Gemma squeezed his hand.

After lunch, they walked his mother home, he checked to make sure everything in the house was still safe and secure, and then he walked Gemma back to the bar so she could open up for the day.

"I didn't realize," Gemma said as they walked hand in hand down the sidewalk.

"Realize what?"

She shook her head. "When you told me what she was like after your dad died, and all you had to do to keep your family going, I was so mad at her. I thought she was selfish, leaning on you that way. But she really can't help it, can she? She's so helpless."

"She was never what you'd consider a tough woman. Nothing like you."

She smiled and nudged his shoulder with hers.

"If my dad hadn't died... I don't know, maybe she'd be different. But losing him that way destroyed her, and she was never the same afterward. Then Harry... That just did her in." He paused before he continued, because Gemma needed to understand that his mother would always be his responsibility. She wasn't suddenly going to get her shit together and go traveling through all the European capitals with her girlfriends. "I don't think she'll ever be any different, Gem."

"Probably not," Gemma conceded. "So I guess it's good she has you."

"She always will. She's always going to be my responsibility."

"I get that now. You're a good son. I'm sorry it had to be you, but I'm glad you're looking out for her. She's lucky to have you."

## Chapter Thirty-Four

Gemma was late. Not like there'd be anyone waiting to get into Romano's at noon on a weekday, but still, Romano's was never late opening.

It had just been too hard to climb out of bed on time this morning after the night she'd had. Mrs. Simonsen's birthday dinner for the ambassador had been exhausting and stressful. This time, she didn't have Kendra to run interference for her. It was just her and Mrs. Simonsen's Upper East Side moneyed friends. Fortunately, despite the higher stakes and the tension, it had gone off well. Everything turned out the way she'd practiced it, and—at least judging from the reports from the servers—everybody loved it. At the end of the night, Mrs. Simonsen had declared herself delighted. She'd taken the job solely because she needed the money, but it was deeply satisfying to know she'd done the job well.

But while enjoying herself was all well and good, the best part of the night had definitely been that fat check Mrs. Simonsen handed her. Now they could pay off Tony Santini's electrical upgrades in the apartment without asking for a loan from Uncle Richie. Despite her bone-deep exhaustion and the ache in the back of her neck, Gemma felt downright optimistic as she hurried toward the bar.

As soon as Tony finished the wiring and the drywall guy finished up, they could list the apartment and get another tenant in there. That income would cover the property taxes and a few other things this year. Romano's wasn't raking it in, but if she could keep this up, they'd manage to keep their heads above water for a while.

And to top it all off, there was this incredible, intoxicating thing with Brendan. They hadn't yet discussed where this might be headed, but with each day that passed—and each night she spent in his arms—he worked his way further into every image she had of her future, and she liked the way he looked there.

She rounded the corner onto Court Street, but what she saw a few blocks ahead stopped her in her tracks.

Fire trucks. In front of Romano's.

*Oh, no no no no no…*this could not be happening. Oh, please, *no.*

Her heart broke out in a panicked gallop as she sprinted down the sidewalk toward their building. When she was still half a block away, she saw Tony Santini standing out front, his cell phone to his ear.

She screamed his name as she veered around a dog walker and a few people milling around watching the action. Her voice was ragged with breathlessness.

Tony turned and held his phone up. "Just left a message for you and your dad," he called as she darted in front of an oncoming car and reached the far corner. "Calm down, it's okay."

"What happened?" Her chest felt like it might explode with each heartbeat and her throat burned as she panted for breath.

"Sparks from an old wire. Caught that newspaper insulation on fire. Lucky thing I was in there working when it happened or the whole building would have gone up."

"Shit." *Shit shit shit.* Jess had called this place a fire-trap and she was right. "What's burning? How fast is it moving?"

"Gemma, it's okay. I carry a fire extinguisher in my kit. Soon as I saw the smoke, I put it out. It was out before the firefighters even got here."

"So it's okay?" She sagged with relief.

"Well, not so fast. There's damage."

"How much?"

Tony shrugged. "Didn't look too bad from the out-side, but who knows how far it went into the walls, and how much of the wiring got fried. The guys are up there now checking it out. They'll let you know what they find."

"Gemma! What's going on?"

She turned as her dad sprinted across the street, ducking around a car turning the corner.

"Fire in the wall. Tony got it out. Now we're wait-ing for the fire department to come down and tell us how bad it is."

John tipped his head back, looking at the shabby, fa-miliar facade of the Romano's building. "Ah, hell. This is the last thing we need."

She touched her Dad's arm. "I'm going to call Jess, just so she doesn't hear about it from somebody else."

Dad dropped his head, squeezing his eyes shut and

rubbing a hand over his face. "Yeah, I'd better call Teresa. Thanks for being here, Tony."

Tony shrugged. "Glad I was there to put it out. Let's just hope the damage isn't too bad."

Gemma was trying to stay optimistic, but secretly she was eaten up with dread. She'd just clawed them back from the brink of financial ruin. There was no way of telling if they'd be able to withstand this latest blow. And if they couldn't...well, she wouldn't let herself think about that just yet.

Mrs. Kim from the green grocery came with cups of coffee, clucking at the sight of the flashing lights and the firemen stomping up and down the stairs to the apartment. Joe walked down from Sal's with a tray of subs for the firefighters. They weren't supposed to accept, but few would be able to say no to an Italian sub from Sal's. Amen came, pacing up and down the sidewalk, shaking his head sadly. Maria DiPaola brought over a box of Italian Wedding cookies.

Gemma sat huddled on an empty plastic crate, arms wrapped across her stomach, watching the firefighters complete their inspection, waiting for the verdict.

Maria squeezed her shoulder. "Hang in there, hon."

"I just don't know what we'll do if it's bad, Maria."

Dad was a few feet away, pacing as he spoke into his cell to their insurance company, so he couldn't hear her voicing her fears.

Maria wrapped her nubbly cardigan more securely across her stomach. "You'll do whatever it takes to get through it as a family. That's what we did."

Gemma let out a humorless laugh. "Except you're closing up shop."

The older woman was quiet for a moment. "Sometimes that's just what you have to do."

"I don't know what I'd do without this place," she whispered, feeling cold to her bones, and not because of the brisk, early spring breeze. "It's my whole life."

Maria crouched at her side, tucking a wisp of hair behind her ear in a comforting way. "Doll, your whole life is your *family*, and you still have them. This? It's a business and a building. You're young. You have no idea what life has waiting for you. Isn't that exciting?"

"Exciting? No, it's terrifying. Whoever said the unknown was exciting should be shot. This place is in my blood, and I don't want anything else."

Maria was about to respond when the fire chief came down the stairs and strode over to join her father and Tony Santini. The fire chief was Alan Ferranti, who was distantly related to them on Mom's side in some way Gemma couldn't quite remember at the moment. She scrambled to her feet and darted over to stand behind her father.

"Smoke damage is minimal," Alan was saying. "But the wiring is all fried. And with that old newspaper insulation…you're gonna have to tear out the walls and rewire the whole place, John."

Dad sighed and shook his head. "What about the bar?"

"You're in luck there. No damage in the walls or the ceiling. It'll take a few days to sign off on the inspection, but you should be able to reopen again by the weekend."

Her father nodded grimly. "Thanks, Alan. I appreciate it."

"Anytime, John. Sorry, I don't have better news. These old buildings…"

"I know. These old buildings."

"You gonna stick around a bit? Got a few things for you to sign before we go."

"I'll be in the bar."

Dad watched Alan head upstairs before turning to Gemma. "Gem, why don't you go on home and call your sisters? I'll finish up here."

"You sure?"

He forced a smile for her. It was decidedly unconvincing. "Sure."

Gemma started to go, but paused and reached out for her dad's hand, squeezing it in both of hers. "We'll figure this out, Dad. I'll call Kendra, have her work all her contacts. I'll get some more catering gigs. We can manage."

He hesitated then squeezed back. "I know we will, honey."

## Chapter Thirty-Five

Alan had originally thought it would be at least Friday until they got the all-clear to reopen, so Gemma was pleasantly surprised when the call came on their home phone that the paperwork had processed quickly and they were okay to reopen Thursday.

But now she was behind schedule. There hadn't been any smoke damage in the bar itself, but the place smelled decidedly toasted. She'd intended to scrub down the tile floor with lemon cleaner to banish the smell, but she hadn't gotten around to it yet. If she got a jump on it, she could scrub down everything and prop open the doors for a few hours today. By tomorrow, they'd be good to go.

She was surprised when she rounded the corner onto Court Street and saw the metal security gate had been rolled up on one side. Dad had spent the night at Teresa's last night, but he must have come over to clean up, too. Well, with two of them, they'd get the place whipped back into shape in no time.

"Did Alan call you, too, Dad?" she said as she swung through the front door, but she stopped short when she realized Dad wasn't alone.

Brendan was there. Which would be a nice surprise,

except for that expression on his face when he looked over his shoulder and spotted her. Then there was the look on her father's face. And the fact that the two of them were there alone, bent over the bar, conferring intently over a stack of papers. Her blood went cold.

"Hey, what are you doing here?"

"Just talking to your dad about some stuff." Brendan slid off his bar stool and stood. "John—"

"We'll talk," Dad said quietly.

Gemma's heart started to flutter in her chest.

Brendan crossed to the front door, pausing beside her long enough to touch her hand and kiss her cheek. "I'll talk to you later," he said, and then he was gone.

Gemma couldn't make herself move away from the front door. Her feet felt like cement, rooting her where she stood. "What's going on, Dad?"

"Come have a seat, Gem. We need to talk."

Her throat felt tight and it was hard to draw a full breath. A tinny little ringing started in her ears.

"About what?"

He said nothing at first, just watching her with those sorrowful dark brown eyes of his, and the poker face that made it impossible to read him. Forcing her feet to move, she crossed the room. "About what, Dad?" she repeated, her voice going slightly shrill at the end.

Dad pressed his eyes closed very briefly, and when he opened them again, she knew. She just knew, before he even said a word. "I've made a deal to sell the building to Brendan."

"Dad, no!"

"Honey." He pushed off his elbows, bracing his hands on the bar the way he'd done a million times before in her life. Seeing Dad behind the bar that way had always made her feel safe and secure, like he was her fixed point in the universe, the one thing she knew would never disappear, never change. Now she felt like the world had tilted sideways and she was scrambling to hang on before she fell over the edge. "We both know what we're facing. There's too much to do and the bar just doesn't pay for itself anymore."

"So you're giving up? Just like that?" She'd never, ever in her life been angry at her father, but now it felt like her rage was choking her. She had plenty of fight left, but she couldn't do it on her own. He had to fight, too, and here he was, throwing in the towel right when she needed him most.

"No, *not* just like that," he said sharply. "I've given my whole life to this place."

"So how can you just walk away from it now?"

"Because I'm not about to let you give up your life for it, too."

"That's *my* choice, Dad. *Mine*. It's my legacy, and you're selling it out from underneath me!"

"Listen to me." Dad leaned forward. "This bar is my legacy, too, but a legacy doesn't mean shit if it steals every other dream from you."

She blinked as his words sunk in. "Oh, I get it. You and Teresa want out. You're tired of the hours and the struggle and you want to start over and leave all this shit behind, is that it?"

"This has nothing to do with Teresa or what I want. It has to do with what *you* want."

"I already told you I want *this*!" In the empty bar, her voice echoed off the tile floor and mirrored wall.

Dad crossed his arms over his chest and examined her in that all-seeing way he'd been using all her life.

He might be unreadable, but he could always tell what his girls were thinking. "Are you really going to stand there and tell me there's nothing else you want out of your life, Gem?"

"Yes," she snapped, although with a lot less conviction than she had a second ago. Because it felt like she was lying. But imagining something was not the same thing as wanting it. People imagined shit all the time that they had no intention of ever doing. That's what fantasies were for. But this bar…this bar was the only thing she'd ever *wanted*.

"I know you, honey. I know you better than either of your sisters because you've been a lot more than a daughter to me. You've been my best friend and my business partner for years. I *know* you, inside and out. And I know you've never let yourself want more because you didn't think you could have it, and that's my fault."

"What are you talking about?"

Dad looked down, shaking his head. "When your mother died, I'm not sure if we'd have made it through in one piece if not for you. You stepped up and held this family together when I couldn't."

"Because it's my family, too."

"Yeah, but I let you keep doing it. I relied on you too much. So much that I didn't notice that you'd never even bothered to dream for yourself. You were too busy dreaming for your sisters. What kind of kid grows up without a dream?"

"*This* was my dream."

"Because it's the only one you let yourself have. Your sisters went off to Ivy League colleges and careers while you did what you thought you had to do. You chained yourself to this bar as it crumbled into the ground."

"It was my choice. It's *still* my choice."

He looked her in the eye. "I'm not letting it happen again. You might hate me for this, but I'm doing what I should have done for you years ago. I'm setting you free, Gem."

Her eyes were burning with unshed tears and her throat ached, either with a sob or a scream, she couldn't tell which. All she knew was that she was burning up with helpless, frustrated rage and there was only one person to aim it at. "I *do* hate you. How can you do this to me? How can you do it to *us*? Do you know what he's going to do with it? He's going to tear it down! The building we've owned for nearly a hundred years. Torn down!" Her eyes flicked to the mirror behind the bar, with Romano's written in flaking gold paint, and the pain in her throat coalesced into a sob. *Gone.* It would all be gone. She couldn't bear to think about it.

"Nothing lasts forever, honey. This place has been good to the family, way beyond what Grandpa Romano could have ever envisioned. But it's time."

Gemma shook her head frantically. "No, not if we don't let it be. Not if we keep fighting."

Immovable as a mountain, Dad watched her. "We've fought all we can for this bar, but now it's done. I'm picking a new fight for the next generation. I'm fighting for you this time."

She tried to draw a breath but ended up choking on a sob. The tears were crowding her eyes now, turning every well-worn, familiar corner of this place into a watery blur, like it was already fading into memory. "Keep your damned fight," she spat. "I don't want it."

And because she couldn't bear to spend another moment surrounded by everything she'd ever wanted and just lost, she turned and fled.

## Chapter Thirty-Six

As the afternoon crept on and the light grew longer, it got colder, but Brendan didn't move from his post on Gemma's front stoop. If he knew her—and he did— this was the first place she'd come after whatever was going down with her father.

He'd fucked up. He'd known it the instant he met her gaze in the bar and saw the realization sink in.

When John had called him up to talk it through, once he'd gotten over the shock, it had seemed like the best possible solution for everybody. He needed the plot, John needed to sell, and selling to him was bound to be easier for Gem than seeing her building go to a stranger, with no control over what happened to it. At least if he bought it, she'd still be a part of it, in a way. John had convinced him to leave Gemma out of it for the moment. He'd thought it would be easier for her.

At the time, it had all made sense, but maybe that was just because he'd wanted it to. John's proposal had so neatly solved all Brendan's problems that he'd convinced himself the rest—Gemma—would work out somehow. Now he could see with crystal clarity how this looked to her, and it was bad. It didn't matter what he planned to do with her building, her bar. She was losing it, and that's all that mattered. Losing it to *him*. That wouldn't make it easier; it would make it worse. He'd just become her enemy.

It was too late to undo the damage. All he could hope now was that she loved him enough to give him a chance to explain, apologize, make it up to her. If she didn't…well, he'd face that when he had to.

He was staring between his feet at a crack in the concrete step when her shadow finally fell across him. His head jerked up.

"Gemma—"

Her face was pale and blotchy, her eyes red and puffy with tears. "I don't know what the hell you're doing here, but you'd better go."

He scrambled to his feet. "Look, we need to talk—"

"What do we have to talk about? It all seems pretty clear from where I'm standing. You needed a property, so you swept in when we were down and made my dad an offer he couldn't refuse."

"That's not how it happened—"

"I don't care!" she screamed, her ragged voice echoing off the front of the brownstones all the way down the block.

Moving down the steps toward her, he held up his hands. "This was your father's idea—"

She staggered back several steps, so he stopped his advance. "And you just happened to be there with your checkbook out. How fucking convenient."

He stopped short, stunned at the venom in her voice, and at what she was implying. "I hope you're not suggesting that I got involved with you to get your bar."

"You sure were in the right place at the right time."

Her accusation hit him like a fist in the chest. Not

once had he expected her to think him capable of something like that. "That's not fair."

"Fair?" she cried. "What's fair about me losing the bar? My family losing its legacy? *That's* what's not fair. But here you are walking away with exactly what you wanted. Seems if anybody's coming out of this on top, it's you."

*Yes, yes, and yes.* What was she saying that wasn't true? But he had to try to explain, had to attempt to reach her before it was too late.

"The bar was going to be sold one way or another. If it wasn't me, it would have been somebody else. Somebody who doesn't give a shit what gets built there. Where Romano's once stood, one of those god-awful glass and aluminum pieces of shit from up the street, full of a bunch of people who aren't part of this neighborhood, who contribute nothing. Is that what you want?"

"What I *want* is my bar! The bar that was my father's, and my grandfather's, and my great-grandfather's. It was supposed to be *mine*!" The tears started again, streaking down her cheeks. He never could stand to see her cry.

"Gem," he said carefully. "The writing has been on the wall for a while now—"

"Shut up! You don't understand—"

"I understand what your father is trying to do. He's trying to take what's inevitable and make something good out of it. For you. That's what I want, too."

She threw up her hands and spun away. "Oh, God, save me from all these fucking men in my life who think they know what's best for me!"

"Nobody's trying to tell you what to do, Gem." Except they had, he realized with a sinking feeling. He and her father had gone behind her back and made a deal she should have been a part of.

She spun back, eyes blazing, as she thrust her finger at him. "No, you're all just taking away my choice."

"Your father is trying to *give* you choices. Choices you never had before. That's what I want for you, too."

"Right. Just like you took away my choice when you didn't tell me what was happening with your family. You just left and broke my heart."

"I told you I was wrong about that—"

"And you're wrong about this!"

"Wrong for thinking you're destined for a hell of a lot more than pouring beers for a bunch of old men? That you can do better than some forgotten old bar in Brooklyn?" As soon as the words left his mouth—no matter how true they might be—he knew he'd fucked up.

Her expression went icy. "Those old men are my family. That place is my home."

He took a step toward her, reaching out a hand. "I'm sorry. That's not what I meant. I just wanted to make things better for you—"

She slapped him away. "Yeah, that's what you said last time. For the last goddamned time, I am not your mother. I didn't need you to protect me from this, to fix this for me. Whatever happens to the bar, it should have been *my* choice to see it through. Mine!"

"Look, I know you don't want to talk to me now, so I'll go. When you're ready, we'll talk—"

She took another step back, her face closing up like she'd just locked herself away in a vault. "I'm not going to be ready to talk to you. I'm never going to be ready."

There was something cold and final in her voice,

something that sent a shaft of fear through his heart. "Gem—"

"Leave! I mean, you got what you came back for anyway, right?"

She was baiting him, lashing out in her anger and pain, but that didn't stop the barb from landing and digging in. All his life, all he'd done was try to help—his mother, Gemma. He tried and tried, and somehow he always managed to screw it up. The people he tried to protect got hurt anyway, or he wound up hurting them himself. "I didn't come back here for your damned bar and you know it. I came back here for you."

"Well, you should stick to real estate, then, Brendan, because you can't buy me as easily as you bought my bar." Her eyes flashed with fury, and her rage twisted up her beautiful face. "I don't want to talk rationally about how you've destroyed my future. I have nothing to say about that, Brendan, so you'd better just leave and keep on going."

It was hard to draw a breath, but somehow it kept happening without his willing it to. His heart kept beating even as it caved in on itself. "I suppose," he finally managed to say, "it doesn't matter that I love you?"

Her throat worked as she swallowed, those hard, glassy eyes never leaving his. "I've heard that one before. But I'm not dumb enough to fall for it twice."

Once again, he'd managed to hurt Gemma, and this time, he knew in his bones he wouldn't have another chance to make it up to her. Everything that had happened since he'd come back to Brooklyn, everything they'd done to find their way back to each other—he'd undone it all with one stupid, thoughtless, self-serving action. It didn't matter what his intention had been, it didn't matter that he'd wanted to protect her. All he'd done was devastate her life. Twice. He should have just stayed gone. That's what would have been best for Gemma Romano.

Drawing as deep a breath as he could, he looked into her face for what was probably going to be the last time. She deserved to hear this from him, whatever she decided to do with the knowledge once he was gone. "I love you, Gemma. It was the truth then. It's the truth now."

Then he did as she asked and he left.

## Chapter Thirty-Seven

Brendan was gone.

Because she told him to leave, and he left. Which was good, because she couldn't bear to look at him right now. She couldn't bear to hear that gentle voice as he tried to explain he'd done all this for her, that he *loved* her… What a joke.

She looked up at the front of their dark house. That's what Dad had said, too. All of this was for her, so she'd have her fucking *freedom*, whatever that meant. Her skin crawled with anger she had no outlet for. Her guts twisted with a pain she'd never get over. The betrayal was bitter in her throat.

One thing was for sure, she couldn't stand the sight of either of them right now. So she didn't go inside. She turned and left, headed for the subway entrance and escape.

Fifteen minutes later, she was banging on Jess's bright blue front door. After all the wrangling over where they'd live—the luxury Upper East Side four-story townhouse Dan Drake tried to buy them, versus the studio apartment with sloping floors and a mouse problem that Jess had advocated for—they'd compromised with this place. It was small, an old carriage house in Brooklyn Heights, but by no means shabby. The outside might look straight out of turn-of-the-century Brooklyn with the old barn door and the red-brick facade, but it was an understated masterpiece inside.

"Hang on!" Jess called from inside.

A second later, she threw the door open.

"You should always ask who it is before you open," Gemma said automatically.

"Did you come all the way over here just to scold me?"

Abruptly, Gemma crumpled, the tears starting up again and a ragged sob tearing its way out of her throat.

"Gem!" Jess reached for her, pulling her inside and nudging the door closed. "What is it? Has something happened to Dad?"

"Other than him being a heartless bastard?"

Jess absorbed that, eyes wide. "Okay, inside."

She dragged Gemma by the hand through the house. It still nominally looked like the barn it had once been, with rough-hewn dark beams overhead and white-washed walls. But the wood floors were polished to a high gleam, with a bright Turkish rug making the room feel homey. One wall was exposed brick with a fire-place, where a small log crackled on the hearth. The back of the open-plan space was given over to their enviable kitchen. The skylight overhead was dark now that night had fallen, and the garden on the other side of the wall of glass doors was dark, too. An open circular staircase on one wall led to the second floor, where the bedroom was. Jess had managed to navigate the line between Alex's astounding wealth and her own down-to-earth sensibility admirably. The house was small, cozy, and perfect.

When they reached the big squishy bright red sofa, Jess nudged her until she sat. Then she went to the kitchen island where an open bottle of wine stood on the counter, and fetched two glasses from the overhead rack, which she could only reach by kneeling on a bar stool. After pouring two healthy glasses, she came back and handed one to Gemma before sitting next to her on the sofa, angling her body to face her.

"Okay, what's going on?"

It took Gemma a minute to get the words out. Every time she said them or thought them, it seemed to make them more real, more irrevocable, something she'd never be able to undo.

"Dad's selling the bar."

Gemma waited for Jess's outraged explosion, for the hysterics, but it never came. When she looked up at her baby sister, Jess was watching her with sympathetic eyes. "I'm sorry."

"You're not even a little bit upset?"

Jess bit her lip and looked down. "I'm devastated, of course. The bar is like home. But I'm also not surprised. Gem, I keep the books, remember? I'm amazed you guys have kept it going this long."

For the first time since Dad dropped the bomb on her, it occurred to her that he might have had a point. Maybe all the determination and fight in the world wouldn't have been enough to save it. If anybody would know the truth of their situation, it was Jess. The thought gave her no comfort. It just made the whole thing feel more final, like the door had just been slammed and locked, and there was no opening it again. Her eyes burned with yet more tears. Right now, it felt like they'd never stop falling.

"He's selling the building, too."

Jess nodded sagely. "Makes sense. It needs so much work, and with only the one rental unit upstairs, it can barely pay for itself."

"But…they're going to tear it down, Jess. It'll be *gone*."

At that, Jess's features crumpled slightly. "I know. And it's going to kill me to see it go, but nothing lasts forever."

"You sound just like Dad."

"I'm guessing you didn't take the news well?"

Gemma thought back to that horrible confrontation in the bar… She'd yelled at Dad. She wasn't sure she'd ever done that before. And she'd told him she hated him. A sob rose up and choked her.

Jess reached for her, slipping an arm around her shoulder. "Oh, sweets, I'm so sorry. This is going to be hardest on you."

"I'm just so *mad*."

"Of course you are."

"I can't even look at Dad right now. If I do, I'll start screaming, or I'll say something I'll regret later."

"So maybe stay here for a couple of days. Or you could go to Brendan's."

The mention of his name was like a punch in the gut. "He's gone," she whispered. Then another wrenching sob wracked her chest.

"Gem, what happened?"

"He's the one buying the building. He *knew*! He knew how much it meant to me, but at the first chance he got, he swept in and scooped it up. And now it's all gone. And everywhere I turn, there's somebody who helped take it from me. Dad and Brendan and…"

She couldn't finish, bending over until her face was against her knees, letting the sobs roll through her unabated. Jess was silent at her side, just rubbing her back. Then abruptly, she stood and walked away.

Gemma sat up. "Jess?"

But she was turned away, her cell phone against her ear. "Hey. Gemma's here and there's, well, there's a situation. I know I've never asked you for this before, but I need a favor from your dad."

Gemma listened to Jess's one-sided conversation for a moment in confusion. Then Jess hung up and turned back to face her. "Okay, we're going to St. Croix."

"I...*what*?"

"Dan's estate in St. Croix. We're borrowing it for a few days. And his private plane. We're leaving as soon as the pilot can file the flight plan."

"Jess, what the hell are you talking about?"

Jess came back and sat next to her, reaching for her hands. "This is going to be hard for all of us, but especially you, especially how it happened. What you need is a little time somewhere far away to let it all sink in. Someplace *not* our neighborhood, where it's all in your face every second."

"So we're going to *St. Croix*?"

"I'd have picked the apartment in Paris but you don't have a passport."

"But—"

Jess squeezed her hand. "Look, I never ask Dan for anything. But we need this. You need this."

"I can't just go to St. Croix."

"Of course you can. Alex says there's a whole bungalow full of bathing suits and beachwear. And anything you need that they don't have, we'll buy when we get there. Now I have to call Livie."

"Livie? Why?"

"Dan's secretary is emailing her a plane ticket and sending a car to her apartment as we speak, and she's going to be really confused if she doesn't hear from me first."

When Gemma would have protested again, Jess shushed her. "This is for the Romano sisters. We need this. Just us."

Gemma collapsed back, letting the sofa swallow her up. "When did you get so smart?"

Jess smirked as she scrolled to Livie's contact. "I learned it from you, the very best."

## Chapter Thirty-Eight

"This is a nice way to start the day." Jess stretched on the chaise lounge, arms over her head, toes wiggling.

Gemma took a deep breath of warm, tropical, flower-scented air, feeling the gentle midmorning sun bake her closed eyelids. "Agreed. Thanks for this, Jess."

"No problem."

The conversation went no further because the three of them had decided last night during their chauffeured drive to Dan's estate not to discuss what had brought them to St. Croix for a full twenty-four hours. First, relax. Then talk.

Right now, Gemma was perfectly content to do just that. When they'd staggered into Dan's vacation mansion well after midnight, they'd done little more than sort out which of the eight bedrooms they'd claim and then they'd all fallen into bed.

This morning, she woke late, wrapped in a cocoon of silky white sheets, with bright morning sunlight streaming through the plantation shutters on the French doors in her bedroom. When she'd swung them open, it was to a spectacular view of a perfect crescent of sandy white beach and an endless expanse of startlingly blue water.

The cove, their driver last night had informed them, was private. Dan owned the whole thing.

Downstairs, she'd encountered Jess, and together they'd discovered that someone had come in during their flight and fully stocked the kitchen. After the coffee was made and some delicious pastries were eaten, they'd rummaged through the pool house, which was as big as some New York apartments, and found a whole room of assorted swimwear and water gear. Gemma chose a tiny black string bikini, slathered herself up with sunscreen, and deposited herself beside the glistening aqua pool, happy to think about nothing more than sun, water, and maybe lunch later on. When Jess emerged with a tray of mimosa fixings, Gemma decided maybe a liquid lunch would suffice.

"I'm no expert," she said, taking a sweet, bubbly sip of her drink. "But I think we could pay off your student loans with that bottle of champagne you opened. Dan won't mind us drinking it?"

"He'll be delighted. He's always trying to get me to indulge in all his expensive stuff. He's like a drug pusher, but with luxury retail items."

They'd been out there about twenty minutes when Livie wandered out, blinking in the bright sun like a mole.

"She's up." Jess grinned up at her, passing her a champagne flute of plain orange juice. Livie might have changed in many ways during the past year, but she still didn't drink.

"That bed was so comfortable," Livie sighed, staring out at the shimmering ocean.

"God, yes," Gemma groaned. "I haven't slept so well in years."

Which was surprising. She'd thought she'd lie awake all night, crying and freaking out, thinking about the carnage she'd left behind in Brooklyn. Dad's face when she said she hated him. Brendan's eyes when she threw his "I love you" back at him. Everything she ever thought she knew about her future, gone, destroyed... *Nope.* No thinking yet. Just baking.

Gemma cleared her throat. "So, Livie, was Boy Genius upset that you cut out of town so fast yesterday?"

"Oh, he's not in Greenvale." Livie laid herself out on the chaise lounge next to Jess and reached up to tighten her ponytail.

"If that little shit bailed on you again—"

Jess cut her off before she could get really colorful. "Livie, where's Nick?"

"NORAD."

Gemma and Jess exchanged a look. "NORAD?" Jess echoed.

"Well, he works for the government now, pitching in wherever they need help."

"Right."

Livie shrugged. "They need help at NORAD. He's there a lot lately."

"I didn't realize that," Jess said.

"He likes it because it's pretty close to Greenvale and he can drive back home most nights."

Gemma burst into laughter. "I can't believe it. That reprobate hacker is commuting to a computer programming gig like a regular working stiff."

"He does it because he loves me," Livie said.

Which made Gemma smile, because she was right. She might have had her reservations about Nick, but he was more than just fast talk and grand gestures. He'd given up a lot just to lay Livie's dreams at her feet. He loved her sister, which said something very good about his judgment.

"That's a cute suit, Livie," Jess remarked.

Livie looked down at the slightly retro one-piece, made out of a navy blue cosmos-patterned fabric. "Thanks. I found it on Etsy. The woman who owns the shop is an astronomer, but she makes stuff like this as a hobby. A friend in the department told me about her store."

Jess and Gemma exchanged a look.

"Etsy?" Gemma said.

"Friend?" Jess added. "Who are you and what have you done with our sister?"

Livie laughed as she stretched her arms over her head. "Very funny. Yes, I have friends and I do things outside of school now." She closed her eyes, tilting her face into the sun. "You know, I spent so much time staring at the stars, and I didn't even realize there was stuff all around me here on earth. I just had to pick up my head and look for it."

"That's great, Livie," Gemma said. "I'm glad you're so happy."

This time, Jess and Livie were the ones to exchange a look, which Gemma caught out of the corner of her eye.

"Spit it out, you two."

"Nope," Jess said. "Today is for relaxation. Tomorrow we talk."

Gemma blew out a frustrated breath and sat up. "I'm not going to relax *now*, knowing the two of you are exchanging worried looks about me. Yes, I saw that."

Jess sighed and sat up, too. "Okay. I know closing the bar is a big deal—"

"It's been in the family since 1934, Jess."

"I *know*. It's breaking my heart, too."

"And mine," Livie added.

"But, Gem, what did you tell me when I offered to ask Dan for the money?"

Gemma shifted on her chaise lounge. "I said Romano's was a business, not a charity."

"And sometimes businesses fail," Jess said gently. "You and Dad have worked so hard. It's not your fault."

"The neighborhood has changed so much," Livie said. "Even since we were kids. Everybody's moving away."

"I know all this."

"So?"

"It's just…it happened on my watch. Nearly a hundred years of Romanos behind that bar and it goes under on *my* watch."

Livie and Jess protested in unison.

"Oh, come on."

"Gem, you know that's not true."

"And I'm mad. Dad should have talked to me first. I should have been part of this decision."

"Okay," Jess conceded, "I can see how you'd be mad about that."

"Furious."

"But Gem, how would that conversation have gone?"

"'Gemma,'" Livie said in her gruff Dad voice. "'Have a seat. I want to discuss selling the bar. What are your thoughts?'"

"'Of course, Dad,'" Jess replied, in what Gemma supposed was meant to be her Gemma voice. "'Let's sit down together and rationally discuss a pros and cons list.'"

Gemma rolled her eyes. "Okay, you have a point. I was never going to handle this well. Still, he should have told me first."

"Yes, he should have. But you know Dad. He still sees us as his little girls. He was just trying to protect you. I think Dad knew it would be awful for all of us no matter what, especially you. So he figured he'd spare you the agony of the discussions and get it done."

Deep down, she knew Jess was right. Dad had messed up, but he meant well. Despite what she'd said the day before in the heat of the moment, she didn't hate him. She could never hate him.

"Look, I know the reality," Gemma explained. "We've been running in the red for ages."

"When was the last time you could cut yourself a paycheck?" Jess pressed.

"I can't even remember, it's been so long. So yeah, in my head, I'm aware of all that. The neighborhood changed, the new market didn't want to buy what we were selling… I know all that up here." She tapped her temple. Then she pressed a hand to her chest. "But here…all I feel is loss. I've just lost everything I've ever known, every plan I ever had for my life."

Livie got up off her chaise lounge and came to sit next to her, reaching for her hand. "I'm so sorry, Gem."

"Except…" Jess murmured.

"What?"

Jess heaved a sigh, her eyes dancing away toward the expanse of blue ocean on the other side of the pool. Gemma knew her well enough to know she had something controversial to say. "Just say it, Jess."

She looked back at Gem, her face full of determination. "Maybe that's the problem."

"What's the problem?"

"It's everything you've ever known and every plan you ever had."

"Planning to spend my life running Romano's was a problem?"

"No, but you never let yourself consider anything else, which *is* a problem. Now that plan is gone. So it's time to come up with a new plan for the rest of your life."

Gemma huffed, falling back on her chaise. "I wish people would quit telling me that. I don't want a new plan."

"Really?" Jess hiked one eyebrow. "There's *nothing* else you like doing? *Nothing?*"

"Okay, yes, smartass, I love cooking. But I'll tell you what I told Kendra. It's not that easy. Cooking professionally isn't the same thing as cooking for you guys. I'd have to go back to school. There are food safety courses and stuff."

"So? Now you can do that."

"You might even qualify for financial aid," Livie said. "We'll help you with the forms."

"Then what? I still don't have any experience."

"So get some!" Jess said, her eyes lighting up with enthusiasm. "Come on, Gem. It's time to think outside the box. Take the classes, get a job with somebody to get some experience under your belt, and then go for it! What's stopping you now?"

Nothing, she realized. Absolutely nothing. Except…

She swallowed hard, looking down into the pulpy dregs of her mimosa. "I'm so scared," she whispered.

Livie leaned forward, until she could make eye contact. "Believe me, I know. Change is scary. Some days, all I wanted to do is run back home to you guys. But it gets easier with every step you take."

"I'm almost thirty. Who the hell starts a new career at my age?"

Jess rolled her eyes. "These days? Everybody. Sticking with one career until you die is a Baby Boomer fantasy. Now people switch all the time. I guarantee you won't be the oldest person in your classes."

Gemma swiped the champagne bottle off the side table and took a hefty swig straight from the bottle. This conversation was rattling her straight to her bones. A dainty mimosa wasn't going to cut it. In fact, this might call for scotch.

"And what if I'm terrible at it? Let's face it, you guys aren't the most discerning food critics."

"Your food is amazing, Gem," Livie protested. "Everybody says so."

"Didn't everybody at Kendra's fancy dinner party go nuts for it?"

Okay, Gemma had to concede that one. A room full of people who knew good food had eaten her dinner and loved it. At Mrs. Simonsen's, too. That was a tiny bit encouraging. Still, everything about this left her quaking with fear. Romano's—the taps, the bottles, the grizzled old patrons—all of that had been baked into her DNA. She could work the bar in her sleep. This—it was all new and absolutely terrifying.

"Gem, what did you say when I told you I stayed in Brooklyn for grad school because I was afraid to move away?" Livie challenged.

Gemma grumbled out an answer under her breath. "I told you to get your ass out there and fulfill your potential."

Jess reached out and patted her knee. "It's tough love time, Gemma. Get your ass out there and fulfill your potential."

The expressions on their faces were what finally did her in. Compassionate but tough, and full of so much love. Really, how badly could she fuck up when she had a family like this at her back? She swiped at her suddenly watery eyes and let out a shaky laugh. "When did my little sisters get so much smarter than me?"

"Shut up," Jess said fondly. "You've always been brilliant. But it's time for more people than just us to see that."

Gemma sniffed back her tears. "Well, this was a super fun first morning in paradise."

"You know what I'm ready for?" Livie said.

"What?"

"A dip in that amazing pool. The three of us are here together in paradise. We should enjoy it."

Gemma reached for Livie, pulling her into a hard, brief hug. "You're right, Liv. No more heavy stuff or worrying about the future. Let's have fun."

## Chapter Thirty-Nine

He'd lost her. As the long night dawned into a cool, gray morning and every call to Gemma's cell went straight to voicemail, he had to accept the fact that she was gone and it was all his fault. As hard as he'd tried to do the right thing, to make the unbearable as bearable as possible for Gemma, he'd still failed. She was never going to forgive him. He was never going to forgive himself.

Well, as much as he wanted to spend the day hiding in the dark, maybe with a bottle of scotch for company, there was another woman in his life to feel guilty about and he'd promised to see her today. His mother was waiting for him. At least he could make sure she was taken care of. One woman he wouldn't let down.

The workmen had finished the repairs to his mother's broken gutter yesterday. He stood on the sidewalk in front of the house taking stock of the work. It looked as if the guys had done the job well. The gutter was secure and looked like it'd drain properly in the next big storm. As he examined the house, he couldn't help but mentally note everything else that needed to be done. It really needed a new roof and all the windows needed to be replaced, but fuck if he was doing any of that. He'd do exactly what was necessary to keep his mother safe and comfortable there and not one inch more. If, one day, he turned the house over to Jimmy a wreck, then so much the better. Jimmy Walsh had squeezed the last dollar out of Brendan that he was ever going to get.

Suddenly the front door opened to reveal Jimmy Walsh himself, as if Brendan had just conjured him into being. A second later, his mother appeared at his side, all smiles. She glanced up and spotted Brendan at the end of the walkway.

"Oh, good! You're just in time! Look who surprised me with a visit!" Claire Flaherty beamed up at her older brother, adoration positively radiating from her pores.

It was remarkable how the same features on two different people could have such opposite results. The Walsh black hair, pale skin, and delicate features gave his mother an air of fairy-tale fragility, like Snow White who'd just been awakened from a hundred-year sleep. Jimmy wore his black hair slicked straight back, and those dark blue eyes and sharp cheekbones gave him the air of a dangerous predator, a shark with a taste for blood.

Brendan made his way cautiously up the walk. "Hey, Jimmy," he said, voice utterly neutral. "What brings you to Brooklyn?"

"Just a visit to my only sister." Jimmy smiled down at her. Brendan marveled at the guy's ice-cold blood. How had he ever been fooled, thinking there was a human being in there? The insincerity was plain as day to him, now that he knew what Jimmy really was.

"You're so good to me, Jimmy," his mother said, ducking her chin.

"Yep," Brendan said. "That's Jimmy. What a prince of a guy."

Jimmy's gaze swung back to him, his dark eyes hard and flat. *There* was the sociopath asshole Brendan knew so well. No way he'd come back just to visit his little sister. After all, when had he ever done it before? Jimmy was there to gloat and nothing more.

"What brings you by, Brendan?" his mother asked.

"Just came to make sure the gutter was fixed."

"Oh, yes. Nice young men. They came yesterday."

"Taking care of the place for your mom?" Jimmy asked. Brendan could see the glee hidden in the depths of his eyes. The bastard had no idea that he knew.

"Just a few odds and ends."

"Jimmy was just taking me out to lunch," his mother said brightly. "Isn't that nice of him?"

"He's a saint." Brendan stepped to the side. "Really, don't let me keep you."

"Why don't you come?"

Jimmy frowned at his sister, but there was no real way to protest without looking like a jerk, and that was the one thing he didn't want to do. Jimmy reveled in his little sister's hero worship. So even though sitting across from Jimmy for a meal would feel like choking down glass, he wasn't going to miss this for the world. They were long overdue for some real family togetherness.

Jimmy took them to one of the more upscale new restaurants along Court Street. A place like Sal's wouldn't even register on his radar. His mother protested that it was too fancy, and that Jimmy shouldn't spend all his money on her that way. Brendan said nothing at all as Jimmy grandiosely declared that she deserved to be treated like a queen.

They sat down near the front window, his mother

oohing and ahhing over everything, oblivious to the brittle silence between Brendan and Jimmy. Jimmy busied himself pressing his sister to order an extra appetizer, to treat herself to a glass of wine, and not to worry about the money. When the server got to Brendan, he ordered a side salad and a glass of water, staring Jimmy down as he did so.

"Jimmy, tell us how your business is doing," his mother pressed, when the three of them were alone again.

Jimmy leaned back in his chair and spread his hands. "It's like the money makes itself these days."

"I sure wish you could convince Brendan to come back to Chicago with you. A perfectly good job with family, and he just threw it away."

"I'm busy with my own company here, Mom."

"I heard you hit a few bumps in the road," Jimmy said slyly before taking a sip of his vodka tonic.

"There was one, but it wasn't really much of an obstacle."

"Is that so?"

He shrugged, holding Jimmy's gaze. "I know the neighborhood. Something worked out."

The slight tightening at the corners of his mouth was the only indication that he'd gotten to Jimmy. Jimmy hated to be bested, and Brendan fully expected him to hit back in some passive aggressive way.

It didn't take long. "It sure is a shame, Claire, that I couldn't convince your boy to stay in Chicago. The firm's not the same without him."

Brendan bit back a laugh. As salvos go, that one was spectacularly transparent. The guy really wasn't nearly as clever as he thought he was.

But Brendan waited it out as his mother got antsy, reaching out to touch his arm, full of concern. "I know you've got this crazy idea about owning your own business, Brendan, but honestly, how could you walk away from your own family like that?"

Brendan answered his mother, but he kept his eyes on Jimmy. "I walked away from Jimmy's business, Mom. You're my family. I'm not walking away from you."

"But…" Her hands fidgeted with her napkin. "After everything Jimmy's done for us—"

Okay, enough was enough. No way was he sitting through another paean to Jimmy Walsh's saintly attributes with the guy right there, preening and eating it up. Not when he knew the truth. He hadn't planned on doing this now, but why not? A nice public scene should suit Jimmy's sense of the dramatic.

He leaned forward on his elbows, still staring Jimmy down. "Yes, let's talk about everything Jimmy's done for our family, Mom." There was a flare of alarm in Jimmy's eyes, and his face settled into a warning scowl, but Brendan barreled ahead. "He offered me a job, making enough to eventually pay off your debt, which I did."

"Taught you everything you know," Jimmy said harshly.

"Yes, you did. And I am grateful for what I learned under you. I thanked you for it before I left. But see, Jimmy, *because* of all the things you taught me, I know my way around property records."

Jimmy went still.

"Please don't start that again," his mother whispered.

"What? I'm just talking about a little family business. Jimmy knows what I mean, don't you, Jimmy?"

"Don't upset your mother like this." His eyes were full of fury.

"Mom's going to be a lot more upset when she accepts the truth, that you had her sign her house over to you and never told her."

"Brendan—"

"Mom, just ask him. He's right here. Ask him what he had you sign."

"Jimmy would never—"

Brendan reached into his messenger bag hanging over the back of a chair and pulled out a slim folder. "I know you didn't want to believe me when I showed you the paperwork from the lawyer, so I pulled the city property records." He drew out a piece of paper and laid it on the table between the three of them. "It's a copy of the property records, according to the City of New York. Look what it says, under Owner, and right next to your address, Mom."

Her eyes flickered unwillingly down to the paper, but this time, she didn't turn her face away in denial. Documentation from a lawyer she'd never heard of would have been easy for her to brush aside as a misunderstanding, but this was as clear and simple as it got, and it wasn't Brendan telling her, it was the City of New York.

"Jimmy," she murmured. "I don't understand."

"I was just trying to make things easy on you, Claire. Clear out all the paperwork so you didn't have to worry about anything."

"But you didn't clear out anything," Brendan said. "*I* paid off her mortgages, and the credit cards, and every other bill that came up for the past fourteen years. You didn't take anything off Mom's hands except her house."

"You told me you'd take care of things for me," his

mother said, lifting her eyes to Jimmy's at last. "You said you'd handle everything so I didn't have to worry."

Brendan let out a bitter scoff, pushing back from the table. "You really are a piece of work, Jimmy. She'd probably never have figured it out if I hadn't come back home and started poking around. Why'd you do it, anyway? I mean, yeah, the place is worth a mint as far as houses go, but it's not like you need it. Was it just a control thing? You wanted to make sure I had no way out?"

"You ungrateful little shit," Jimmy hissed. "I *saved* you. I offered you a job when you were nobody and knew nothing. For all I knew, you'd end up a disaster. I was covering my ass."

"Oh, yes, I see." Brendan nodded slowly. "You needed an insurance policy, just in case I didn't pan out into a stellar partner in the business, bringing in millions of dollars for you. Wouldn't want to risk a dollar on something as worthless as family, am I right?"

"You were nothing but the son of some idiot knuckle-dragging firefighter. Without me, you'd have turned out just like your old man. I should have been *paid* to take a chance on you."

Brendan saw red, imagining the future that had been stolen away from him, the one he'd chosen for himself, the one with Gemma at his side from the start. "So you made sure you *got* paid, no matter how things turned out. You're not a tenth of the man my father was, Jimmy. Look at you, you small, desperate, little tyrant, resorting to stealing a dead man's house from your own sister, and running a harmless old woman into an early grave just so you could say you won."

"Oh, Jimmy." His mother's eyes filled with tears. "Please say you didn't do it."

Jimmy muttered a curse under his breath and threw his napkin on his plate, shoving himself to his feet. "Fucking ungrateful family. Don't call me the next time you need help."

Brendan leaned forward, pulling his mother into his arms. She bent her head toward him, weeping into his shoulder. "Don't worry, we won't. She's my responsibility. She always has been. You can go back to Chicago and forget we ever existed."

"With fucking pleasure," Jimmy snapped, before storming out of the restaurant. And Brendan was left on his own with his mother, just as he'd always been.

"Come on, Mom. Don't cry. We don't need the house. You'll be okay, I'll take care of you." Seemed nothing much had changed since he was twelve. He was still reassuring his mother that everything would be okay, he'd make sure of it.

But his mother's response was not what it once would have been. She abruptly sat back, looking up at him with red, watery eyes. "I want my house back," she whispered.

"What?"

"That was your father's house. He left it to me. To you boys. It's supposed to be yours."

"I know, Mom, but it's okay."

"Can you get it back?" she pressed. "With, I don't know, lawyers or something?"

"Uh, maybe?" In truth, there might be something he could do, but it would take his mother's cooperation, her willingness to turn on Jimmy, which he'd never thought he could count on. "I can look into it and see. But, Mom, you'd have to testify that Jimmy did this without your knowledge. That he tricked you. That he *lied* to you. Are you sure you want to do this?"

Her mouth wobbled, and tears spilled down her cheeks. But there was also a tiny flicker of anger in her eyes, the first spark of anything he'd seen there in years. "I want my house back," she said, low and fierce. "I want *your* house back."

"Then I'll help you get it back, Mom." He pulled her into a hug, feeling her thin shoulders shaking against him. He wasn't fooling himself. Mom would always need to be taken care of. But right now, fired by a mother's righteous anger, she wanted vindication. She hadn't been able to do anything about losing her husband. And she hadn't been able to do anything about Harry's betrayal. But this she could do something about. And he could help her. If that's what she needed, he'd go to the ends of the earth to make it happen for her.

As he held his mother, absorbing her tears and anger, he thought about Gemma, about the power that he'd unwittingly helped to strip away from her. Well, he couldn't turn back the clock and do it differently, but maybe there was something he could do to put control of her future back in her own hands. If it made her happy— even if that happiness didn't include him anymore—he'd go to the ends of the earth to make that happen, too.

# Chapter Forty

"I can't get over how warm the ocean is down here," Jess said, wringing the salt water out of her hair over one shoulder.

"It's like a bath." Livie wrapped her beach towel more securely around her waist.

Her sisters' voices floated back to Gemma as she followed them up the winding path from the beach to the house. It was bordered on either side with lush tropical flowers, and the shade from the trees felt good after baking in the sun on the beach. A warm breeze dried the water from her skin as she walked, leaving her feeling refreshed and new. These days had been perfect. Spending time with her sisters in paradise had been just what she needed as she began the terrifying process of staring down the rest of her life.

Already it wasn't quite so scary. Yesterday, Jess had gotten her laptop out and they'd spent some time researching culinary schools. There were plenty of great programs right in New York, and if she went full time, it wouldn't even take that long. Gemma had to admit to feeling a frisson of excitement as she read through the course listings and saw some of the places their graduates interned. Her excitement was tempered a bit when she saw the price tag, but Livie wouldn't let her worry about that yet. Right now was just for dreaming. Practicalities would come later.

Tomorrow morning, they'd fly home, and then it would be time to start dealing with the real world. It would also be time to face the mess she'd left behind. But one thing at a time.

When they got back to the cool, shady patio, Gemma saw a missed call icon on her phone, which she'd left by the pool this morning. For the first day, Brendan had called constantly. She declined every one. But this time it wasn't Brendan; it was Kendra.

It only rang once before Kendra picked up.

"*There* you are. Now I've got Tuesday at two or Wednesday at eleven, but he's got a lunch meeting on Wednesday, so that would be a hard exit time."

"Kendra, what the hell are you talking about?"

"Your sit-down with Carlos. Do you want to do it Tuesday or Wednesday? Personally, I'd say Tuesday."

"Carlos your boss?"

"Of course Carlos my boss. Who else?"

Gemma squeezed her eyes closed. "Kendra, you know this is *Gemma*, right? Why would I need to meet with Carlos? Does he have another dinner party coming up?"

"No, this is about the investment, you idiot."

She was starting to feel like she and Kendra were having two entirely different conversations, and she wasn't even sure what *hers* was about, never mind Kendra's. "What investment?"

"*Carlos's* investment," Kendra said with exaggerated patience. "In the bar."

"Kendra—"

"Wait. You've talked to Brendan, right?"

*Brendan?* "What the hell has Brendan got to do with anything?"

Kendra sighed. "So you haven't talked to him?"

"Um, we're not exactly on speaking terms right now. Maybe you'd better start from the beginning."

"Yeah, I guess I'd better. So Brendan called me and told me your dad decided to close the bar."

"And Brendan's buying the building. Did that traitor tell you that part?"

"Yeah, he did, Drama Queen. Just listen, will you?"

Gemma sank down onto a chaise lounge. When Jess and Livie motioned to find out what was going on, she waved them off and they retreated to the house to rummage for lunch. "I'm listening. Go ahead."

"He isn't buying the building."

"What?"

"He called me to see if he could talk to Carlos about investing in the bar. So I worked my magic, and yes, Carlos is going to invest in the bar."

Gemma blinked in disbelief and fury. It turned out a few days in paradise hadn't quite taken the edge off her anger and resentment. "So Brendan just waltzed in there and set this up with Carlos? He didn't even ask me first?"

"You just said you're not speaking to him."

Okay, fine, Kendra had a point. He *had* called. She just hadn't answered. "Still, he had no right to talk to Carlos about *my* bar."

"No, *I* did that part. Because I'm, you know, family. It was Brendan's idea, but I put together the business plan, and I pitched it to Carlos. As far as investments go, it's a little small-time for him, but he's in, because he listens to me and he does what I say."

"How did *you* write a business plan?"

"Hello? I did go to college."

"You dropped out after three semesters."

"Yeah, but while I was there, I paid attention. And I pay attention to all of Carlos's business shit, too. I've learned a thing or two."

"So…" She had to pause and shake her head to clear it. "Carlos wants to invest in the bar? *Our* bar? I don't understand."

"You need an infusion of cash. He'll give it to you in return for a cut of the profits. He's going to want to make a few changes. Come up with a concept for the place…you know, something other than 'we're really old.' Do some renovations to freshen the place up, update the cocktail menu and bring it into the twentieth century, expand the beer list, that sort of stuff. You guys can work it all out at your meeting. So Tuesday or Wednesday?"

For a minute, everything vanished. The big white house, the glittering pool, the cove off in the distance… Gemma couldn't see any of it. All she could see was everything she wanted suddenly handed to her.

The problem was, in the course of the past few days, she'd picked up something else, and now her hands were full. She was going to have to set something down.

"Kendra, I have to call you back."

"But the meeting—"

"I'll call you as soon as I'm home, I promise."

"Wait—where are you?"

"St. Croix."

*"St. Croix?"*

"Yeah, it's a long story. But we're flying home tomorrow. Jess has to get back to work and Livie's got school."

"So—"

"I *promise*, I'll call. I just… I need a minute. A lot has happened." Her whole life had been tipped sideways, and now it was tipping back in the other direction. She was dizzy with it, and she had no idea which way to turn. But one thing she knew for certain. "Kendra, I have to go talk to my sisters."

## Chapter Forty-One

"Jess, I don't think I thanked you for this."

Gemma bumped her sister's shoulder as the three of them waited in line for a taxi at LaGuardia airport.

"You did." Jess grinned. "But you can do it again if you want."

She snagged Jess's hand and squeezed. "Thank you. Thanks for taking time from work. And you, Livie, for bailing on classes and flying all the way across the country to hold my hand while I melted down."

"You owe me one," Livie said. "This time *I* was the one with the fake dead grandmother."

"So," Jess said. "What are you gonna do?"

"I need to talk to Dad first."

"Makes sense. Just remember, Livie and I are behind you one hundred percent, no matter what you decide."

"I know. And thank you." She really did have the best sisters. "I texted Teresa. She said they're on City Island with Richie right now."

Livie held out her hand for Gemma's bag. "Go. We'll meet you back at the house. We can hang out tonight before I have to fly back."

Spring seemed to have finally arrived in earnest while they'd been away. Or maybe it had been coming on for weeks and she just hadn't noticed it. As the cab drove across the low, green-painted, steel bridge to City Island, Gemma lowered the window and let the soft, cool air hit her face and clear her head. She had a lot to do now that she was back, but Dad came first.

On a hunch, she directed the cab driver to the pier where Richie kept his boats moored. After she'd paid and gotten out, she wandered down the wide wooden dock toward Richie's berths. One was empty, but his second boat was tied up at the dock, and sure enough, there was Dad, moving around on deck.

Gemma paused for a moment, just watching him work. He looked so different here, outside in the sun, the wind whipping his dark hair. He looked younger, infinitely more relaxed. She'd grown so used to the sight of him behind the bar that he only existed that way in her mind. But he had his own life, didn't he? Things he wanted outside the bar. Maybe this was it.

He was in the middle of folding up a blue tarp when he turned and spotted her.

"Gem... Is everything okay?"

"Yeah, everything's fine. I came out to talk to you."

John looked down at the deck briefly, then set the tarp aside and dusted his hands off against his jeans. "Come on up." He came to the edge of the boat and offered her a hand as she made her way up the rickety little portable wooden steps he'd set on the deck.

She'd been going over what she had to say for the whole of the cab ride, but now that she was here, starting was hard. Stuffing her hands in her back pockets, she looked out across the marina, at all the boats bobbing at the docks, and at the sun dancing on the water of the bay.

"It's nice here."

John looked out across the water, too, the corner of his mouth twitching with what might have been a smile. "Yep."

"You working on the boat?"

"Helping Richie get her into shape for the season." He motioned to the empty berth next to them. "He's got the other one out on the water."

Gemma nodded, but said nothing. *Okay, coward, get to it. It's just Dad. He's not going to bite your head off.*

Taking a deep breath, she forced the words out. "Dad, I'm sorry. I was upset and I said things I didn't mean. You know I didn't mean any of that, don't you?"

"'Course I know that, Gem. I wasn't mad at you. Not for an instant." He paused again, looking at his feet. "I owe you an apology, too. The bar might be in my name, but it's as much yours as mine. I should have talked to you first before I decided anything. I just... I knew how much it was going to hurt you and I wanted to spare you that. Guess I was still trying to take care of my little girl. But you're not a little girl anymore, are you? You're all grown up and it was wrong of me not to see that."

She'd never heard her dad say so many words all at once in her life. Especially not ones about feelings. Her eyes burned. It was impossible to stay mad at him. He was only trying to protect her, even if he'd gone at it all wrong. A little voice in her head told her Brendan had been doing the same thing, but it was one thing for your dad to be overprotective. It was another for your boyfriend to do it. "It's okay, Dad. I know you did it because you love me." Her words came out a pinched little whisper because her throat had closed up.

"Come here, sweetheart." John reached for her, pulling her into a firm hug. Gemma squeezed her burning eyes shut and gripped the warm, worn flannel of his shirt. "I love you, Gem. And I'm sorry. Sorry for everything."

With a sniff, she pulled back, swiping at her eyes. Dad's eyes looked suspiciously red, too. "Here, sit down," he said, motioning to one of the benches alongside the deck railing. "We've got some things to talk about."

"Yes, we do." She took a seat next to him, leaning forward, knees on her elbows, realizing as she did that her posture mimicked his. Working side by side for so many years really had made them much more than father and daughter. She needed to tell him about Kendra and Carlos, but it felt important to hash out what was between the two of them first. Clear the air and set things right before they decided how to move forward.

"First things first," he said. "I approached Brendan about buying the building, so any ideas you might have that he was just using you to get at the bar are wrong."

"I know that." As soon as she'd had a moment to think clearly, she'd realized that was probably the case. Whatever she thought about Brendan—and right now, that was a complete muddle—he wasn't that underhanded, that heartless. Her accusation had been made in the heat of the moment, but she'd never really believed that. But one problem at a time. First, she fixed things with Dad. Then she'd think about Brendan.

"The other thing…" Dad trailed off and was silent for a minute. "The legal settlement we got after your mom died…at the time, I did what I thought was right, what would serve you girls best in the future. Buying out Marianne and Richie… I had the money and it seemed like the smart thing to do."

"I know, Dad. We've been over this. You did the right

thing. That insurance company put us through hell. If all we got from it was money, then at least we could do something good with it. For our family."

Dad nodded pensively. "The business was solid back then. Not flush, but dependable. Then the stock market crashed and everything changed."

"I remember." She'd just graduated high school and started working full time at the bar. It seemed half their business dried up overnight. Some of it had eventually trickled back, but a lot of it hadn't. Looking back, that had been the beginning of the end, really.

Dad inhaled and sat up. "Still, I set money aside out of the settlement for each of you girls, and I hung on to it. But then Livie and Jess went to college within a year of each other. And even with financial aid, those Ivy Leagues cost money. It ate up your share, too, and I'm sorry about that."

"I'd have insisted you spend it on Livie and Jess. No way were they not going to get a shot at the best just because of money."

"Still thinking of everybody else first."

"Dad, they're my sisters—"

He reached out and laid a hand over hers. "It's one of the best things about you, Gem. Still, there's something I want you to know. A portion of the money from the building is going to you. It's the share you should have had years ago."

"Dad—"

"I don't want to hear it. I'm paying off the debts and your sisters' student loans; then a piece of that money is coming to you. Your sisters got their shot and now you will, too. That money is yours, for travel, or school, or starting a business, or whatever it is you think you might want to do."

*Oh.* And suddenly all those new plans she'd been toying with glowed brighter in her hands. But Dad was right. They were partners. This decision was theirs to make together. "Dad, we need to talk about the bar. Kendra has this plan."

And so, as briefly as she could, she outlined what Kendra had done, the business plan, Carlos's investment, the changes that would have to be made. Dad sat back, listening and staring out over the water.

"So," she said when she finished. "We'd have to change some things. It wouldn't be the same, but we could keep it going. If you want."

His jaw worked as he thought. Finally, he looked over at her. "Is that what you want, Gemma?"

And now it all came down to this. It was her choice to make. In the end, when she opened her mouth to respond, she realized she'd already made it, because the answer was right there, bursting to come out. "No. I can't believe I'm saying this, but no, I don't want it anymore. I want to go to culinary school."

"Culinary school?"

"Yeah, I looked at some programs with Jess and Livie. And I've been thinking about what I could do afterward…opening a catering business of my own, maybe…and yeah. That's what I really want to do." Saying it out loud was terrifying. It was one thing to dream. It was entirely another to plan. She felt like she'd just walked off the edge of a cliff, but oddly, that breathless feeling of falling was just a little bit thrilling, too.

Dad smiled, the first genuine smile she'd seen on his face in ages. "That's fantastic, honey."

"But if you want to keep the bar," she hurried to add. "We can figure something out. I can go part-time and still cover shifts. Maybe we could afford to hire more staff. We could—"

His hand came down to cover hers and he squeezed. "Gem, I'm ready to let it go, too."

"You are?"

Dad nodded his head at the nearby boat. "Richie's asked me to partner in the business with him."

"Charter fishing?"

He was smiling again, staring out over the water, the wind ruffling his hair, and Gemma could see it in his eyes. He loved it there. He loved it out there on the water. "I'd captain one and he'll captain the other. Teresa would run the office and handle the bookings with Sheila."

"Wow." The implications of that settled into her brain. "So are you guys are going to *move* out here?"

"You know our house is always going to feel like home," he told her. "But yeah. Teresa's going to sell her mother's place and we thought we'd look for something out here."

Her heart was aching, but she smiled through it. How could something be so sad and so great at the same time? "That's really good, Dad. It's a fresh start for you."

"It's a fresh start for both of us. It's the start you should have had and never got."

"Dad, I don't regret a second I've spent behind the bar. Part of me still doesn't know how I'm going to bear losing it."

He slipped his arm around her shoulders. "I know, honey. But what you've got in store for you…" He paused and shook his head. "I'm so damned proud of you."

She laughed softly, swiping at her damp eyes. "Well, I haven't done anything yet. I might suck at it."

"You won't," he said. "Not you. You're going to be amazing."

As much as it hurt to end this part of both their lives, it also felt right. Dad was finally, after all these years, getting a chance to be truly happy again, and she was, too. Dad was right. For first time in her life, every path lay open to her.

Dad paused for a moment, clearly considering what he was about to say. "Gem, just so you know, the house is safe. That's part of why I wanted to sell the bar now. I wanted to make sure the house was secure for you girls. It'll always be yours."

"I know."

"But if that's not what you want…if you want a clean start, too—"

"No! No, I want the house." She didn't know much about what her future looked like, but she knew it was happening in the Romano house. She couldn't consider anything else.

"Well, since you'll be the one living there, if you want to fix it up, change anything…just…you don't need to ask for permission. It's yours. Yours and your sisters'."

She laughed, but then that idea settled in and…oh, *yeah*. Last year, she'd decorated Nick's new apartment for him for free, just because she was so desperate to fix up somebody's house, and her own was just a hodge-podge of choices made by long-gone generations of Romanos. Before she knew it, she was imagining ripping up scuffed linoleum and stripping faded wallpaper, updating the kitchen… *One thing at a time, Gemma.*

"So," he said. "I'm guessing things blew up with Brendan before you left?"

She let out a humorless chuckle. "Yeah, you could say that."

He was silent for a moment then inhaled deeply. "The last thing I want to do is stick my nose in your relationship, but maybe think about hearing him out. You cut me some slack, maybe you could cut him some, too."

"But you're my dad."

"He cares about you a hell of a lot, Gem. Maybe he and I were a little pigheaded about how we handled it, but we both did it for the same reason."

*Because you both love me.*

"I know," she murmured. "I'll think about it."

"Good enough." Dad squeezed her shoulders again. "You gonna be okay, kid?"

Gemma thought about that for a minute. Everything was changing. Things that had seemed set in stone for the entirety of her life were crumbling into dust all around her. And at first, that had been terrifying. But now that the dust was settling, so to speak, she could see so much farther than she could before. There were possibilities on the horizon that had been out of sight before. And that was good.

"Dad, I'm going to be great," she told him, and she absolutely meant it.

## Chapter Forty-Two

Spudge was just making his slow way out to the front door to greet her when she let herself into the house later that afternoon. Spudge, who'd been her faithful friend since high school. Brendan had brought him to her and then disappeared. Spudge had sat by her side through all the years since. Brendan had come back, saved Spudge's life, and now he was gone again. And still, Spudge was here.

Crouching down, she scratched behind his ears, earning a long, throaty groan. "You're the only man I can depend on, aren't you, buddy?"

Spudge lumbered behind her as she made her way back to the kitchen in search of her sisters. She found Livie and Jess sitting at the kitchen table, heads bent together as they talked, like they'd been doing since they were toddlers. They both looked up as she came in.

"Well?" Jess asked. One little word asking such a huge question.

"The bar is staying closed," she said. "Dad and I decided together."

A long beat of silence met her pronouncement.

"I'm going to miss it," Livie finally said.

"*So* much," Jess said. "But Gemma, this is good."

"I know," she replied. Amazingly, she wasn't crying. Any time she'd ever imagined closing the bar in the past, it was enough to strike terror in her heart. Now it felt—well, *right* was maybe the wrong word. It was happening as it should happen. "Part of me is going to miss the bar for the rest of my life."

"But the rest of you?" Livie asked.

"The rest of me is excited to see what comes next."

Jess and Livie broke into wide smiles. "There you go," Jess murmured.

"So," Livie said, sitting back in her chair. "What about Problem Number Two?"

"What's that?"

"Brendan?" she said. "What are you going to do about him?"

"Oh, I don't know. It's complicated, Liv." Brendan was still a big black hole of conflicting emotions, confusion, and pain, and she didn't have a clue how to begin untangling it.

"Didn't seem so complicated to me," Jess said. "He's clearly crazy about you."

"But what he did…"

"He made a mistake," Livie interjected quietly.

"And then he called Kendra and did his dead level best to undo it," Jess said.

Livie leaned forward, wide dark eyes imploring. "Maybe you should just talk to him."

"After all. You love him." Jess looked up at her questioningly. "Don't you?"

Gemma's heart gave one fierce thud and she bit her lip at the emotions welling up in her throat. "Yeah, I do."

"And you've been in love with him since you were sixteen. Haven't you?"

There was no use in denying it. She'd loved Brendan at sixteen. She'd never really stopped loving him, even though he'd given her plenty of reasons not to. The truth was, she would probably *always* love him. So she probably owed it to herself to see what he had to say for himself.

"Guys, I know we said we'd hang out tonight before Livie has to leave—"

Abruptly both of her sisters pushed themselves to their feet. "Livie wants to go get subs at Sal's before she has to head back to the wilds of Colorado. So we'll be gone for—" She looked at Livie, who shrugged and looked back.

"A while."

"A while," Jess confirmed. "So if you need to go… take care of stuff, you should go do that."

"Um, I need to make a phone call."

Turned out, she didn't have the guts to call him, so she texted.

Meet me at the bar?

His reply came in under a minute.

Be right there.

# Chapter Forty-Three

The thought of going to the bar sent a shaft of pain straight through her heart, but she'd never been one to shy away from the tough stuff. Sooner or later, all traces of Romano's would be gone. The sooner she faced that head-on, the better.

So she made the familiar walk one more time. Her feet could probably find the way to the bar in her sleep. Once there, she got out her well-worn key ring to unlock the padlocks on the metal roll gates. Then she cursed and sweated as she forced the Court Street one open. Well, at least she didn't need to bother with getting it replaced now. Uncooperative piece of shit. Grabbing hold of the age-worn brass handle, she opened the front door, and it let out an ear-splitting screech. She never had gotten around to dealing with those hinges.

Inside, Romano's already felt like an artifact. The flat-screen TV was dark and the stools were all empty. Dust motes floated in the shaft of late afternoon sunlight pouring in through the front window. Already it looked more like a memory than someplace in the here and now.

She ran her fingertips down the brass rail, marveling at the light coating of dust that had settled after just a few days. Near the cash register, where Dad had been standing on that last day, when they'd had their awful fight, a stack of papers was left abandoned. The papers he and Brendan had been looking at together when she'd come in. Curious, she shifted through them.

The top one was a drawing of a building. Nothing so polished or official as architectural renderings. These were very rough sketches for an idea of a building—three stories high, with big, arched windows and wrought iron balconies. She flipped through the rest of the pages. Some were whole buildings, some just a window, or a bit of cornice, or a doorway.

There was something familiar echoing in every page. Something in the shape of the windows, which looked like a smaller version of the bar's windows, or the stone lintel over the doorway, which was the same as the one over the bar's front door. There was a detail of the bar's white and black hexagon tile floor with a scribbled note in Brendan's handwriting, "bathrooms and kitchens," and a big mirror feature in the middle of what looked like a dining room.

"You can throw those out."

She spun around to see Brendan filling the doorway, thrown into silhouette by the bright golden late afternoon light behind him. He'd ditched his usual jacket and tie. His white dress shirt was open at the neck, sleeves rolled above his elbows, and his red-gold hair was in disarray, as if he'd been running his fingers through it all day.

As she took him in, Gemma was hit with a pang of almost unbearable longing. She would give anything— *anything*—to rewind and go back to where they'd been just a week ago, when being with him had been so effortless. But there was no rewinding time or hiding in the past, she'd learned. Nothing to do but face the future head-on.

"What are these?"

He shrugged as he moved inside. "I like to brainstorm like that before I meet with an architect. So they know what I'm after. I brought those to show your dad… before. But it doesn't matter now. Just toss them."

These were his ideas for the building he'd planned for this spot. And Romano's was woven through every inch of it. He'd let this go to give her back her bar.

"It's the bar," she finally said. "The building looks like the bar."

"I wanted what came after to reflect what came before." Abruptly he stopped, squeezing his eyes shut. "Gem, I'm so sorry. I know that doesn't mean much to you now. Your dad called me and it seemed like the best thing for everybody. I needed the building and your dad needed to sell. I don't know… I thought that if it had to happen, maybe it would be easier for you if it was me doing it." He waved a hand at the stack of drawings. "Maybe if that came after, it would make it better somehow. Maybe that's just what I wanted to believe. Stupid. I know there was no making it better for you, no matter how much I wanted to."

Gemma toyed with the edges of the stack of papers. "See, this does make it better. What didn't make it better was having my choices taken away. And not just by my dad, but by you, too."

He blew out a long breath, moving closer, until he was just a foot away. This close, she could see the dark circles under his eyes and the lines of strain in his face. "I know." He nodded tightly, his jaw set. "And I'm sorry.

It's no excuse, but I've got a lifetime of experience taking on other people's problems. It's a hard habit to break. But you didn't need me to step in and solve your problems, and I was wrong to try."

She nodded, but said nothing, just absorbing. Yes, he was wrong, but he was also so damned big hearted and caring. A huge part of him was still that overwhelmed twelve-year-old kid, desperately trying to take care of everybody he loved. That kid would probably always lurk inside of him.

"What about this?" She drummed her fingers against the drawings.

"It's just a building. I'll build one somewhere else." This wasn't just a development plan. This was his triumph over his shitty uncle's attempt at sabotage. And he'd given it up without a moment's hesitation to try to get her bar back. That counted for something. It counted for a hell of a lot, really. "It doesn't matter to me," he continued. "What matters is that you hang on to what's important to you, that you get the life you want." He hesitated, eyes dropping to the floor. "Even if I'm not in it anymore."

She didn't think. She just reached for his face, pulled him in close, and kissed him. After a moment of startled stillness, his hands settled on her hips and he kissed her back.

"Sorry," she murmured when they broke apart. "I seem to do that a lot around you."

"I'm still not complaining," he said.

"I don't like my life without you in it."

His face creased up with emotion and his fingers curled tightly into her hips. "I hate my life without you. I always have."

"You have to let me handle things myself. I'm not breakable."

He nodded. "I know. I never thought you were."

"And you'd better not throw these out." She reached out and tapped the stack of drawings. "You're going to need them." When he shook his head and frowned in confusion, she leaned up and kissed him again, this time a little slower and softer. "The bar is staying closed and the building is yours," she whispered against his mouth.

He pulled away in shock. "Gem, no. Carlos—"

"Yeah, Kendra worked it out with Carlos. We could have kept it going, in some form. And I appreciate what you did to make that happen. But in the past few days, I realized something. I don't want to keep it going anymore. I'm ready to see what comes next."

"Are you sure?"

She let out a watery huff of laughter. When had she started crying again? "No? Yes? It was a hard decision to make. It's still hard. I think I'm going to burst into tears about a million more times before it's all out of my system. But…" She turned her head to look over his plans for what would stand here, and imagined the people moving in, the new families putting down roots in the spot where hers had flourished for so many years. "Knowing that this is what will be here instead…it does make it easier. You weren't wrong about that."

"I'll make it the best it can possibly be, for your sake."

"Just make it yours and I know it'll be good."

"I'm sorry about what I said."

She looked up at him in confusion.

"When we fought. I implied you were better than all this, as if there's something wrong with this."

"No, I know what you meant. At the time, I didn't want to know. But I do now. And you were right. Not…" After a pause, she shook her head. "Not that I'm better than this, but there's more out there for me. Honestly, I was too afraid to admit it, because if I admitted there was something I wanted, then I'd have to go for it."

Brendan hiked an eyebrow. "And? What is it you want?" It was a tiny moment of levity, but it sparked something warm and hopeful in her chest.

"I'm going to culinary school. I want to be a caterer." Every time she said it, it felt more real, more like a concrete plan and less like some crazy daydream.

Brendan's grin was as wide as the world. "Gem, that's…it's fucking fantastic. Really."

"For the first time, I have no idea how I'm spending the rest of my life. That's terrifying."

"Also a little exciting, maybe?"

"A lot." She reached for his free hand with hers, until she held them both. "Because I might not be able to predict what's coming at me, but I'm seeing a little light up there at the end of the tunnel."

"Really?" He moved a step closer, until his toes were nearly touching hers. "What's up there in that light?"

"You," she said simply. "You are. Along with the rest of my future."

Brendan's hopeful smile was almost painful to see. "You see me in your future?"

She nodded through encroaching tears. "In my past and in my future, for as long as you want to be there."

In a flash, he'd untangled their fingers and taken her face in his hands, pressing his lips to hers, so gentle and hungry all at the same time. It was a kiss she could get lost in, feast on. For the rest of her days, she'd never get tired of this kiss.

"I gotta warn you, Gemma," he murmured, pulling back and pressing his forehead to hers. "I think I can see forever."

"Forever sounds pretty good to me. See, I'm in love with you, so forever sounds just about perfect."

## Epilogue

"Sorry, guys, the taps are already disconnected. It's bottles only. And all I have left is Molson's," Dad said, handing a couple of cold bottles across the bar to Dennis and Frank.

"Ah, hell. Molson's?" Frank moaned. "I was hoping for one last draft, for old times' sake."

"This'll do, though. Thanks, John." Dennis tapped his bottle against Frank's and the two of them took a drink.

It had been a few weeks since the fire that closed the bar. When Dad told her Dennis had called asking about their future, Gemma suggested that they open back up for one night, just to give folks a chance to come say goodbye. Honestly, she'd figured it would just be their immediate family and Dennis and Frank. One final toast before they turned off the lights for the last time.

But word had spread, and from the minute they'd opened the doors, people had streamed in. Joe brought a platter of subs from Sal's. Pat Russo brought down a stack of pizzas. Maria DiPaola brought boxes of cookies. Amen brought trays of pita and hummus. Mrs. Kim had brought down armfuls of day-old flower arrangements. Suddenly, what was supposed to be a quiet goodbye had turned into an all-night party. Family, friends, neighbors…everybody had turned out to send off Romano's Bar.

Already it looked different in here, partly because the big mirror behind the bar was gone, baring the brick wall underneath. Brendan had had it removed for her. Currently it was wrapped in tarps in the basement of the house. But one day? Gemma was going to hang it in the front office of her catering company. That wasn't a dream; it was a plan.

"It's the end of an era," she heard Willie Fortman say mournfully to her cousin Paulie. They'd heard that one all night, along with "It's not like it used to be around here."

But Gemma refused to be sad about that. No, it wasn't like it used to be, and she was going to miss the old days. They all would. But there was no way they could live in the past. Change was coming no matter what, so best to face it on your own terms.

Jess came over to lean on the bar. "If nobody wants it, I think I'll take the Michelob sign in the window."

"What are you going to do with it?" Livie asked, wrinkling her nose. She and Nick had flown back home for the weekend, so they could be here for this, too.

"Hang it in Alex's office. He'll be *appalled.*"

"I heard that." The man himself came up behind Jess and dropped his arm across her shoulders. "A neon beer sign isn't exactly my taste," he said, eyeing the sign suspiciously. "But it's part of your history, Jess. You should keep it."

"I took the mirror," Gemma pointed out. "Dennis and Frank are splitting the bar stools. And Dad's taking the taps."

"What for, Dad?" Livie asked.

John Romano shrugged. "There's a finished basement in the house we're looking at."

Teresa came up next to him, slipping an arm around his waist. "We're thinking of installing a little home bar down there. Put up a flat screen, get some comfy chairs…make it into a man cave."

"So the Superbowl's at your place this year, John?" Nick asked.

"Sure, why not? We'll start a new tradition."

"Traditions are good," Gemma said. "It's about time we started some new ones."

"So when's the big move, Frank?" John asked.

"As soon as I close on the house, we're heading down to Vero."

The mysterious Veronica had shown up in the flesh tonight, and what flesh it was. Her skin had the burnished bronze of a dedicated sun worshiper, set off to even greater contrast by her bleached platinum-blond hair. She was across the bar, chatting with Uncle Richie and Mariel Kemper, towering over them both in four-inch heels, a leopard print miniskirt, and a hot pink, very tight shirt. Richie and Mariel looked a little shellshocked, because Veronica had one of those huge personalities that sort of hit you square in the face. But Gemma had to admit, the affection between her and Frank seemed genuine. She hoped they made a real go of it down there in Vero Beach.

Dennis shook his head in wonder. "Gonna miss you, man."

"What are you talking about? You're not even gonna be here!"

They all looked at Dennis in question, and he shrugged

awkwardly. "Moving to Toms River with my daughter. She found a little place near them."

"Dennis, that's great," Gemma said, sincerely meaning it. Dennis needed to be closer to his family, to be there as his grandkids grew up. She wondered how long his daughter would be able to hold out before she invited her dad and the widow Marjory to dinner on the same night.

"Glad to hear that, Dennis." John reached across the bar and shook his hand.

"Brendan and Dan seem to be really hitting it off," Livie observed.

Across the bar, tucked into a corner behind her cousins Amber and Nicole, Brendan and Dan Drake were deep in conversation. Gemma's heart gave a silly little pulse of happiness as she watched Brendan.

"He looks like he's going all George Bailey again," she sighed. He was so hot when he went off on one of his impassioned rants about affordable housing. She swooned every time.

Jess elbowed Alex. "Has your dad ever considered investing in middle-class housing? Because it looks like that might be in his future."

"Diversification is good, and Dad knows a solid plan when he sees one," Alex said.

"We're going to turn your dad into a philanthropist yet." Jess grinned up at him.

Kendra approached the bar, busily typing on her phone. "You guys still going to be here in an hour? Mikey wants to come by when he gets off his shift at the station."

Gemma looked around at the crowd. No one seemed to

be in any hurry to leave. "Tell your brother he'd better get his ass over here. And tell him to bring Christopher, too."

"Oh, he's coming," she said, checking her texts. "So's Nathan and Tony. Jimmy, too. Pretty much everybody." She pocketed her phone. "So, when do classes start?"

"May fifteenth. And I'll be full-time for nine months. Then I'll do an internship somewhere." Every time she thought about it, her stomach erupted in butterflies, but they were the good kind, nerves and anticipation, not dread and fear. She was doing it—cooking school.

"I'm so proud of you, Gem," Livie said.

"We all are," Jess chimed in.

"Thanks, guys." A couple of weeks ago, she'd have immediately protested that she was probably going to fail, that she was too old, too minor league, to succeed at this. But she was doing her best to turn off that destructive little voice in her head. This was her big chance, and she wasn't going to defeat herself before she'd even started. She wanted it too much.

"She's going to be amazing," Brendan said, appearing at her side and draping his arm across her shoulders.

"And very busy," Kendra added.

She had two more dinner parties lined up this summer. Experience was good, right? At least, that's what she was telling herself. And the more contacts she made now, the better positioned she'd be when she eventually launched her own company.

"Between school, catering, and finishing the kitchen, you're going to be swamped," Brendan said.

She hadn't meant to start tearing the house apart, she really hadn't. But in those early days after the bar closed, after she'd sent in the first payment for her culinary classes, she was left home alone with too much time on her hands, full of optimism and energy, and ready for change. And suddenly that tired old harvest gold linoleum in the kitchen was too much to bear. When Brendan had stopped by hours later, he'd found her dirty and sweaty, and the kitchen floor stripped down to the original wood.

The wallpaper in the downstairs rooms went next. Brendan helped with that one, spending the weekend shirtless and sweating, steaming it off in great, long strips. Gemma had been grateful for his help for more than one reason.

Brendan was spending an awful lot of time with her in the house. They'd finally christened her bedroom, although his bed was still more comfortable. So maybe they'd move his bed to her place. The way he listened to her ideas for fixing up the house, suggesting upgrades she could make, or period-appropriate fixtures she could install, she suspected he could see himself maybe living there one day soon. Which was good, because Gemma could see him living there, too. Maybe with his mom. After all, they had plenty of room, and family was family. And she was very much hoping that they'd be part of the *same* family before too much longer.

But that was all in the future, a future she was no longer afraid to face. Tonight was about honoring the past.

"Dad," Gemma said quietly, reaching out to touch his hand. "You ready?"

He looked to Teresa apprehensively, and she gave him an encouraging smile. "You can do it, John."

When they'd discussed this, Dad had thought he'd be making this speech to family and a couple of friends. Now the bar was packed with dozens and dozens of people. But it was still the right thing to do, maybe now more than ever.

Gemma tapped the side of her beer bottle against the brass rail to get everybody's attention. Gradually the hum of voices subsided, and everyone turned to look. Nick had flipped a crate over behind the bar, and now Dad climbed up on it, so he stood head and shoulders above the crowd.

He cleared his throat, running the palm of his hand across the back of his neck. Gemma felt such a rush of love for him, she didn't know what to do with it all. She was lucky, so very lucky, to have this man for her father, and these strong, amazing women for her sisters. With them at her back, she felt like she could accomplish anything.

"I want to thank you all for coming tonight," Dad began. "It means more to me and the girls than I can say. As you know, this place has been in the Romano family since 1934." He motioned to an old black-and-white photograph propped up on the bar, Great-Grandpa Romano out in front on the sidewalk, taken the year the bar opened. "Prohibition ended and Grandpa Angelo knew an opportunity when he saw one. He sank his life savings into this place. And it's been good to us. Four generations of Romanos have stood behind this bar. Countless generations of your families have come through that door and sat on the other side."

Dad paused, looking down, his mustache twitching slightly. Poker-faced as always, but Gemma knew he was fighting back his emotions. She felt Jess reach for her hand, and she reached for Livie's in turn. Her eyes burned with tears as Dad got himself together enough to keep speaking.

"It's been an honor to be a part of this neighborhood," he said at last, looking to Maria DiPaola, Amen Shadid, Pat Russo, Soo Jin Kim, Leo Vinelli, and Joe Caruso. "This community has been our extended family, and that'll still be true, long after Romano's Bar is gone."

Maria DiPaola dabbed at her eyes with a tissue. Mrs. Kim sniffled loudly. Even Joe Caruso looked a little red eyed. Gemma wasn't even trying to hold it back anymore. Tears streamed down her cheeks.

"Angelo Romano, my grandfather, came to this country all alone when he was just sixteen, with nothing but the clothes on his back. He worked hard for what he had, but neighborhoods like this, neighbors like you, made his success possible. Immigrants…they banded together and built a future for themselves, and for us, their descendants. Thank you for the past ninety years," he said, lifting his beer bottle. "And here's to the next ninety. Here's to the future. May it be as successful as our past."

The bar erupted in cheers. Dad stepped off his makeshift stand and wrapped his arms around Teresa, kissing her soundly. Gemma pulled her sisters into a clumsy three-way hug, all three of them weepy, laughing messes.

When she let them go, Alex was there to wrap Jess in his arms, and Nick pulled Livie into a tight hug, too. Brendan was right there, right behind her, waiting for her moment with her sisters to finish.

He slid his arms around her waist and she looped her hands behind his neck. "You okay? Not too sad?"

She shook her head, smiling up at him. "Sad, but happy, too. Does that make sense? It's good. All of this. It's been good. And now it's over."

"And the future's just beginning."

She leaned up and pressed her lips to his. "And that future looks so very bright."

\* \* \* \* \*

*Reviews are an invaluable tool when it comes to spreading the word about great reads. Please consider leaving an honest review for this or any of Carina Press's other titles that you've read on your favorite retailer or review site.*

*To purchase and read more books by Amanda Weaver, please visit the author's website at www.amandaweavernovels.com/books.*

# Acknowledgments

This is my sixth book with Alissa Davis, my Carina editor, and I am so grateful for her hard work and insights. She sees things in my characters that I didn't see myself, and then she pumps up my ego and convinces me that it was my idea all along. She makes every book so much better.

Many, many thanks to my agent, Rebecca Strauss, who's been out there fighting for my books for three years. I feel so lucky to have her.

Thank you, thank you, thank you, Anne Forlines, for still reading everything I send you and giving me such great feedback every time. Seven years of stories! And thanks to Dr. Zaira Lopez for help with the specifics of medical school and residencies.

*Love Around the Corner* is a work of fiction, but almost every location mentioned in the book is closely based on a real Brooklyn business. Without their inspiration, this book would lack all its color and life. Thanks to Sal's Pizza, Sam's Restaurant, Esposito & Sons Pork Store, and Caputo's Bakery of Carroll Gardens, Brooklyn, and J&H Farm of Windsor Terrace. And thank you to Farrell's Bar & Grill of Windsor Terrace, Brooklyn. Without Farrell's, there would be no Romano's Bar.

## About the Author

Amanda has loved romance since she read that very first Kathleen E. Woodiwiss novel at fifteen. After a long detour into a career as a costume designer in theatre, she's found her way back to romance, this time as a writer.

A native Floridian, Amanda transplanted to New York City many years ago and now considers Brooklyn home, along with her husband, daughter, two cats, and nowhere near enough space.

You can find her online at:
http://www.amandaweavernovels.com/

You can find out all about her next release here:
http://eepurl.com/bvgkEv

She's on Facebook as @AmandaWeaverAuthor here:
http://on.fb.me/1W6LnGS

She's on Twitter as @AWeaverWrites here: http://bit.ly/1Zkf6MF

She's on Goodreads here: http://bit.ly/1KcRpPu

She's on BookBub here: https://www.bookbub.com/
profile/amanda-weaver

As a former visual artist, Amanda adores Pinterest.
Check out her profile for pages of visual inspiration for
all her books, plus costume history, textile arts, Wonder Woman, rock stars, and more! http://bit.ly/22Z0JlB